Break Every Chain

Qiana Rae

Beautiflaw Books

Beautiflaw Books

Cover Design:
SelfPubBookCovers.com/RLSather

This book is a book of fiction. Names, characters, places, and incidents are products of the author's imagination or are used fictitiously. Any resemblance to actual events locales, or persons, living or dead, is entirely coincidental.

ISBN: 978-1-7372696-0-1

<u>Dedication</u>

This book is dedicated to one of the strongest women I know, the first person I loved, my best friend . . . My Mother.

Ma, I thank God for your strength and resilience, which has carried you through this life, allowing you to overcome each and every obstacle that has tried to defeat you. No matter what, you've always prevailed, as you never lost your faith, and continued to allow God to order your steps. Because of your unconditional love, unwavering faith, and continuous prayers, I've made it through some of the most difficult times of my life. I will be forever grateful to you, and to God for creating such a beautiful woman, and entrusting her with me.

Love Always,

Kiki

Table of Contents

Prologue

It's said that God knows everything about us before we're even conceived and placed into our mother's womb. He knows every single person in which we will come into contact with, and every situation or challenge that we will encounter within our lives. God knows all of our secrets, even before they become secrets. That includes our innermost thoughts and desires. The things that may be causing us stress, anxiety, pain, sadness, or even that feeling we can't describe, He knows all about it. Nothing comes as a surprise to Him. Not even our sins.

1 "O Lord, you have examined my heart and know everything about me.
2 You know when I sit down or stand up.
You know my thoughts even when I'm far away.
3 You see me when I travel
and when I rest at home.
You know everything I do.
4 You know what I am going to say
5 even before I say it, Lord.
16 You saw me before I was born.
Every day of my life was recorded in your book.
Every moment was laid out before a single day had passed."
– Psalms 139:1-4, 16 NLT

For a large portion of my life, I had a problem believing any of this. If God knew all of this beforehand, why would He allow me to go through all the things that I had gone through, beginning at such an early age? I had so many questions, even though we're told in several different ways throughout the Bible to never question God.

20 "But who are you, a human being, to talk back to God?

"Shall what is formed say to the one who formed it, 'Why did you make me like this?' 21 "Does not the potter have the right to make out of the same lump of clay some pottery for special purposes and some for common use?"
– Romans 9:20-21 NIV

I looked at the world around me and wondered, *Why me, Lord? Why does everyone else get to live such simple, uncomplicated, happy lives, full of so many people who love them unconditionally? Was I not on the list to receive one, and if not, why not? Why did I get stuck with people who seemed to only tolerate me, use me, or downright hate me? When would I get a break?*

I felt guilty for thinking this way, but I couldn't help it. My mind was always at war over things that I never had any control over. The way that I looked at it was that God, for some reason, had chosen to place me in a life that would be full of chaos, hate, dysfunction, evil, and suffering. How did this happen, how would I get out of it, and if ever, when? I resented everything about myself and my life. I prayed for God to save me from the bad hand that I'd been dealt, every single day, for years. I wondered when I would have the breakthrough that I needed so badly. Nothing ever seemed to get better. The more I tried to tell myself that things would get better, it seemed as though, each time, I believed it a little less.

28 "And we know that all things work together for good to them that love God, to them who are the called according to his purpose." – Romans 8:28 KJV

I just needed for God to tell me what I needed to do in order to be released from those chains of bondage, and he finally did. He'll tell you, too, but you have to be willing to listen.

Sincerely,

The Ones Who Listened

Lena

Chapter One

My mom gave birth to me at the tender age of fourteen. When most girls think of that age, they think about having sleepovers, being dropped off at the mall with friends, and going to the movie theater and theater hopping all day until they've seen every movie playing. They think about eagerly awaiting to talk on the phone with friends about that boy they like, why he's with the girl that they don't like, or how they wish that boy would kiss them. Well, from what I'd heard others say about my mom, I could confidently assume that she was no typical fourteen-year-old girl.

My Aunt Donna, who was my mom's older sister, always told stories when she would have too much to drink, and they always seemed to focus around her childhood. According to her, my mom was the definition of trouble. Skipping school, smoking, and getting high seemed to be her only interests. My aunt was five years older than her, and tried to keep her on the right track, but as soon as she was old enough to move out from with their parents, she did, leaving my mom behind. She always talked about how their parents were a nightmare to live with. Their mom was bipolar, and their dad was physically and emotionally abusive towards both them and their mom. Aunt Donna admitted she was no angel either, but could no longer stay around to watch and endure the abuse. Soon after she moved out, my mom became pregnant with me.

She was able to hide the pregnancy from everyone almost until the very end, by wearing loose clothing. She didn't go to any doctors, or reach out for any medical advice or emotional support from anyone, including her sister. One day, when she was around eight and a half months pregnant, her mom walked in the bathroom on her as she was stepping out of the shower, wrapping her pregnant body into a towel. Her mom looked at her in disgust. Her eyes filled with anger, and she charged at my mom, knocking her to the ground.

"You are nothing but a worthless whore!" her mom, my grandmother, shouted as she straddled my mom on the floor. "You'll never be nothing!"

She finally climbed off of her after staring into her eyes, which were filled with tears.

"Get dressed and get out of my house! You or that thing are not welcome here," she said, without an ounce of shame in her voice, as she walked out of the bathroom.

As my mom struggled to stand up, she looked up and saw her dad standing in the doorway with his arms folded, shaking his head.

When he saw that she'd finally noticed him standing there, he coldly said, "Get out," and walked away.

My mom didn't waste any time packing as much as she could get into two trash bags. With her pregnant belly no longer hidden from the world, she walked three miles, dragging the full heavy bags all the way to her sister's house. When Donna opened the door with her one-year-old daughter, Lily, standing by her side, her mouth dropped as she looked down at my mom's belly.

"What did you do, Tera?" Donna asked.

She pushed Donna out of the way, and said, "I need somewhere to stay. Your parents put me out."

Donna rolled her eyes, and slammed the door after my mom walked in.

"Have you seen a doctor? The way you drink and get high, how could you do this?"

"I quit," she said, as she shrugged her shoulders.

"You might lie to mom and dad, but do not lie to me. Especially when you need me to help you!"

"I'm not lying. I quit as soon as I found out about eight months ago. I'm clean, and quit being a hypocrite! You act like you don't do the same stuff that I do, and Lily is fine, isn't she?"

"I'm an adult, and I wasn't doing those things while I was pregnant, so don't try to turn this around on me! You're fourteen years old! What are you going to do with a baby?"

My mom plopped down on the blue beat up sofa and said, "Take care of it."

"You have a lot to learn," Donna said, again, rolling her eyes.

Donna made sure that my mom got all the care she needed during her last month of pregnancy. Their parents were tragically killed during a home invasion only a few weeks after they kicked my mom out. I often heard rumors about how my mom may have had something to do with that, but I couldn't imagine a fourteen-year-old being so evil, even if they had treated her badly. People thought that maybe my father helped her, but no one ever even knew who he was. There was always talk about it maybe being her twenty-five-year-old dope man. Whoever he was, she never spoke of him, and no one ever saw any random men come around to see me after I was born.

The first and last actual memory I had of my mom was when I was around four years old. At that time, we were still living with my Aunt Donna. My mom was working at the McDonald's that was down the street so that she could take care of me, and obviously support her habits that she had resumed immediately after I was born. She never went back to school once she got kicked out of the house, which wasn't very surprising. Aunt Donna would watch me during the day when my mom worked. She'd had two more kids by then, which were a set of twins named Zoe and Zion, who were practically only a few months old. Aunt Donna had become the more irresponsible of the two, sitting around the house getting drunk and high every day, and living off of the system. Random men would often come by, who she would entertain, and looking back on it, I would suspect that they were helping out with the bills in exchange for her entertainment.

When my mom got off work this particular day, she came home and changed out of her work clothes, which always immediately filled the house with the scent of old cooking oil. She always brought home bags of food for everyone, since no one seemed to cook, or had extra money for food. Lily and I were out of control, as always, running around the house playing. The babies sat in their infant seats on the floor next to Aunt Donna, in a cloud of smoke, as she barely paid us any attention while entertaining one of her guests.

After sitting me and Lily down at the table to eat, my mom walked over to Aunt Donna and said, "I'll be back later. The kids are eating."

"Where do you think you're going?"

"I just need to get away for a little while," she answered.

At that point, Aunt Donna stood to her feet, and said, "I watch your kid all day long so you can work, and now you want me to continue to watch her so you can go out and have a good time? Maybe I want to go out and have a good time. Isn't that right?" she said, looking back at her guest who was sitting on the couch with a cigarette hanging from his mouth, and feet up on the coffee table.

He took a puff of the cigarette and said, "Girl, you're having a good time right here with me. You don't need to go nowhere."

Aunt Donna rolled her eyes, and said, "Anyway, I'm not watching her, so go ahead and take her wherever you're trying to go."

My mom took a deep breath and walked over to the table where Lily and I were eating.

"Hurry up and finish eating, Lena. We have to go."

I looked up at my mom, nodded my head, and finished eating my French fries. She went and got my shoes, and began putting them on.

"Where y'all going?" Lily curiously asked.

I shrugged my shoulders.

"We'll be back in a little while. You be good and eat all your food," my mom said, smiling at her.

She grabbed my hand as we headed to the front door. Aunt Donna and the man were still sitting on the couch watching television.

"Have fun!" Donna said in a sarcastic tone, and began laughing.

In the middle of pulling the door shut, my mom turned around and said, "YOUR child is eating dinner." She then slammed the door.

My mom didn't have a car. We normally walked to the store, and sometimes to the park. She walked to and from work every day. I didn't know where we were going this particular day, but we walked for quite a while. At one point my mom knelt down and told me to get on her back because I had begun to walk so slowly. The sun was still up when we started, and had gone down by the time we arrived at our destination.

We began walking up to the door of a brown brick home where I heard music being played extremely loud. There were several cars parked in the driveway and along the street. My mom beat on the door with the palm of her hand. We stood there waiting for about a minute or so. She then beat on the door again. She seemed to be getting anxious, tapping her foot as we waited. Just as she was about to knock again, the door swung open. A man holding a bottle of beer stood in front of us.

"And here is the life of the party," he said, as he smiled at my mom. His entire expression changed when he looked down a little lower and saw me.

"Tera, now you know we can't have kids around here."

"Come on, Barry. I promise she won't be a problem. You won't even know she's here."

The man hesitated, then held the door open, and said, "I better not! Come on."

I felt like I had walked into a fog. The entire house was full of smoke. There was a mixture of scents, but none of them were good. In one area I smelled the scent of weed, which I had been accustomed to at home, but then in another area, I smelled chemicals mixed with a stench of something that smelled like vinegar. At one point, I even thought I smelled burning plastic.

Looking through the eyes of a four-year-old, what I thought I saw were people sitting at tables sniffing flour through their noses, wondering why anyone would want to do that. The ones who weren't sniffing, were smoking and drinking. Everyone who we walked past greeted my mom with a smile. Some of them hugged her, and some of the men kissed her on the cheek. Most of the people who were there looked older than my mom, with the exception of a few who may have been a little younger. My mom seemed as though she was on a mission to find someone as we walked through the crowd, and she held on tightly to my hand.

We turned a corner into one of the bedrooms, and my mom instantly became excited.

She released my hand and said, "Hey Malcolm," giving him a hug.

Malcolm was around my complexion, which was mocha brown. The thing about him that stood out, which I would never forget, was the fact that he had a light pigmentation underneath his right eye. It was in the same spot as the one I had, shaped like a heart, as was mine.

"Hey, Baby Girl. I didn't think you were gonna make it."

"I almost didn't," she said, as she looked down at me.

"Oh, had to bring Little Tera with you today, huh?"

"Little Tera, huh? Yeah, well, I think she looks more and more like her father every day," she replied.

As my mom and Malcolm conversed, I looked over in the corner of the room and saw a woman slouched in a chair with her head hanging down. My mom saw me staring and asked Malcolm if we could go into another room. We followed him upstairs and went into a larger room where it was a lot more quiet.

"So, what do you have for me?" my mom asked Malcolm.

"I should be asking what you have for me," he replied.

My mom stuck her hand deep down into her pants pocket and pulled out a roll of money that was secured with a rubber band. Malcolm stuck his hand out, waiting for my mom to hand over the cash. I watched, as I wondered what she was buying.

"Where is it?" she asked.

"Girl, as long as you've known me, you should have a little more trust in me," he said, as he unbuttoned his shirt pocket and pulled out a small plastic bag. "You ordered a little more than you normally do. You must not plan on coming back to see me for a while."

My mom anxiously began rolling up the sleeve of her denim shirt, and that's when I noticed all the scars going up and down her arm. I gasped, shocked at what I was looking at.

Malcolm looked at me, then said to my mom, "You're not going to do that here in front of her, are you?"

My mom snatched the bag from him as she said, "Just give me my stuff and mind your business."

She threw the money at him and rolled her sleeve back down.

"Come on, Lena," she said, grabbing my hand.

She quickly stormed out of the room, and back down the stairs to where the large crowd was. I thought we were about to leave, but as we were walking towards the front door, we passed a bathroom. We then stopped and turned around.

"Wait right here, Lena. I'll be real quick, and then we can go home. Don't move."

"Ok, Mommy," I replied.

She kissed me on the forehead before going into the bathroom, and shut the door behind her.

After I had waited outside of the bathroom through at least three songs that had played on the stereo, I finally knocked on the door.

"Mommy," I said, as I tried to turn the knob, but the door was locked.

I tried putting my ear up to the door so that I could hear her, but I couldn't hear anything over the loud music. Suddenly, I saw Malcolm coming around the corner, and he didn't look very happy.

"Little girl, where's your momma? She owes me some money."

I was afraid to answer, so I just stood there and shrugged my shoulders.

"Is she in the bathroom?"

Again, I shrugged my shoulders.

"Tera! Open this door. I don't want to have to take your pretty little girl as collateral. I just want the rest of my money," he yelled.

He tried to turn the knob and put his ear up to the door as I had previously done.

"Tera!" he yelled again.

Malcolm began to look nervous after he didn't hear anything. He looked at me and said, "Stand back."

I took a few steps back as I watched Malcolm use all of his strength to knock down the door. It took him three times of ramming his broad shoulder into the door before it finally broke off of the hinges. He moved the door completely out of the way and went in. A couple of other men who had been watching the entire time went in after him. One of them was Barry, the man who had let us into the house after my mom had to practically beg. I didn't know what to do, so I didn't move, just like my mom had told me not to.

"How much did you give her?" I heard one of the men say loudly, in a panicked voice.

"Too much for anyone to take at once, and she took it all!" Malcolm said.

The three men came back out of the bathroom, and Malcolm looked at me, breathing heavily, and shaking his head.

"What's the plan?" Barry asked Malcolm.

"We need to get them out of here," he replied.

The two men nodded their heads at Malcolm. While he took me into one of the other rooms and locked me in, the other men turned off the music and began clearing out the house, telling everyone that they had to leave. Once everyone else was gone, Malcolm sent Barry into the room to get me. He took me outside and put me into the back seat of a black car with dark windows, and sat next to me. Malcolm was already in the driver's seat and the other man sat next to him in the passenger seat.

As I looked around and didn't see my mom, I began to panic and cry uncontrollably.

"Where's my mommy?" I yelled.

"Put your hand over her mouth, but don't hurt her!" Malcolm yelled, as he pulled the car out of the driveway.

"What's the address on her ID?" he asked the man that was sitting in the passenger seat next to him.

The man read off the address from my mom's ID, which was the address where we lived with Aunt Donna.

After driving for a few minutes, the car suddenly slowed down. Barry had taken his hand from my mouth once I had calmed down. Malcolm then turned off his headlights and came to a complete stop in front of Aunt Donna's house.

He looked back at me and said, "We're not going to hurt you. We're just trying to help you and your mom, so once we take you to the door, wait until we get back in the car and drive off before you knock, ok?"

With tears in my eyes, I nodded my head. The other two men got out of the car, and I heard the trunk open. Malcolm got out of the car and opened my door, immediately grabbing my hand, in case I tried to run. We walked towards the front door behind the other two men. It wasn't until we got closer to the door that I noticed them lying my mom down on the wood planked porch. She looked as if she was sleeping, but had white foam around her mouth.

"Remember what I said," Malcolm whispered. "Don't knock on the door until we're gone."

As Malcolm and the other two men ran back to the car, I knelt down over my mom.

"Mommy. Wake up. I did what you said. I didn't move. Please wake up. We're home."

I heard the screeching sound of tires and looked up to see that the black car had driven off.

My mom still wasn't responding. I knocked on the door and waited for Aunt Donna to open it. There were no cars outside, so I knew her company had left. I finally heard the door opening, and Aunt Donna was soon standing in front of me.

As she turned on the porchlight, she said "Lena, where is your . . ."

Before she could finish her sentence, she looked to the ground and saw my mom's lifeless body lying there.

"Oh my God! How did this happen? Who did this?" Aunt Donna shouted, as she fell to the ground, cradling my mom.

Lily came outside in her pajamas and began crying when she saw her mom crying. The neighbors filled the street trying to see what all the commotion was about. After the police and paramedics arrived, the coroner was called out, and it was considered an open and shut case of a young, negligent Black mother who overdosed while her child was in her care. Those cases were oftentimes looked at as just another problem off the street. I didn't understand everything that had happened at that time, but at that age, all I knew was that my mom who loved me and took care of me had suddenly been taken away from me. As I became older and was able to better comprehend the situation, I began to despise everything about her, and blamed everything bad that ever happened to me on the fact that she didn't care enough about me to take care of herself so that she could keep me safe. Because of her, I had been stripped of a normal childhood, which would continue to have an effect on me for the rest of my life.

Chapter Two

After my mom died, my Aunt Donna became my legal guardian since there wasn't anyone else around to accept responsibility. Since my mom was gone, I would probably never know who my dad was. She took that secret to the grave. My aunt made sure she reminded me on a regular basis that she wasn't thrilled about having to take care of an additional child. I wouldn't even consider what she did for me as "taking care of me". My mom was the one who always made sure we had something to eat. Since Aunt Donna couldn't depend on that anymore, she would have her male friends to come over to the house with dinner for the two of them, and when they would leave, she would give us the leftovers. We never had food in the refrigerator, and some days, we would go the entire day without eating. Later in life, I often wondered if she even knew who her own kid's father or fathers were, and if she did, why didn't they want to help take care of their kids? When I was a kid, I didn't think anything of it because I didn't have a father either, so it seemed normal at the time. Aunt Donna was on welfare and received food stamps, so there was no excuse as to why the refrigerator was empty. Instead of buying food, she would sell her food stamps for cash so she could buy cigarettes, liquor, weed, and whatever else she desired.

My cousin, Lily, was the first of all of us to be enrolled in school since she was the oldest. I was jealous, not because she got to go to school and learn new things and make friends, but because she got to get out of that filthy house and get a couple of good meals each day. She would come home and brag to me about the different types of fruits and cereals she would have for breakfast, and things like pizza and chicken nuggets for lunch. Some days she would save a pack of cookies, or a piece of fruit for me, just in case it was one of those days that we wouldn't get a meal. Zoe and Zion were still only babies, so they would get the baby formula and food that the government provided for them, but there would soon come a day when they would be in the same situation that Lily and I were in.

Things didn't get any better as we got older. They actually got a lot worse for us, especially when we became teenagers. Other kids hadn't been that cruel when we were younger, but as we got older, the other kids began to notice that we weren't the cleanest kids around. Every month we would have to go at least a few days without water because Aunt Donna would be late paying the water bill. Our clothes were too small because we had grown out of them, and dirty because Aunt Donna wouldn't do laundry for weeks. Because we didn't have a washer and dryer, she would have to take them to the laundromat. Clean clothes obviously weren't on the top of her list of priorities because she never had money to make sure we had something clean to wear. Lily and I would attempt to wash them in the tub a few times, but each time, we would break out in rashes from not rinsing all of the laundry detergent out of them. If we weren't being made fun of for being dirty, it was because our pants were too short, shirts too tight, or hair not combed.

By the time I was sixteen, I'd had enough. I couldn't continue to go to school each day, dealing with being bullied and harassed by the other kids. I was tired of holding my head down in shame every time I walked through those doors, so I stopped going. I wanted to finish school so badly, just so that I could say that I did something that my mother didn't. I wanted to be better than what she was. I never wanted anyone to ever be able to say that I was just like my mother. She was the reason that I had to live life the way that I did, and there was nothing anyone could tell me that would change my disposition about her.

Aunt Donna never asked us about school. Not about our grades, or if we had homework. When our teachers would call to discuss our grades, or even tell her we were failing a particular subject, she would just say whatever the teacher wanted to hear, and act as if she was going to talk to us and resolve the problem. What the teachers failed to realize was that us and our grades were the furthest things away from Aunt Donna's mind than anything. As long as we left the house Monday through Friday, and she didn't have to see us for at least eight hours, she didn't care what we were doing.

During the school day, I would just aimlessly walk the streets. It just felt good to be able to be away from it all. I didn't have to deal with watching Aunt Donna as she did absolutely nothing with her life, and I didn't have to go through the daily ridicule of being the laughingstock of all of my peers. Most days, I was hoping that I would just somehow walk into a miracle. I wanted to know what it was like to live a normal life like the other kids at school. My cousins and I had lived through years of misery, and I believed that if there was a god, he didn't like us very much. To tell you the truth, at that point, I didn't believe there was a god because if there had been one, he wouldn't have allowed us to be subjected to all of the things we had seen and been through.

Lily would always try to skip school with me, but I wouldn't allow her to. She was a year older than me, and closer to finishing high school than I was. Even though I had given up, I didn't want her to. She had her siblings to think about. I figured if she could finish school, she would be able to get a decent job, and help get her sister and brother out of that house. I only had me, so I didn't feel responsible for anyone else, but in the meantime, I was going to try to find a way to make life a little easier for the four of us.

One morning, as I walked my normal route, wearing my too small jeans, t-shirt that was once white, but now looked gray, and my bookbag on my back, a fancy white car pulled up on the side of me, and slowly followed me as I continued to walk, picking up my pace. A man wearing dark sunglasses was driving. He stared at me for a moment, and finally sped off. As I kept my eyes on the car, I noticed it stopping at the next street, preparing to make a U-turn. I saw a convenience store ahead, and quickly ran towards it, trying to get inside because the white car made its way back around.

When I got inside of the store, I walked around trying to look as though I was really looking for something. The clerk watched me from behind her plexiglass window, as if she was waiting for me to try to steal something. At that time in my life, yes, I was a thief, but for a good reason. I had to steal to survive, but that wasn't on my mind at that moment. I was just trying to stay safe until I felt like whoever the man was who was stalking me had gone about his business.

A few minutes later, as soon as I felt it was probably safe, I was about to walk towards the door, when suddenly, I heard the sound of the chimes on the door jingle. I went and hid around the corner and faced a rack of potato chips. I heard footsteps getting closer and closer. They then stopped, and I felt a hand on my shoulder.

"Lena, is that you?"

My heart was pounding so hard that it felt like someone could've seen it through my tight t-shirt. I didn't know who the man could've been. There were no men that had been a part of my life outside of my teachers at school, and the random men that Aunt Donna would have around. I, however, really didn't consider them being a part of my life. They probably didn't even know my name.

I took a deep breath, trying to calm down, and slowly turned around. It was the man from the white car, and he was still wearing sunglasses. Even up close, I still didn't recognize him, until that moment he took off his sunglasses. I saw the heart underneath his eye that matched mine, and I instantly had a backflash of the night my mom died. It was Malcolm, and I couldn't understand what he possibly could've wanted from me. I honestly couldn't even believe that he'd had the audacity to approach me.

As soon as he removed his sunglasses, my mouth almost hit the floor before I said, "Malcolm."

He squinted his eyes and said, "You remember me?"

"How could I forget?" I asked.

He grabbed my arm and said, "Come with me."

"No! Let me go!" I said, as I looked over at the clerk to see if she was still watching.

"Lena, please come with me."

"Why should I?" I asked with an attitude.

Malcolm looked me up and down and said, "You look like you might need my help."

I became furious and said, "My mom needed your help that night!"

Malcolm put his index finger up to his lips gesturing for me to quiet down.

"Ok. I'm going to go out to my car. I'll wait out there for five minutes. You decide. I'm just trying to help you."

Those words "just trying to help you" lingered in my mind. I heard those words almost every day for years because those had been the same words he had said to me on that horrific night. There were so many things I had remembered about that night, and it took so many years to try to forget most of them. Now, suddenly, Malcolm showed up, making me relive everything all over again.

Malcolm walked out as I stood there in the middle of the store, feeling more confused than I had felt in a long time. I tried to think of how this situation could in any way turn out good for me. This was the same man who had given my mother the drugs that killed her, and put her in the trunk of his car. Not only that. He had thrown her body on the porch like she was a dead dog. After reliving those memories, I decided I needed to get as far away from Malcolm as I possibly could.

I waited five minutes to see if Malcolm would realize I wasn't coming out, and drive off, but he didn't. I realized then that I would just have to gain enough courage to walk out and keep walking, so that's what I attempted to do. As soon as I walked out of the store, Malcolm rolled down his window and stuck his head out. I walked in the opposite direction.

"Lena. Come on. I'm not going to hurt you."

I kept walking, trying to ignore everything that was coming out of his mouth. I was sure that my mom didn't think that he would've done anything to hurt her either, but in my eyes, he did.

"Look, I'm sorry about your mom. It hurt me, too!"

At that moment, I felt something strange move through my body. It was almost like electricity. His words had fueled something inside of me. I stood still without turning around.

"I was young and stupid, Lena," he continued. "I should've handled things a lot differently. I've changed. I've changed my life."

I could hear Malcolm's car starting to move. Next thing I knew, he had pulled up on the side of me.

"Just get in. If you don't want to hear what I have to say after a few minutes, you can go, and I won't ever try to talk to you again."

I cut my eyes at Malcolm and took a deep breath as I walked towards the passenger door. I got in and folded my arms as I looked straight ahead.

"Stubborn, just like your mom," Malcolm said, as he giggled. "You look just like she did at your age."

I glanced over at Malcolm, and rolling my eyes I said, "She always said I looked like my daddy, but I guess I'll never know."

Malcolm bypassed what I'd said and began telling me again how sorry he was for what happened. He told me that he knew my mom had a drug problem, but really didn't understand how bad it was because he was too deep into what he was doing, and saw everything as a business deal. He said he should've treated her situation differently because he really cared for her. He wouldn't, however, take responsibility for her death. He said if he wouldn't have sold her the drugs, someone else would have, and it still would have resulted in her overdosing. She had a problem, and no one could make her quit.

"The only time she did quit was when she found out she was pregnant with you, Lena. That's how much she cared about you," he proclaimed.

"I'm not trying to hear that! If she cared that much about me, she would've cared enough to stay away from it after I was born! I wouldn't be living the life that I'm living right now if she would've just done that one thing for me!"

"I get it, and as close as your mom and I were, I should've tried harder to help her, but like I said, I wasn't mature enough. I was a man, age-wise, but mentally, I was still a boy. I think about what I could've done all the time, but that's not going to help the situation. I feel like I do owe you something, though. I can't bring your mom back, but let me do something for you."

"What can you possibly do for me?"

Malcolm reached over and opened his glove compartment. I jumped as soon as I saw the gun inside.

"I'm not going to hurt you," he said, as he grabbed his wallet out of the glove compartment.

He opened it and pulled out a large wad of cash. I watched him as he counted the one-hundred-dollar bills, one by one. He tried to hand me ten of them, and I refused to take it.

"I don't want your money."

"I know it's not enough for all you've lost. No amount of money will ever be enough. I just don't want you on these streets without having anything. It's rough. Just let this help you get on your feet. Get some new clothes and maybe try to find a job. I'm assuming you're not going to school because if you were, you would be there right now."

Malcolm was right. I needed that money badly. I had nothing, and without that money, I would probably never have anything. I didn't need to think about it any longer. I snatched the money from Malcolm, jumped out of the car, and slammed the door. Before walking away, I knelt down and stuck my head through the window.

"One question," I said.

"What's that?" Malcolm asked curiously.

"Are you my father?"

Malcolm stared at me dead in my eyes, as our matching birthmarks faced each other, and hesitantly said, "No, I'm not. I'm just helping out the daughter of someone who was a very special friend."

I wasn't sure what I felt at that moment, but now when I think back on it, I guess I might've been a little disappointed. Instead of showing it, I just nodded, and walked away with the miracle I had been hoping for.

Chapter Three

knew that the money that Malcolm had given me wasn't a whole lot, but it was a start. It was way more than what I had to begin with. I knew I had to use that money to get as much done as I possibly could, so I needed to make a plan. I was in survival mode, and I knew that the first thing I needed to do was get a continuous cash flow going, but I also knew that no one was going to hire me looking the way that I did. That made it very clear as to what I needed to do first, so that's what I did. I caught the bus to the mall and went shopping for new clothes. Every store that I walked into, the salesclerks looked at me as if I needed permission to be there. I finally walked into a store where the woman at the cash register, who looked to be in her mid-twenties, gave me a friendly smile and asked if I needed help. I told her that I needed to buy a few things to help me get a job. She told me that her name was Myra, and she helped me find everything I needed, from pants that actually fit, to cute tops, and stylish shoes. I didn't go on a shopping spree. I just needed enough to keep me looking descent long enough to get my foot in the door somewhere. Then, I would be able to make enough money to try to make a life for myself.

After I finished shopping, Myra suggested that I go to the hair salon that was a few doors down and let them do something pretty to my hair, which had been in one long French braid that Lily had done for me for over a week. I didn't know about that. I had to spend the money wisely, and a visit to the hair salon wasn't exactly in my budget.

"I don't think so," I told Myra. "I've already spent way too much money on clothes and shoes."

Myra looked like she felt sorry for me. She told me to wait there and she'd be right back. She went to the back of the store and returned within a couple of minutes. She then stood in front of me and took my hand and opened it up.

"Take this," she said, as she placed money into the palm of my hand, and gently closed it.

I was confused. I didn't understand why this woman who didn't even know me was being so nice to me. I didn't know whether to say thank you, or hand the money back to her, and not accept it.

"I don't know what you're going through, but it looks like you're having a rough time and could use some help. We all fall on hard times at one time or another. I know I have, and when I did, there was always someone there to help me. I think I owe it to someone else to help them."

I put the money into my pocket, and said, "Thank you, Myra."

17 Whoever is kind to the poor lends to the Lord, and he will reward them for what they have done. – Proverbs 19:17 NIV

After leaving the salon, I felt pretty confident, and knew that someone out there had to hire me. It had crossed my mind to apply at some of the stores in the mall, but it was too far away from home. I couldn't afford to catch the bus back and forth to work every day, so I thought I'd begin my search closer to home. I caught the bus back to my side of town, and the entire way there,

I was trying to figure out how I'd get into the house without Aunt Donna seeing me walk in with shopping bags. She would then question where I got money, and try to take it from me, or even try to sell the clothes that I'd bought for myself. Something led me to a restaurant a few blocks down from the house, called Nora's Diner. I figured I could stay there until it got dark, and then I would be able to go home and sneak through the back door.

When I got to the diner, I walked in and slid into an empty booth. There were four girls who looked only a year or two older than me already sitting in the booth in front of me. Wearing slinky clothes, and a lot of bright makeup, they looked like a girl's singing group that was about to perform. They were talking loudly and having a good time, while I sat there not even knowing what that felt like.

"Can I get you something?" I suddenly heard a voice say out of nowhere.

I had been so fascinated by the girls in the other booth that I hadn't even noticed the waitress walking over.

"Do you want to order?" she asked, after I didn't respond the first time.

I hadn't planned on ordering anything, but I hadn't eaten all day, and had no idea if I would get a meal when I got home, so I decided to treat myself.

"I'm sorry," I said, apologizing to the waitress for seeming as though I was ignoring her.

"No problem, Hun. What can I get you?"

"I'll take a cheeseburger, large fry, and a large chocolate shake, please."

Chewing her gum and mumbling my order back to herself, she quickly wrote on her notepad. As she got ready to walk away, I thought about my cousins. I couldn't think to have a good meal when they would probably get scraps for dinner, if anything, for that matter. I knew they'd had breakfast and lunch at school, but I knew they would appreciate getting a nice dinner. I stopped the waitress as she was about to walk away, and ordered three more burgers and fries to go.

After the waitress walked away, I began eavesdropping on the girls again, imagining myself sitting at the table with them, laughing about whatever came to mind.

I overheard one of the three girls say, "Girl, I saw this bad outfit at Green Valley Mall the other day, but I have to work a few more nights before I can go get it."

The girl was so beautiful. All of them were. She had beautiful, smooth, caramel skin, and a dark-brown shoulder-length bob. I figured their parents must've been rich in order for them to look so well put together, but after I heard what she said about working a few more nights, I wondered where she worked.

"Girl, now you know you have enough money to get it now! You're just too cheap to buy what you want," her friend, who was sitting directly across from her, said.

"Right! She can buy ten of those outfits after one night of work!" the third girl said, who looked to be of a mixed descent, and the oldest out of the three.

They all began laughing, and continued eating their meals.

The waitress soon came over with my food and told me that she would wait to put in my to-go order so that the food wouldn't be cold. As the waitress was talking to me, the girl with the bob stared at me as if she knew me. I tilted my head as to say, "Do I know you?" but I didn't say a word. She then rolled her eyes and continued her conversation with her friends.

The waitress saw what happened, but she also didn't say anything. She told me to enjoy my meal and let her know if I needed anything else. When I looked down at the food in front of me, I could feel my mouth salivating. I hadn't had a full, hot dinner in a long time, so I was going to enjoy it to the fullest. In the middle of eating, I saw the three girls starting to move around, getting their belongings together. They all threw a tip on the table before sliding out of the booth, one by one. They walked in a single file line as they strolled past me. The girl with the bob was last in line.

As I was about to take a bite of my burger, she stopped and said, "I was just looking at how pretty your hair is. I wasn't trying to be rude."

The other two girls realized she wasn't behind them and walked back over to wait for her.

"Thank you. I wasn't trying to be rude either."

"Is there a problem?" her friend that had been sitting across from her, said.

"No, Danielle! You're always trying to fight. I was just telling her how pretty her hair is. Isn't it pretty?"

"Yeah, it's ok," the girl, whose name was obviously Danielle, said, turning up her nose."

"Don't mind her. Have a good night."

As they walked away in their tall heels, I heard Danielle say, "Did you see what she was wearing? She looked like she was wearing her little sister's clothes!"

The girl with the bob slowly glanced back over her shoulder to see if I had heard what was said. When she realized I had, she quickly pushed the others out the door.

The waitress came over to check on me.

"Are you ok?" she asked with concern.

"Yeah. She just wanted to compliment me on my hair."

"Ok. I was going to tell you, don't mind them. They come in here all the time flaunting their bodies and their money. If they were my children, they would not be walking out the house like that, but it's none of my business. They can't be much older than you, and they work up the street at Club Venus. They leave me a good tip every time they come in, so they're all right with me," she said, smiling, showing off the huge gap between her two front teeth.

"They work at Club Venus?" I asked.

"They sure do. It's a shame, she said, shaking her head. "Let me let you finish your meal, and I'll be right back with your to-go order." She walked over to the booth where the three girls were sitting and snatched up the tip they had left.

I couldn't believe that they worked at Club Venus, but that explained the way they were dressed. Club Venus was a strip club a few blocks from the diner, so it wasn't very far from Aunt Donna's house either. My mind began churning. I'd never considered working anywhere like that, and it certainly wasn't the most conventional job for a sixteen-year-old, but it might've been the answer to all of my problems.

When the waitress came back over with the rest of my food to take home to my cousins, I thanked her for everything.

"You're welcome, Baby. Make sure you come back by!" she said, as she began cleaning off my table.

As I was walking away, with my shopping bags, and now a takeout bag, I turned back around and asked, "How often do they come in here?"

"Oh, they're here at least every other night. I assume they come in right before they go to work, like tonight. Why do you ask?"

"Oh, just wondering," I said.

I had my own agenda in asking that question, but she didn't need to know. She probably just assumed that I was trying to avoid them, when I was really trying to make sure I ran into them again. When I walked outside, it was pitch dark, just as I wanted it to be when I headed home. When I got to our street, I took the route through the alley so that I could sneak in through the back. I was hoping the back door was unlocked, but it wasn't, so I had to knock on the bedroom window where all of us kids slept, in hopes that someone was in there.

Lily came to the window and raised it up.

"Where have you been?" she whispered.

"I had to take care of some stuff. Is she awake?" I asked.

"No, but she was looking for you, so you better have a lie ready in the morning."

"Just come open the door," I said, with an attitude.

Lily came and opened the door. I walked in, trying not to make any noise with the shopping bags I had in my hand. Lily quietly shut the door, and we tiptoed to the bedroom.

"You've been shopping? And look at your hair!" Lily said with excitement, as she ran her fingers through my silky, straightened hair.

Lily's sister, Zoe, and their brother, Zion began sniffing around with their nose in the air.

"What's that smell?" Zoe asked.

I had forgotten that I'd brought food home for them.

"Oh," I said, as I pulled out the bags of food. "I brought you guys something."

Zion grabbed the bag and began pulling the food out.

"How did you get all of this stuff?" Lily asked, folding her arms, trying to act like the big cousin for once.

"I'm trying to figure some things out for the benefit of all of us."

"Ok," Lily said, looking at me suspiciously.

While they ate, I hid my new things in the back of the closet, and snuck down to the basement while no one was paying attention. "I hid the majority of the money that I had left behind one of the wooden panels on the wall. No one ever went down to the basement, so I knew no one would ever find it there.

The next morning, I got up with everyone else, and got dressed as if I was going to school, as usual. I woke up feeling extremely impulsive, which I did on a regular basis. The difference between before and now was the fact that I no longer felt stuck. I actually felt like I could get some things accomplished, and there were actual possibilities for me. Possibilities of having a different life from what my mom had and the one that I'd been living up to this point.

I put on one of my new pair of white jeans and a top that Myra had helped me pick out. I was about to be on a mission, and I was determined to be set free from what I'd begun to feel like was bondage. Lily always seemed pretty content and accepted the way that she and her siblings lived, but I never was. I always felt like I was a little different. I was different in how I looked at the world and envisioned my life to be regardless of how I was currently living. My mind seemed to always be all over the place, trying to think of ways to change my situation. My brain never shut down. Not even when I slept. Whatever I went to bed thinking about the previous night, I always woke up the next morning with the same exact thing on my mind. It was a continuous cycle that seemed to never cease. I oftentimes wondered if other people's minds worked the way mine did, but from what I'd experienced from the people that I'd encountered during my lifetime, it didn't seem that way.

When I came out of the bathroom, fully dressed, Lily looked at me and asked, "Are you going to school today?"

"No. I'm going to find us a way out of here."

"Lena, it's a waste of your time! This is all we have right now. You should just go to school like the rest of us and wait it out. Like you told me, you need to get your high school diploma."

She then looked me up and down and said, "And whatever you're doing to get money to buy these things, you need to stop."

"You don't need to worry about what I'm doing. Come on. Get your sister and brother and let's go."

As we walked through the living room to the front door, we walked past Aunt Donna, who was passed out on the couch. Bottles of liquor were all over the table, and a few empty ones on the floor next to the couch. That had become the normal everyday scene for us over the years. She was never awake when we left for school, which was why I wasn't concerned about answering to her about where I was the previous night. All that she worried about was that we weren't there to bother her when she woke up. We never even asked her for anything. What she considered "bothering her" was just being in her eyesight.

As I parted ways from my cousins as they walked through the schoolhouse doors, I walked the same route that I'd gone the previous day, wondering if I would run into Malcolm again. I wasn't expecting to, and really didn't have the desire to, but I couldn't help but wonder if he would ever admit what we both clearly knew. I would've been ok if I never saw him again.

I stopped and picked up breakfast for myself at a pancake house in the area, then went and sat in Mayson Park to eat. As I sat there with my food sprawled across the park bench, I noticed a young mother pushing her daughter on the swings. They were smiling, and laughing, and I could tell they were enjoying each other. It made me smile. Something that I didn't do much of those days. I looked down for a brief moment to take a bite of my bacon, and when I looked back up, I gasped for air. I suddenly became dizzy, and couldn't catch my breath, as I looked at the mother and daughter, whose appearances had suddenly changed to those of me and my mom. I then had a vision of my mom's face right before she went into that bathroom, not realizing that would be the last time I saw her alive. I put my hand on my chest due to my heart beating so rapidly, but I couldn't take my eyes off of them. I felt like I was having a heart attack.

The young mother looked over and saw me in distress, and quickly grabbed her daughter off of the swing.

"Are you ok?" she asked, as she stood over me.

I quickly nodded my head, as I took deep breaths and tried to get my mind back into a peaceful state. I had learned that remedy on my own after I had begun experiencing, what I later learned were panic attacks, right after going through the trauma of my mom's death. Anytime my Aunt Donna had been around during one my attacks, she would lock me in a room by myself, as if I was going to hurt someone. She had seen her mom, who was my grandmother, go through it, and she would become violent. After realizing what was going on with me, she thought that by locking me up, she was protecting herself and my cousins. However, she was much more concerned about herself. Lily and the other kids had never been exposed to my attacks. I would only have them when I was around Aunt Donna, or something else that upset me, so I quickly learned what triggered them, and tried to stay as far away as possible from any stimuli.

Once I began to relax a little, I replied, "I'm fine," as I looked at the pretty little girl who was looking at me directly in my eyes, smiling.

"Are you sure? Do you need me to take you to home, or to the hospital?"

I repeated, "No, I'm fine, but thank you for checking on me."

"You're welcome," she said, as she gently patted me on the shoulder. "Come on, Lena. Let's go home to see Daddy," she said, as she grabbed the little girl's hand and walked off.

I could feel my eyes well up with tears, and I immediately held by head back and closed my eyes until they went away. I wasn't good at expressing my emotions, partly because I didn't know how to comprehend sadness, or any other emotion.

After my panic attack, I didn't feel much like eating, so I put my food away for later, and sat, watching people come and go for the next couple of hours. I didn't really have a plan for the day, but was just hoping for the best. I thought about going back to the diner later that evening to see if the three girls were there, but even if they had been, I had no idea what I'd say or do. I was just so fascinated by them and felt there was a purpose for them in my journey.

I let that entire day go by without accomplishing anything. In all reality, I didn't know what I was doing, or even where to begin, but that next evening showed me how fast things could change.

I went into the diner where I'd seen the three girls a few days before, and sat at my same booth. The same waitress was there, whose name I'd learned was Valerie. She greeted me with her smile and told me it was nice to see me again. I only ordered a soda and sat in the booth looking out of the window. After sitting there for a little over an hour, I was just about to grab my bookbag and head home, when I heard the diner door open, and a few familiar voices.

I turned around to see the same three girls coming through the door.

"Shae, did you see his smile?" one of the girl's said to the girl with the bob.

"Yes! It was gorgeous," Shae replied, grinning from ear to ear.

They sat in the same booth right in front of me. My mind was racing. I'd had a couple of days to work out everything in my mind, and it was all still a jumbled mess. I sat there the entire time, getting refill after refill, and going to the bathroom at least five times. I wished one of them would've sparked a conversation with me, but then I thought, *Why would they do that?*

Valerie, the waitress, came over asking if I wanted another refill.

"No, thank you."

"Well, do you want to order something to eat?"

As Valerie was grilling me, I saw the girls getting up, grabbing their things so that they could go. They dropped their tip onto the table and walked around Valerie, trying to get through the aisle.

Valerie continued to talk, and I put my hands up to my head, sighing.

"What's wrong?" she asked.

"Nothing. I just need to do something, and I just don't know how," I said as I watched the girls walk towards the exit.

"Well, when I need to do something, and I'm afraid of how it might turn out, I just try to tell myself, if it doesn't work out, at least I tried. That's what I did before I applied for a waitressing job here. I was twenty years old, two kids, and didn't even have a high-school diploma. I wondered who would hire someone like me. Now look at me. I'm the owner of that same diner."

I quickly turned back around, taking my focus off of the girls, and looked at Valerie with a stunned look on my face.

"I might have to bust tables and serve customers because my staff doesn't show up half the time, but it's still mine, and if I had let fear overcome me, I don't know where I would be today. To be honest, I'm sometimes glad when people don't show up for work. If they don't show, I don't have to pay!" she laughed.

I had thought Valerie was just a waitress when she actually owned the entire diner, and she had done it all without a high-school diploma, and with two kids. After hearing her story, I thought about my Aunt Donna. There was no excuse for her to be living the way that she was. She actually had a high-school diploma, but still chose to sit at home on her butt and get something for nothing.

After talking to Valerie, my entire mindset changed. After seeing those three girls for the first time, seeing how nice they dressed and how happy they looked, I wanted to be like them. I had planned on trying to talk to them and figure out how I could get a job as a dancer, like them. That was my reason in waiting to see if they would show up at the diner that night. Valerie showed me that I could be better than that.

"Valerie?" I said, as she was walking away.

"Yes?" she said, still smiling as she turned around.

"Um . . . Are you hiring?" I asked inquisitively.

Valerie's smile got even brighter.

"I thought you'd never ask! There's one thing I'm going to ask you to do, though."

Nervously, I said, "What's that?"

"Please call me Miss Val. You're a child, and should never call an adult by their first name."

The very next day, I started working as a waitress at Miss Val's diner.

Chapter Four

had planned to only work at the diner for a few months. I knew I wouldn't make enough there to accomplish everything I wanted to do. My plans obviously didn't matter. I ended up working at the diner with Miss Val for a couple of years. Aunt Donna eventually became curious about where I was going every day, and I ended up having to tell her I had a job. After that, I became another stream of income for her. She made it seem as though she was charging me for rent. She told me since I wasn't going to go to school and still lived there, I had to pay. It wouldn't have bothered me so much if she was actually using the money to keep food in the house, or pay her actual rent, but she wasn't. There was still never any food in the refrigerator, and an eviction notice on the door every month. I wished I could've afforded to get my own place, but I couldn't. That's what made me begin to question my decision to settle for the job at the diner. It especially didn't make matters any better when Shae and her two girls came into the diner just days after I started working there. I, of course, had to serve them because the rest of the crew didn't show up.

"Hey, girl with the pretty hair," Shae said, with a smile.

The other two looked at me and rolled their eyes. I felt so humiliated. They sat there with their freshly styled hair, perfect makeup, and fancy clothes, while I stood there wearing an apron and Miss Val's shoes that she'd let me borrow because I didn't have any that were good enough for standing up in all day.

"Hi. What can I get you?" I asked Shae.

She hesitated and looked at the other girls.

"Are y'all thinking the same thing I'm thinking?"

The other girls shrugged their shoulders as to say they had no clue what Shae was talking about.

She continued, "I know I'm not the only one. Look at how pretty she is! Why in the world are you working here?"

I was flattered by Shae's compliment, and answered her the best way that I could.

"Because I need money," I said in a sarcastic tone. I didn't know what she wanted me to say. Why else would someone be working, outside of making money?

"Well, Honey, there are other ways to make money without having to serve people, isn't that right, girls?"

"Well, we do have to serve . . ." one of the girls said, before she was interrupted by Shae.

"We go to work looking nice every day, get paid for doing what we enjoy, don't do anything we don't want to do, and buy ourselves whatever we want. It doesn't get better than that. You should come check us out down the street at Club Venus when you got off tonight, or you can pull off that apron and those grandma shoes, and join us. You can be our special guest for the night."

"Lena, there are some guests over there. Can you go take their order? I'll handle this one," Miss Val said, as she quickly came over from behind the counter.

She looked at me sternly, telling me with only her eyes that she didn't like what was going on.

Before I walked away, Shae said, "Just think about it."

When I walked over to the table where I saw a mid-aged couple sitting, I asked them if I could get them something.

"Oh, no, thank you. The lady over there was just over here and we told her we're waiting for a couple of friends. We'll wait until they get here before we order," the woman said.

I glanced over at Miss Val who was over at Shae's table taking their orders. She glanced at me for a quick second and continued with what she was doing. She knew exactly what Shae was up to, and made sure she stepped right in the middle of it. Although Miss Val didn't say anything about what had happened, knowing that she knew what Shae was talking to me about made the rest of the evening a little uncomfortable. I knew Miss Val was just trying to look out for me, but she wasn't my mother. I barely even knew her, and she just needed to let me pave my own way. She didn't know anything about my situation, therefore, she didn't realize the pennies she was paying me didn't make it hard for me to be persuaded to go elsewhere if it meant there would be an easier way out for me.

I couldn't help but to be curious after thinking about everything Shae had said about her job before Miss Val had intervened. When I left work for the evening, I decided to take the long way home. The "long way" involved walking past Club Venus. I didn't plan on trying to get in. I knew I wouldn't be able to anyway, because I was underage. I wasn't sure how Shae and the other girls worked there, or how they were going to get me in, but obviously, whatever they were doing was working for them. I just wanted to get a quick peek inside to get a vibe of what it was like.

As I stood in front of the club, I stared at the multi-colored bright lights, and heard the loud music playing from inside. Suddenly, I heard a loud horn coming from out near the road.

"Lena!" Miss Val yelled out the window from the inside of her car.

I took a deep breath and shook my head. I quickly walked over to her car and said, "What are you doing here? There's an hour left before the diner closes."

"No! What are you doing here? And it's my diner so when I say it's time to close, it's time to close! Get in this car!"

I rolled my eyes, but did as I was told. As I sat in the car, I looked straight ahead with my arms folded. There was so much I wanted to say, but I wasn't disrespectful. Especially not to my elders. I could feel Miss Val's stare burning a hole in the side of my face.

"Lena, look at me."

I slowly turned my head towards Miss Val.

I'm not trying to be your mother, but I know she wouldn't like what's been going on through your mind. I'm just trying to save you. You don't want to go down that road. Trust me. I've been there," she said, as her stern expression turned into a look of shame.

She then had my full attention. I unfolded my arms and sat up in my seat as she put the car into drive.

As the car began to slowly pull off, she said, "From the moment I saw you a few days ago, you reminded me so much of myself. You came into the diner looking lost. Just like I did thirty years ago. I walked in and sat in that same booth that you sat in. I couldn't do anything except cry. It felt like my life was over and I had nowhere to turn. I'd had two kids by two different grown men by the time I was seventeen. My mom and I didn't get along, so I had left home a little over two years before I walked into the diner that morning. I knew I couldn't take care of the kids on my own, so I even left my babies."

Miss Val began to cry. I handed her some tissue that I found in her center console. She wiped her tears and continued.

"Even though I felt like she hated me, I knew she would take good care of my kids. I didn't know if I would ever be able to take care of them, or if I really even wanted to. I walked the streets for a few months, sleeping at bus stops, shelters, or wherever I could find. I washed up in restaurant bathrooms and took food off of customer's leftover plates on my way out. I thought all of that was the worst of it."

"What happened?" I asked.

"I hope you don't mind me pulling over for a minute. I don't like talking about all of this, but something in my spirit is telling me that this is necessary to help you. Sometimes you don't know why you're going through certain things, but there is always a reason. I truly believe you are my reason," she said, as she parked in front of a random house.

"God put us in each other's paths so that my testimony can help you," she said.

2 "Has the Lord redeemed you? Then speak out! Tell others he

has redeemed you from your enemies." – Psalms 107:2 NLT

I was hoping she wasn't about to get all religious on me because I wasn't trying to hear any of that. She shut the car off and turned her body completely towards me. Her eyes were full of tears as she looked at me.

"I ran into some girls that I knew from school, and they had found a way to make some quick money. They just so happened to be exotic dancers. They told me how easy it was to make money, and I was easily influenced. At that point, I was willing to do about anything to get off the streets. I wanted a clean bed to sleep in and a decent meal. My kids weren't even on my mind anymore. Anyway, they introduced me to the owner of the club where they danced. It used to be in this area, but that was a long time ago and it's not open anymore. The owner was really nice and agreed to let me come on board as long as the other girls taught me the ropes. I turned out to be pretty good at it. That wasn't such a good thing, or anything to brag about, but I did it "successfully" for a little over two years. I made really good money. I rented a nice apartment and furnished it all on my own. I was even able to buy a car."

"So why did you quit? You had the life you wanted. That's what I want for myself."

"All money isn't good money. Money isn't worth selling your soul to the devil, and that's what I'd done. Everything was going so well, and suddenly, it was all taken away within a matter of minutes."

36 "What good is it for someone to gain the whole world, yet forfeit their soul?" – Mark 8:36 NIV

"One night, or I should say, early morning, I was coming out of the club with a few of the other girls. It was a rule to never leave without a buddy, so we normally left in groups. We got all the way out to the parking lot, and I realized my keys weren't in my purse. Everyone was tired and didn't feel like waiting, so they left while I went back inside to get my keys. I scanned my keycard, walked inside, and down the hall to our dressing room. I looked all over, and my keys were nowhere in sight. I decided to go check the bathroom, so I stepped out into the hallway, and immediately noticed a man who I recognized from the crowd that night. I was wondering what he was doing back there, and who had let him in. He started running towards me, telling me how beautiful I was and how he enjoyed watching me on stage dance for him. I was running and screaming, hoping someone would hear me. After closing, the owner would normally still be inside the building for a while, making sure everyone was gone. I don't know where he was that night, but if he had been there, things may have not gone so badly for me. As I tried to run in my heels, I fell and twisted my ankle. I took my shoes off and threw them at the man, but he still continued to get closer and closer as I tried to run on my injured ankle. Next thing I knew, I felt a strong arm grab me around my waist. I tried my best to get away, but I was so small, he just overpowered me."

Miss Val paused, held her head back, and took a few deep breaths. I grabbed her hand and held it as she tried to regain her composure.

"He took me into the laundry closet, and he raped me. He looked at me afterwards like I was a dirty dog, and he spat on me. I had never felt so degraded in my life. Not even dancing on that stage. I had no keys, no shoes, and my clothes were ripped. Mascara ran down my face as I walked the streets once again. At that moment, I realized when I had walked the streets for months, it had been by choice, and I was in control, although it didn't feel like it at that time. That night, it was not by choice, and I had lost all control. As I walked, I felt empty inside. I didn't have any direction. It was dark, and everything was still closed. Well, I thought everything was closed, until I saw lights on in a building straight ahead. It was the diner. That's when I walked in and sat in that booth, and Miss Nora changed my life."

Miss Val went on to tell me that Miss Nora was the owner of the diner before it became hers. She didn't have any children or a husband. The diner was her life, but when Miss Val went into the diner that early morning, she became a big part of Miss Nora's life. She took Miss Val in and gave her a job waitressing at the diner, just like Miss Val had done for me. Miss Val admitted that she'd lied to me about applying at the diner because she was desperate to make sure that I didn't make a decision that I'd regret.

She said she never looked back at the strip club after that night. She just focused on trying to better herself. She had told Miss Nora about her children, and she replied by telling her that she needed to bring her kids to live with her, and be a real mother to them. Miss Val felt ashamed of herself and couldn't face her mother after she'd realized how unreasonable, selfish, and unappreciative she had been towards her. She'd had two kids at a young age, yet, her mother was still supportive. Miss Val admitted that she just wanted to do what she wanted to do, and her mother wasn't allowing that. They fought and fought, until Miss Val decided to leave her mother and her kids behind.

After about a year of living with Miss Nora, Miss Val finally felt like she was in a good place mentally, emotionally, and financially. She wasn't making great money at the diner, but it was enough to give her the ability to fully care for her children. She was nervous, but Miss Nora helped to encourage her to go to her mom's house one Saturday afternoon. The entire drive to her mom's house, she talked to herself, trying to hype herself up. The more she did, the more excited she became.

When she turned down her mom's street, she noticed an ambulance in the cul-de-sac where her mom's house was located. As she got closer, she realized it was right in front of her mom's house, and she saw one of her mom's longtime friends standing outside talking to one of the paramedics. Miss Val quickly parked and jumped out of the car. She ran over to her mom's friend, Beverly, interrupting the discussion that was in progress. She noticed Beverly had tears in her eyes.

"What's wrong?" she asked nervously.

"Oh, Val. I'm so sorry. I should've come and checked on her earlier when she said she wasn't feeling well," Beverly said, as she wrapped her arms around Miss Val.

Miss Val's mom had been sick that morning, but didn't think much of it. She had talked to Beverly on the phone and mentioned it. Beverly asked her if she needed anything and she told her that she would be ok. She tried calling her a little later to check on her and she didn't answer, so she decided to stop by. When she rang the doorbell, she could hear Val's two kids crying, and the oldest, which was her five-year-old daughter, opened the door. Val's mom was lying on the kitchen floor, unresponsive. They found out later that she had suffered a heart attack. Beverly told Miss Val that her mom had been looking for her, and would talk about her all the time. She would say how things could've been easily resolved, and blamed herself for being too hard on Miss Val. Sadly, she died feeling as though maybe she hadn't shown her daughter enough love. She was hoping that she would someday come back home. She did, but it was too late.

After losing her mom, Miss Nora built an even stronger relationship with Miss Val. She became like a mother to her, and a grandmother to her kids. When Miss Nora became too old to live on her own, Miss Val moved her into her mom's home with her and the kids. She lived until she was eighty, and when she died, Miss Val found out that she'd left her entire estate to her, including the diner. In remembrance of her, Miss Val never changed the name of the diner.

"Lena, my mom died of a broken heart because of me," Miss Val said.

After being silent for a moment, she said, "I don't know what your situation or relationship is with your mom, but whatever it is, please fix it. I don't want you to end up with the same regret that I had. It took me a long time to stop blaming myself all the time. I have my days that I still feel like it's my fault, but again, I also know everything happens for a reason."

I had never really talked to anyone about my mom, but that night after Miss Val had shared so much with me, I decided to share the part of me that I didn't share with anyone, with her. When I finished telling her about what happened to my mom, she looked more in shock than I did after she had told me all that she'd experienced. I even told her about my Aunt Donna, and the reason why I needed money so badly. Miss Val was the first person to be able to earn my trust since my mom had died. Before then, no one had made me feel loved. I knew it hurt Miss Val to tell her story, but it made me feel more special than I had ever felt to anyone. For her to put herself through the pain of recounting what she had gone through just to make a point to me and try to help save my life meant a lot. No amount of money could've ever bought what she had given me that night. She had provided me with a sense of acceptance and security. I continued to work for Miss Val, and I became so close to her and her kids that I finally felt like I was a part of a real family. Miss Val had become by Miss Nora, and I was grateful for her.

Chapter Five

"Table four is ready to order!" Miss Val yelled from the register, as more and more people rushed into the diner.

I had been working there for a little over a year, and it had been one of the busiest days I'd seen since I'd been working there. Miss Val was running a special of buy a breakfast, lunch, or dinner entrée, and get one free. It seemed like everyone was looking for a free meal. I had promised Miss Val that I'd work the afternoon and night shift because we had assumed it would be super busy.

After my first couple of hours, my feet were killing me from running from table to table. There were three other waitresses working, including my cousin Lily, but they were all pretty new since Miss Val had to fire most of her previous staff because they weren't reliable. Lily decided to come work with me after she graduated from high school. She could've gone off to college, but didn't want to leave her sister and brother who were only thirteen. We planned to save up enough money together to get our own place, because not only was Aunt Donna getting part of my paycheck, she was also taking part of Lily's. Since Lily had just started working at the diner, we'd agreed to wait six months before making our move, so she could get her half of the money. We knew Aunt Donna wouldn't make it easy for us when the time came, but she would have no choice. Lily was just worried whether or not she would be able to get the twins away from her. I told her we would just have to face that battle when the time came.

Miss Val saw how tired I looked, running around the diner, trying to do everything, so she said she'd cover for me on the floor while I took a break. I had told her about my panic attacks when I started working for her so that she didn't become alarmed if I ever had one in her presence. She just always tried to make sure I didn't get overwhelmed. I was so relieved, and always so grateful that I had Miss Val to always look out for me. She always made sure I had everything I needed before I went home every night, including food for my family. I sat in the back of the diner and took off my shoes to rest my feet for about fifteen minutes, and took a deep breath before going back out into the madness.

When I got back to the front, it seemed like things had calmed down a bit. I sighed in relief, and went over to Miss Val and asked her if everyone had been taken care of.

"There's a family that just came in and sat at the table over by the door. You might want to go help them. I've never seen them in here before, and I know you'll give them a good first impression. Maybe they'll come back," she said, as she smiled and winked at me.

"I got you, Miss Val!" I said, as I walked over to the family's table.

There was a woman who looked like a supermodel sitting there with a little girl who looked to be around ten years old. They were both looking at their menus.

"Hi! Can I get you all something to drink while you look over the menu?" I asked.

"Yes, please. Can I have a sweet tea?" the woman said, as she smiled, showing off her gleaming white, perfect teeth.

As I started writing on my order pad, the woman said, "Wow! That is so weird!"

I raised my eyebrow and said, "What's wrong?"

"Is that a birthmark?" she asked.

I immediately became offended that the woman would say that my birthmark was weird.

"Yes, it is, and why would it be weird? I asked with a slight attitude.

"No, I'm sorry. I'm not saying weird in that sense. It's just so distinctive."

She then turned to the little girl, who was still looking down at the menu, and said, "Laila, look up for a second."

The little girl looked up at me, and I gasped as my mouth almost hit the floor.

"Hey, Babe! You got back right in time. Look at this," the woman said, looking behind me, gesturing for someone to come over.

"My husband was in the bathroom. He's coming over now. He has to see this," she said excitedly.

When I turned around, the man stopped in his tracks, looking like he had seen a ghost.

"Malcolm?" I said.

"Wait. You know her?" said the woman, who I assumed from the huge rock on her finger, was Malcolm's wife.

Malcolm took a deep breath as he stood there speechless. He slowly sat down in the empty chair across from the woman. She sat there, looking back and forth, waiting for one of us to say something. I could feel my body heating up, and my blood boiling over. I couldn't believe Malcolm wouldn't even claim me as his, but had an entire family with a new daughter. It made me wonder what was wrong with me. Why could he accept her and not me? The only emotion I felt was anger. Malcolm had felt like he could buy me off with a thousand dollars and never see me again. Now I could see the full picture. He didn't want me to cause any problems in his perfect little world with his perfect wife and perfect daughter who I shared the same birthmark with.

The woman became impatient, and angrily said, "Malcolm! Are you going to tell me who this is?"

He finally replied by saying, "This is Lena."

"I know that by her nametag! Don't treat me like I'm stupid. You know I can't stand that, so how do you know Lena?"

He took too long to respond, and I was tired of playing the games, so I said probably loud enough for the entire diner to hear, "Look lady! It's not rocket science. Look at us! Look at the three of us with our weird little birthmarks! How do you think he knows me? I'm his daughter! His first daughter! The one he tried to pay off a year ago to try to keep you happily in the dark! Well, everything done in the dark comes to light!"

I couldn't hold back my tears any longer. I was so upset, I could barely breathe. I looked around and it seemed like everyone was looking at me. The room began spinning, and I then felt myself hit the floor. All I could hear was the woman and Malcolm arguing back and forth. I was hyperventilating when suddenly I felt someone pick me up. I was being carried by someone, and I didn't know by who, or where they were taking me, so I tried to fight them and wiggle my way out of their arms, but whoever it was, held me so tight that I could barely move. My vision was completely distorted.

"She has panic attacks. She needs to calm down," I could hear Miss Val say, but I couldn't see her.

I suddenly heard a calm, manly voice in the midst of all the commotion.

"Just breathe. Focus on one breath at a time."

I closed my eyes as I tried to control my breathing, hoping that when I reopened them, I'd have a clear view of who this person was.

"Come on. Let's count to ten. Breathe with me," the man said.

As we counted to ten, and my breathing calmed down, I repeatedly blinked my eyes. Coming into clear view was a very attractive guy who looked like he may have been in his mid-twenties. He knelt in front of me on the floor, holding my hands until my breathing sounded normal.

"Thank God!" Miss Val said.

I looked around and saw Lily standing in the corner looking scared. She had never seen me like that, and I could tell she was worried and felt helpless.

The man put his hand over my heart, and asked, "How do you feel, now?

Before I could answer, Miss Val said, "Thank you so much young man. I've never seen her have an attack before, but I'm so glad you were here and knew what to do. What's your name?"

"I'm Karter, and you're very welcome. It was actually my pleasure," he said, looking at me as he smiled.

He then took his finger and wiped the tears from my eyes.

Miss Val's expression of gratitude quickly faded, and she went into protector mode.

"Where are you from?" Miss Val asked as she folded her arms.

"I'm from around here. You don't have to worry about me. I heard about the diner and the special you were running, and thought I'd drop by. It just so happened that I was in the right place at the right time."

Speaking of right places at the right time, I had remembered what caused me to lose it. I quickly jumped up and ran to the front of the diner. I looked at the table where Malcolm and his family had been sitting, and it was empty. I looked all around and didn't see them anywhere in sight. One of the new waitresses came over and asked me if I was ok. I asked her if she had seen where the family went that was sitting at that table. She told me they walked out without ordering anything right after I was taken to the back. I had thought Malcolm was really trying to help me when he stopped me on the street that day, but he was actually just a coward hoping that his past didn't catch up with him. I was absolutely nothing to him except a skeleton in his filthy closet. In that one moment, I felt so much hate develop in my heart for him that I was afraid of what I might've done if I'd ever seen him again. He had implanted a subconscious fear of rejection within my mind that would cause me to never be the same.

10 "**Even if my father and mother abandon me, the Lord will**

hold me close." – Psalms 27:10 NLT

Chapter Six

After that evening full of unwanted excitement, the diner's business boomed. We were busy every single day, and each day, there was a different crowd. The one thing that the crowds did have in common each day was Karter. There was not a day that went by that he didn't show up, and Miss Val kept her eye on him. He never did or said anything out of the way. He just came and had a meal just like everyone else, but he was sure to take his time eating. Most days he would bring in a bookbag full of books, and dug into them while he ate.

I would always catch Lily walking over to his table batting her lashes, trying to spark a conversation with him, but he didn't seem the least bit interested in whatever she was saying. She didn't care. She would just continue talking, and sometimes she would take her break and sit down right across from him without an invitation. It was a little entertaining to watch, and would actually put a genuine smile on my face.

"You know he comes here every day to see you, right?" Miss Val whispered in my ear as I stood behind the register, watching Lily grin in his face.

"He does not, Miss Val! I think he gets a kick out of Lily throwing herself at him," I laughed.

"Yeah, ok. Believe that if you want to. I'm watching him, though. I don't trust anyone I don't know anything about. Especially when I see them every day."

"Well, you don't have to watch him on my behalf. I don't have time to be involved with anyone. I have to stay focused on what I want in life. And besides, after how my own "dad" did me, I trust no man!"

"Lena, you can't put all men in the same category just because of your experience with Malcolm. Believe me, he doesn't know what he's missing. You are a wonderful person."

Miss Val used to always compliment me, but they would go through one ear and out the other. I just always felt like she said those things to make me feel good, or she just felt like it was the right thing to say. If anyone who didn't know me had heard the way she complimented me, they would've thought I was someone special. If I had been that special, I was sure life would've been a whole lot easier for me.

"Look!" Miss Val said, rapidly tapping me on the shoulder.

Lily was walking towards us, away from Karter's table. We watched Karter as he shook his head. I felt bad for Lily. She tried so hard, but she couldn't make that man show any interest in her.

Lily came behind the counter with me and Miss Val and said, "I'm trying to loosen him up. He's so shy. I know he likes me, but he's just scared to tell me!" she said, sounding frustrated.

Miss Val and I glanced at each other, probably thinking the same thing. Lily walked towards the bathroom, and as soon as she was out of view, Karter got up from the table and came up to the register.

"You ready to pay?" I asked.

"No," he said, without saying another word.

"You need something else?"

"Yes," he replied.

Miss Val and I stood there looking confused.

"Ok. What do you need? And please don't give me a one-word answer," I said, sounding just as irritated as I felt.

Karter took a deep breath and said, "You. I need you. I'm tired of playing these games and spending all of my money here just so I can have a good reason to see you." He looked at Miss Val and said, "No offense. I love this diner and the food is delicious, but, Lena, I don't want to have to have a reason to see you. I just want to see you just because."

Just then, we heard the door to the backroom slam.

"I'll handle it," Miss Val said, rushing to the back to console Lily after hearing the man she had a crush on express his feelings for me.

I didn't know what to say to Karter. I wasn't interested in being anything more than friends with him. I appreciated his interest in me, but not enough to let my guard down for him.

"I'm sorry, Karter. You seem like a nice person, but I really don't have a place in my heart for you. Not just you. For anyone. I'm a different kind of person. I've been through different kinds of stuff that'll cause me to probably never be able to have feelings for anyone."

Karter looked down at the counter, looking defeated. I didn't feel good about having to let him down, but I didn't want to lead him on. Miss Val and Lily still hadn't come back from the back, and we had more customers coming in.

"Again, I'm sorry. I have to help these customers, but I hope you understand."

As I began to walk away, Karter said, "You know what I understand? I understand you need me as much as I need you. I saw what you went through when you had that panic attack, and I understand I was there to help you for a reason. I'm supposed to be there to continue to help you."

I felt my heart do something strange, and I didn't like it. I had to get out of the situation I was in, and fast. I wanted absolutely no parts of it.

"If you need to help someone, try helping Lily. I think she actually wants your help. Now excuse me. I have people that I need to help," I said, as I walked over to one of the tables that had recently become occupied by two women.

"Hi ladies. Can I get you two something to drink?"

As I spoke to the women, out of the corner of my eye I saw Karter sadly walking towards the exit. Shortly after he left, Miss Val and Lily finally reappeared. As Lily walked past me looking disappointed, I looked back at Miss Val and she shrugged her shoulders. She later told me what we already knew. Lily had a huge crush on Karter. Miss Val tried to make her feel better. That seemed to be her specialty, but Lily wasn't trying to hear anything she had to say. Lily had it in her mind that Karter was interested in her, just as she was in him, but I, somehow, came in between their connection. From hearing what was going on through Lily's head, I knew that it would be a long walk home that evening.

After the diner was empty, I went to tell Miss Val good night while she finished up some things. I then went looking for Lily. She normally waited for me outside, but I didn't see her anywhere, so I began walking. After walking for a few minutes, I soon saw her in the distance.

"Lily!" I yelled.

I knew she had to have heard me, but she never turned around, so I began to jog to catch up to her. When I finally did, I began walking next to her, trying to catch my breath. She still didn't say anything, and never turned to face me.

"Lily. Talk to me. We're cousins. More like sisters. Do you really think I'd try to be with someone who I knew you liked? You know I've always looked out for you. I've wanted more for you than I've wanted for myself."

We stopped at an intersection where cars were flying by.

Lily finally faced me as we waited to cross, and said, "What is it about you that he likes so much? What do you have that I don't have?"

"I don't have anything you don't have," I said, throwing my arms out to the side. "In fact, I think you have more than what I have. I surely don't have a high school diploma. It really doesn't matter. I told him I wasn't interested, which I'm not, and even if I was, I would never ever do that to you."

"Really?" she said.

"Really. You never have to question my loyalty. You, Zoe, and Zion are all I have. Oh, and Miss Val."

Lily and I were not only like sisters, but we also looked like sisters. What I felt turned Karter off from her was that she was being so aggressive, but I didn't know how to tell her that without her taking offense. She was already in a sensitive state, and I didn't want to exasperate that.

"Thank you, Lena. Sorry for being such a brat," she said as she hugged me on the corner of the busy intersection.

When we got to the front of Aunt Donna's house, there was a car parked outside. I checked the hood to see how warm it was. That would tell us about how long she'd had company, and in turn, how drunk and high she probably was. The engine was cool, so with that being said, we didn't know which of her personas we would be dealing with when we walked in. The twins were probably closed up in the bedroom, just waiting for us to get home so they could eat.

Lily used her key to open the door. As soon as the door opened, the smoke that filled the house quickly began to escape. When we walked in, we immediately saw Aunt Donna sitting on the sofa, hugged up with one of her male companions, with a glass in one hand and a cigarette in the other.

"Hey girls. What did you bring us to eat today?" Aunt Donna asked with a huge smile on her face.

We both became extremely confused when we looked around at all the shopping bags that were lying around.

"What have you been doing today, and where did all this stuff come from?" Lily asked.

"What does it look like? I've been shopping," she laughed.

"Where did you get money, or did he take you shopping?" Lily asked Aunt Donna, while looking the man directly in the eyes.

Aunt Donna put her cigarette in the ashtray and stood up in front of Lily.

"He took me to the shopping center, but I shopped with my own money!"

The more and more questions that were asked, and the answers that Lily was getting from her mom, caused me to become more and more nervous. While they were still going back and forth, I quickly ran to the kitchen and flew down the basement stairs, skipping over half of them. I immediately saw that all of the paneling had been torn down off the walls, including the panel where I used to keep my stash of money. I had told Lily about it when I had first started hiding money there, but I had begun giving my money to Miss Val to hold on to because I knew I could trust her. Lily then began using my secret spot, keeping her entire savings there. It was gone. All of it.

I heard someone coming down the stairs. It was Lily, and as soon as she saw what I was looking at, she began crying and screaming. Aunt Donna then came walking slowly down the stairs.

With her speech slurring, she said, "The landlord came by here today to get started on getting this nasty basement remodeled, and he found my money I had forgotten that I'd stashed down here. Ain't that a blessing?"

Lily walked up on her and said, "You know that wasn't your money! How could you spend my money?!"

"Don't forget who you're talking to! This is my house, so it was my money! Y'all owe me more money anyway. If it wasn't for me neither of you would have a place to lay your heads."

She began walking back up the stairs, tripping on every other step before she finally got to the top. I felt sorry for Lily, and myself for that matter. That money was to help us get out of there, and now it was gone. I was trying to keep myself from becoming too upset, but it was hard. I just couldn't understand how Aunt Donna could be so uncaring. As I thought about being in that house for even one more day, my heart began pounding, and the room began to spin. I leaned up against the bare concrete wall, and slowly slid down.

As Lily was still crying, she turned around and saw me on the floor.

"Lena! What do you need me to do?"

Breathing heavily, I said, "Just go upstairs. I'll be there soon."

"But . . ."

"Just go, and stay away from your mom," I said.

Lily kept looking back as she walked up the stairs. I just liked being alone when I was having one of my moments. I didn't like feeling vulnerable, or for people to see me in a vulnerable state. At first, I would be afraid to be alone, but Aunt Donna had forced me to learn to deal with the attacks on my own, in my own way. I felt overwhelmed. It seemed like every time I had a plan that seemed as though it would work, or if I felt like I had some control over my life, something like this would happen.

10 "In his kindness God called you to share in his eternal glory by means of Christ Jesus. So after you have suffered a little while, he will restore, support, and strengthen you, and he will place you on a firm foundation." – 1 Peter 5:10 NLT

The next day, I was at one of my lowest points, and when I showed up for work, Miss Val could tell something wasn't right. She kept asking me if I was ok, and I constantly lied, telling her everything was fine. Truth was, I felt so lost. I didn't want to stay at Aunt Donna's for another night, and I wouldn't have if I hadn't been worried about Lily, Zoe, and Zion. I felt like they depended a lot on me to make them feel like everything was going to be ok, and I didn't want to let them down.

Miss Val finally got tired of me lying to her and pulled me to the side. I didn't want to be honest with her because I didn't want her to be worried about me.

"Lena, you know I know you, so I know when something is wrong. Now what is it?" she asked.

"I'm just so tired," I said, shaking my head. "Why do I have to go through so much?"

"The problem is you try to go through stuff alone. You don't have to try to do everything by yourself. I'm here to help if you just ask."

I ended up opening up, telling Miss Val about what had happened the night before when Lily and I got home. She became so upset, she wanted to go talk to Aunt Donna herself. I told her that it would be a waste of her time, and she would leave being even more upset than when she had gotten there.

"How about you come stay with me until you get things figured out? I can even try to find you an affordable place."

"I can't do that. You already do too much, and I'm thankful. I can't leave my cousins there with her anyway."

Miss Val put her hand up to her head and sighed.

"Lena, Lena, Lena. I know you love your cousins, but you have to think about yourself, too. These panic attacks are not normal, and your situation doesn't make them any better. I know you want to, but you can't save the world, so come stay in my extra bedroom. I'll move my clothes out just for you," she laughed.

I stood there thinking. Everything Miss Val had said was true, but it would just feel like I was abandoning my cousins.

"Do it," I heard Lily say in a soft, calm voice.

I turned around, and she was standing in the doorway. I didn't know how long she had been standing there, or what all she had heard, but she had obviously heard Miss Val's offer for me to live with her.

"Lily, I didn't know you were there."

"Go to Miss Val's. I know you want to. Don't stay because of us. We'll be fine. The twins will be eighteen before you know it, and we can all get out of there."

"Lily, they have five whole years before they're eighteen. You can't stay there that long."

"I'll figure it out," she said, as she walked out.

Miss Val looked at me and nodded her head. "It's the best thing for your health."

Chapter Seven

Miss Val lived in a cute, cozy brick home only a few miles from the diner. I had to admit, it was a much different feeling being there than I'd been accustomed to. I was comfortable, and she was happy to be able to give me the level of comfort that she had. She even made me go to the doctor to see if I could find out what was going on with me and those panic attacks. She felt like I was too young to be going through that, but what she failed to realize was that I may have been young on the outside, but I had some old things dwelling within me.

I first went to Miss Val's family physician, who ended up referring me to a psychiatrist. That resulted in me being diagnosed with having early signs of bipolar disorder, and I walked out with a prescription for medication that I would need to take daily to keep it under control. I was already a little familiar with bipolar disorder from what I'd heard Aunt Donna say about it. I hadn't shared with Miss Val that my grandmother was bipolar, and my mother was suspected to be. I honestly even believed my Aunt Donna was bipolar, so the diagnosis really didn't come as a surprise to me. Miss Val got the prescription filled, but I refused to take it. I felt like I had been dealing with it for several years on my own, and I knew how to live with it without putting medication into my body on a daily basis.

Lily and I didn't seem as close anymore. It seemed like she suddenly resented me, and even when I would ask how Zoe and Zion were, she wouldn't go into detail. She would just tell me they were fine, and would then go on about her business. She couldn't have been upset that I went to live with Miss Val. She had told me to go. If she hadn't, I would've never gone. Karter was still hanging around the diner, but not every day like he originally was. Lily would roll her eyes at him literally every time she saw him. If she walked past his table ten times while he was there, she would roll her eyes at him ten times. He and I kept our conversations to a bare minimum which was equivalent to saying hi and bye. I was actually surprised that he had even come back after the way I had rejected him, but he seemed to be over it, and minded his business for the most part, with his head in his books.

I was a little curious about what he was studying. I didn't know much about him at all, but it was probably for the best. Miss Val would sometimes stop by his table and have conversations with him, but she never told me what they would talk about, which I found a little strange. Miss Val and I talked about almost everything. All that I could assume was that she hadn't learned anything interesting enough about Karter that was worth talking about. At least that's what I initially thought.

One Saturday morning, I was supposed to be up bright and early with Miss Val, getting ready to get to work and serve breakfast. I woke up feeling out of sorts. I had been finding myself waking up that way more than often as of late. Miss Val had been noticing a change in me, and constantly worried, asking if I was taking my medication. Of course, I would tell her that I was, but I honestly didn't believe that was the solution to my problem. I would even get the refills when it was time, just so she would believe I was taking it. She told me to just stay home and rest that day. She even sent her daughter, Naomi, to bring me some breakfast by the house. I spent the afternoon drowning in inexplicable self-pity.

What I would experience during those times was hard to explain. My environment was no longer stressful, and I had no reason to really be sad or upset, but I just didn't feel like being bothered with anything or anyone. Some days I wouldn't even want to come out the bedroom all day. Not even to eat. Miss Val would have to drag me out of bed. Other days, I would be pumped with energy and optimism.

As I laid across the sofa staring at the TV, but not having a clue as to what was on, there was a knock at the door. I was hoping Miss Val hadn't sent Naomi back over to keep me company. She was really nice, and I loved her, but I was just not in the mood. I threw my blanket off and jumped up. I was wearing sweats and a tank top, and hadn't put even a finger through my disheveled hair. I was a mess. I ran my hands through my hair, trying to make it look as decent as possible as I walked to the door.

"Who is it?"

No one responded, so I slowly opened the door, peeking through the crack. On the porch was a gift-wrapped box with colorful balloons attached, floating in the air. I began looking around, trying to spot someone who may have left the gifts on the porch. I noticed a car parked in front, but no one was inside.

As I knelt down to pick up the perfectly wrapped box, I heard a voice.

"Hey, Beautiful."

I quickly stood back up, dropping the box. Karter was standing in front of me, holding a bouquet of flowers.

"Karter. What are you doing here?"

"I came to try to brighten up your day," he replied.

At that moment, I suddenly became self-conscious of my appearance, and tried to quickly get rid of Karter.

"I don't think Miss Val would like that you're here at her house."

"How do you think I knew where she lived? She's perfectly fine with it. She told me you weren't feeling well today, so I asked her if it was ok if I came by to check on you. I told you I wanted to be there to help you. I meant that."

I thought I had gotten through to Karter, but apparently, I hadn't. This also explained the conversations between Karter and Miss Val. It all had been a setup. I stood there staring at Karter as he held the bouquet of flowers, hoping that I didn't send him away. All I could think about was the first moment I saw him. The look in his eyes as he calmed me down. Then I thought about the day that he was so genuine in expressing how he felt about me. I had never before had anyone make me feel that way with only words, and it scared me. My life had been full of nothing but abandonment, heartbreak, rejection, and flat-out disappointment. I didn't care to be close to anyone else in my life. It was enough that I had allowed Miss Val to break down my walls in hopes that I wouldn't someday be hurt by her. I was afraid to take that chance with Karter or anyone else.

4 "I sought the Lord, and he answered me; he delivered me from all my fears." – Psalms 34:4 NIV

"So, can I come in, Lena? I promise I'm just here to try to make you feel better."

I picked the giftbox back up off of the porch, and held the door open, welcoming Karter inside.

Before he stepped inside, he stopped directly in front of me and said, "Thank you for trusting me."

At first, I was upset that Miss Val would allow Karter to come over without telling me what was going on, but I actually enjoyed his company. We did a lot of talking in the midst of ordering pizza and watching a couple of movies. I learned a lot about Karter, and I was kind of wishing that I'd given him the opportunity to be a friend to me sooner. He told me that he was twenty-two, and in his senior year of college. He was getting his bachelor's degree in Nuclear Engineering, and already had a job lined up once he finished. After Karter told me that he would soon be graduating from college, I was a little embarrassed to tell him that I didn't even have a high-school diploma. He had accomplished so much, and I didn't have anything. All I could say for myself was that I was the waitress at a restaurant and lived with my boss.

I decided to be upfront with him and tell him the truth. I put my head down in shame as I told him that I dropped out of high school. He put his hand on my shoulder and told me not to be ashamed. He said that I had plenty of time to do the things that I eventually wanted to do. That day, Karter gave me motivation, and a sense of purpose. He made me realize that it wasn't too late to make a difference in my life.

When Miss Val came home from the diner that evening, Karter was still at the house. When she walked in, we were still chatting, learning more and more interesting things about each other.

"Well, hey there you two," Miss Val said, as she walked in the door smiling.

She looked around and saw the pizza on the counter, the beautiful flowers that I'd put in a vase, crumbled up gift wrap on the floor, balloon ribbons hanging from the ceiling, and the fancy bottle of perfume Karter had bought, sitting on table.

"It looks like the two of you had a good day. Karter, it looks like everything worked out just as you planned."

"And how long has this been planned?" I inquired.

Karter began laughing, and said, "Well, Miss Val really didn't want to be a part of any of this at first, but she came around after I kept sweet-talking her."

"I just felt good about it, and I honestly felt that you needed a friend in your life. Especially since you and Lily haven't been talking like you used to," Miss Val said.

I had forgotten about Lily, and how much she liked Karter. The thought of her finding out that I'd befriended him, and that we had spent the entire day together immediately caused me to feel remorseful.

"Lily cannot know about this!" I said with authority.

"I don't think you have to worry about Lily. She had some young man hanging around the diner today. It reminded me of Karter hanging around the diner for you."

I heard what Miss Val said, but I knew Lily would still be upset about me and Karter hanging out. Especially when I told her that I would never do that to her. I would just have to eventually be honest with her, but I wasn't going to rush it. Especially when I didn't know if I was really ready for a full-blown relationship, or if Karter was going to decide that maybe I wasn't what he wanted after all. There was no point in adding more animosity and resentment between us if it wasn't necessary. For now, we would just take it day by day, and just continue to develop a healthy friendship. The way my mood changed, and was all over the place, for all I knew, the next day I might've woken up and dismissed Karter all over again. Only time would tell.

Chapter Eight

As time went by, Karter and I became closer and closer without Lily suspecting a thing. He would still come into the diner, like normal, but we saw to it that we didn't act any differently towards each other than we normally would. It wasn't hard for me because I didn't really feel anything romantic with Karter, but he was a very good friend. I felt a little bad because I knew that he had developed different types of feelings for me than what I had for him. When I would talk to Miss Val about it, she didn't understand how I couldn't have a desire to be more than friends with Karter. She had high hopes for us. Karter was tall, handsome, smart, educated, and very intelligent. He was everything that a girl could ever ask for, and he could've probably had any girl he wanted. I think that was precisely the reason I wouldn't open myself up enough to develop real feelings for him. He was just too good to be true, and too good for me. I knew he was way out of my league, and I just couldn't wrap my head around him wanting me out of everyone else he could've had.

Lily seemed as though she had gotten over being rejected by Karter. She no longer showed any anger towards him. Instead, when she saw him, she acted like she didn't know him. There was a guy who continued to come by the diner who she'd become very friendly with. She seemed happy when he was round, but when I would ask her anything about him, she would change the subject. She had started talking a lot about needing to make more money. She never mentioned that she had a plan, but one day, out of the blue, she didn't show up for work.

After I got off work that evening, I decided to go by Aunt Donna's house just to check on Lily to make sure she was ok. Karter offered to drive me, but I told him it wouldn't be a good idea for Lily to see us in the car together. Before leaving the diner, I told Miss Val I'd see her at the house later. On my way to Aunt Donna's house, I was hoping that nothing bad had happened. I knew how Aunt Donna could be, and I also knew that Lily was probably getting fed up.

I knocked on Aunt Donna's door and no one came. I knew someone was there because I could hear the music playing. I pounded on the door a few more times, thinking, maybe they couldn't hear me over the music. Finally, Aunt Donna opened the door, barely being able to focus her eyes.

"What do you want?" she asked.

"Hey, Aunt Donna. I was looking for Lily."

"Lily!" she yelled, as she walked away from the door and sat on the sofa.

Zoe appeared, and said, "Hey, Lena. Lily's not here. She went to work."

"She went to work?"

"Yeah. She left a little while ago. I think she got a new job though because she wasn't dressed like she normally is." She looked at my clothes and said, "Not like you."

I stood there confused, wondering where Lily could've gone.

"Ok, Zoe. Thanks. How have you and Zion been?"

Zoe looked over at her mom, and said, "We've been ok, as always."

When Zoe added "as always" I knew nothing had changed.

"You have my phone number, so if you need anything, just call me, ok?"

"Ok," Zoe said, as I gave her a hug.

I was about to tell Aunt Donna goodbye, but when I looked over at her, she had passed out. I began walking towards the bus stop to catch a ride home, and suddenly, I heard a car creeping up behind me. I didn't turn around to look, I just began to walk faster.

The car then pulled up on the side of me, and I heard, "Lena."

"Karter! What are you doing here? Why are you following me?"

"Get in. I was worried about you walking in the dark by yourself. I knew you'd need a way home anyway."

I hopped in the car and said, "Thank you, but I don't need you following me. I know how to take care of myself."

"I know you do," he said, smiling as we drove off.

I sat quietly in the passenger seat, even more concerned than I had been before I went by Aunt Donna's house. Lily had come to work every day that she was scheduled since Miss Val had hired her. She never missed a day.

"So, what happened?" Karter asked, interrupting my thoughts.

"She wasn't there."

"Where was she?"

"I don't know. If I did, I would have you driving me there right now."

"Wow. Sorry for asking."

I didn't mean to be rude to Karter. I was just frustrated. I liked being alone to try to figure things out without people asking me a million questions. First would come the questions, then would come judgement and opinions. I didn't need any of it.

I knew Karter's intentions were good, and he didn't deserve to be treated like that, which was exactly why I was immediately convicted by my words and had to apologize to him. I then began looking out the window as he continued to drive, attempting to recollect any conversations that I'd had with Lily that could've possibly given me a clue to where she might've gone. Nothing came to mind, but moments later, I saw something.

"Stop the car!"

"What?!" Karter said, sounding puzzled.

"Pull over."

Karter quickly pulled over on the side of the road. I jumped out and ran across the street. I had seen Lily, half-dressed, with a ton of make-up on, standing in front of Club Venus with the guy who had begun frequenting the diner.

When I approached her, she looked at me like I was small.

"Lily, what are you doing?"

She pointed her finger in my face, and said, "No, what are you doing? I'm not your responsibility. I'm the eldest cousin, remember?"

"I was worried about you! You could've told me what was going on!"

She looked over at Karter's car parked across the street, and said, "Just like you told me what was going on with you and Karter, right? You thought I didn't know? I'm the smart one. I'm the one with the high-school diploma, unlike you!"

"Karter and I are friends! That's it! You need to come with me. You don't have to do this."

The man then interjected. "She's not going anywhere. You had your chance. Didn't my dancer, Shae, try to recruit you? I heard you didn't take her up on her offer, and now you're mad and jealous that your cousin has this wonderful opportunity. I'm still willing to give you a chance. That is, if you want it."

The man that had been coming into the diner, flirting with Lily, happened to be the owner of Club Venus. He had recruited her right in front of my eyes, and I had no idea.

"Go! Get out of here. Go back to your little boy while I tend to my man," Lily said, as she shewed me away with her hand.

"Lily!"

"Go!" she yelled. "And don't try checking on me, or my sister and brother. We're good. I got this."

Hesitantly, I turned and walked away. It took a lot out of me, but I did, only because I heard Miss Val's voice in my head telling me that I couldn't save the world. When I got back into Karter's car, he reached over and gave me a hug, telling me everything would be ok. He was always so optimistic about everything. I guess that was the thing that allowed me to keep him hanging around. He would dissolve a lot of the sadness and anger I would feel, even on my worst days. I knew I couldn't let him go because I felt like my emotions would eventually kill me if I did.

Chapter Nine

An entire year went by, and I had continuously searched deep within my heart for the love that I desired to give to Karter, but I never could find it. I started to believe that I would never find it because it didn't exist. Every time I was around Karter, I felt as though I was trying to force myself to love him. He didn't seem to think anything was wrong, which I was surprised by since an occasional kiss was the most intimacy that we had in our relationship. I barely wanted him to even hug or hold me. I was ok with just conversation. I knew what I felt wasn't love. I wanted desperately to be able to show, and have the same type of unconditional love for Karter that he had for me. I felt guilty because I did feel like I was holding him back from finding someone who would reciprocate that same type of love, because he truly deserved it. I had finally acknowledged and accepted the fact that Karter just wasn't for me, and I planned to make it a priority to tell him just that so that he could start fresh without me being a distraction.

Karter had achieved so many huge accomplishments that he was extremely excited about. He had stayed committed to accomplishing his goal of finishing college, which he did. He had a promising career working at the biggest power plant in the state, and was now purchasing his own home. He had already accomplished all of this, and was only twenty-three years old. I was very proud of him, and made sure I was at his celebration dinner to help commemorate his achievements. I felt honored to be a part of his life during a time when he managed to reach so many milestones.

Karter had made reservations at a fancy steak and seafood restaurant Downtown. He had even invited his mom, who I had never met, because she lived out of town. That made me nervous. Karter kept telling me not to worry, and that his mom would love me. I was afraid that she would see right through me and know that I didn't have deep feelings for her only child. Karter also invited Miss Val to come, which made me feel a little better. She was the closest thing I had to a mom, and if things got uncomfortable, I was sure she'd have my back.

"Hey, you two!" Miss Val said as she arrived, walking up to the table where we were already sitting.

We both stood up and gave Miss Val a hug, as if we hadn't just seen her hours before.

"Where's Mom?" she asked, looking at Karter.

"Oh, she hasn't gotten here yet. She's driving, and said the traffic was pretty thick on the way in. She should be here in the next twenty minutes or so."

"Oh, good. I can't wait to meet her!"

Miss Val continued to talk to Karter about his new home, and how proud she was of everything he'd accomplished. Karter expressed his gratitude to her for being one of the people in his life who motivated him, and showed him support during the short period that he'd known her. He told her that even though she didn't seem too fond of him at first, she ended up being like a second mother to him.

I soon heard the sound of heels clicking across the tiled floor. The sound got closer and closer. It then stopped, and when I looked in the near distance, I saw a well put together woman who was wearing a tan colored pant suit, and black heels. She had short, blonde hair that was beautifully styled, and complemented her light-golden skin tone perfectly. She was speaking with one of the hostesses, who pointed in our direction, informing her of where we were seated.

"There's Mom now," Karter said, as he stood up smiling bigger than I'd ever seen him smile before.

She opened her arms widely before she even made it to our table, anxiously awaiting to embrace her son.

"Hey, Baby!" she said, as she hugged him, and gave him a big kiss on the cheek.

"Mom, this is my girlfriend I've been telling you about, Lena, and our good friend, Miss Val. She owns the diner where Lena works."

Miss Val and I stood up to shake Karter's mom's hand.

"It's so nice to meet you Ms. . . .," Miss Val said, waiting for Karter's mom to tell her what her name was as she shook her hand.

"Mrs. Robinson," Karter's mom said, but you can call me Shari."

I wouldn't have known what to call Karter's mom either, and was a little glad that Miss Val had walked into that one first. I knew Karter's parents had been married, but I also knew that his dad had passed away from cancer years ago.

"Nice to meet you, Shari," Miss Val said.

"You as well, Miss Val," Karter's mom said.

Miss Val laughed, and said, "That's just for the kids. You can call me, Val."

Mrs. Robinson then turned to me, and I held out my hand, and smiled. She looked at me as if she was dissecting every part of me, tearing me apart, piece by piece. I somehow felt violated.

"She then shook my hand, and said, "Hello, Lena. You're not what I expected," she said.

I didn't know if that was a good thing or a bad thing, but I just shook her hand, and replied, "Hi, Mrs. Robinson. Nice to meet you."

Miss Val knew that it had already become uncomfortable for me, so she led the conversation.

"Shari, I just want you to know you have raised a wonderful young man! I love to see our young people go after what they want and get it."

"Thank you, and yes, he's always been a go-getter," she said, as she looked at him, smiling.

Karter made his mom's entire face light up. Seeing other people and their relationships with their parents sometimes made me sad because I knew that I would never have that, but I couldn't feel sorry for myself, and I just had to work with the hand that was dealt to me.

We all ordered our food, and while we waited, I listened to Miss Val, Mrs. Robinson, and Karter converse about a little of everything, from raising kids, to college life, to the housing market. I didn't have any input on any of it because I didn't have any experience in any of it. I felt so out of place, and my heart was pounding the entire time. I tried to smile from time to time just to show I was being attentive.

Suddenly, Mrs. Robinson turned to me and asked, "So, Lena, how old are you?"

"I'm nineteen."

"Nineteen? Karter, you didn't tell me you were robbing the cradle."

"It's no big deal, Mom. Lena is very mature for her age."

"I can vouch for that," Miss Val said. "She's a good girl."

"So, are you a freshman or sophomore in college?" Karter's mom asked.

I hesitated, then said, "Neither. I just work at the diner."

"Oh," she said, as she blatantly cut her eyes at Karter. "So, what do you plan on doing with your life?" she asked.

Just then, two waitresses came over with our food, and began setting plates in front of us. I was wishing at that moment that they wouldn't leave. I didn't know how to answer Mrs. Robinson's question because I had no idea what I was going to do with my life. I, for sure couldn't let her find out that I hadn't even graduated from high school. None of that would even matter very soon because I was going to end it with Karter anyway. I had no business even allowing it to get this far. I had allowed myself to get in a situation that could've easily been avoided.

After the waitresses finished putting our plates in front of us, I excused myself and went to the bathroom. I just needed to calm down. I stood in the mirror, looking at myself, asking myself what I was doing. I took a few deep breaths and splashed water on my face.

"Get it together, Lena. She's just a person just like you," I said to myself.

When I walked back towards the table, it looked like the three of them were having a good conversation. I was hoping that Mrs. Robinson had forgotten about her last question, but she started back right where she had left off.

"So, Lena, while you were in the bathroom did you figure out what your plans are?"

Miss Val and I both looked at Karter, wondering if he was going to speak up for me, but he just held his head down.

"I'm not sure what I want to do yet. I'm just taking my time for now to find what really interests me."

"Hmm. Well, that's what high school is for. You should have the answer to that by now."

I took a deep breath, not knowing what else to say.

"Mom. Everyone is not the same. Everyone doesn't know what they want to do when they finish high school. Isn't it better just to wait if you're not sure instead of wasting other people's time and money?" Karter said.

The table then became completely silent. We all sat there eating our dinner. I only finished half of mine because I no longer had an appetite.

Breaking the silence, Miss Val said, "That was delicious, but the best part of this was getting together to celebrate Karter."

"Most definitely," Mrs. Robinson agreed.

"I thank all of you, but that may not be the best part of the evening," Karter said.

We all raised our eyebrows in curiosity, wondering what could've been any better than the reason for the evening.

Karter suddenly stood up, and we all looked up at him. He then faced me and knelt down right in front of me. I immediately began to feel like I was going to regurgitate the little bit of food I'd just eaten. I wanted to stop what was happening, but I didn't know how. I looked over at Miss Val hoping she could help me, but she sat there with her mouth wide open. She was just as shocked as I was. Mrs. Robinson looked so angry, I thought she was about to jump up and snatch Karter up off of the floor.

He held a small black box that held a beautiful diamond ring, and said "Lena, I know we've only been a couple for a little over a year, but I love you so much. You've been here with me while I finished this part of my journey, but I want you to be a part of the rest of my journey."

"Karter!" his mom interrupted.

Karter turned to his mom and said, "Mom, I'm a man, and as a man I know what I want, so please let me do what I need to do to get what I want."

She looked as if she was going to cry. She began twiddling with the napkin that was in her lap, and looked in every direction except in the direction of where her son was professing his love to me.

"I need you in my life, Lena. I know what life has been like for you, and I want to complement you, and make it better. Please marry me so that we can become each other's better halves."

I stared at Karter, still in shock. No words would come from my mouth. Karter stared back at me, looking as if he was trying to read my mind. If he could've read my mind, he probably would've jumped up off the floor and left me sitting right there in that restaurant, never speaking to me again. All I could think about was how I didn't love this man, and wondered if I'd ever be able to love him. I was about to break up with him after the dinner, and at that moment I felt like I was trapped. I felt like I'd hurt him if I said no, but I'd also hurt him if I said yes and he ended up realizing that I didn't love him. His mom squinted her eyes at me as I quickly tried to weigh the pros and cons of saying yes, and those of saying no.

"Ok, Karter. I'll marry you," I finally said, already having remorse.

Karter stood up and grabbed my hand, helping me up out of my chair, and gave me a hug. Miss Val stood up clapping, and used her napkin to wipe the tears from her eyes. Mrs. Robinson remained in her seat with her arms folded. I knew that she saw straight through my acceptance to Karter's marriage proposal, which gave her even more ammunition to dislike me more than she already did. I didn't know if, or when Karter and I would actually end up getting married, but if we did, something miraculous would've had to happen to make me see Karter as more than just a friend.

Chapter Ten

After that evening, Karter and his mom's relationship was never the same. She told him if he married me, he would be making a big mistake, and he could forget that she was ever his mother. He begged her not to make him choose, but she was uncompromising about her position, and would take the chance of losing him because she didn't want to accept me. That put so much more guilt on me because that was his mother, who for sure loved him, and would be there for him forever. My love for him would always be questionable. Miss Val told me that every couple that got married wasn't in love, and many times, that kind of love came later. She also said that those were oftentimes the marriages that lasted a lifetime. She gave me some hope that I would get through it, and someday I would wake up loving Karter as much as he loved me, or maybe even more.

Karter wanted to get married soon. He told me that his biggest motivation in purchasing a home was so that he would have a place for us. He was so confident that I would say yes when he proposed that he bought a house for us before he even bought an engagement ring. I really didn't want to come in between him and his mom's relationship, and I kept asking him how he felt about the situation to make sure he knew the repercussions of what he was doing. All he would say was that she had made her decision, and if she would end her relationship with him over who he chose to be his wife, then she never cared about him at all. He told me that I would be number one in his life, just like his mom had been number one in his dad's life.

24 "That is why a man leaves his father and mother and is united to his wife, and they become one flesh." – Genesis 2:24 NIV

With that being said, Karter and I had a very small wedding ceremony in the backyard of his home. It became our home after the wedding, and because it was quite a distance from where the diner was located, we decided with Miss Val that it made more sense for me to quit instead of dealing with the commute. It was hard for me to leave the diner and Miss Val, but I knew I could call or visit whenever I felt the need.

Karter invited his mom to the wedding, even though she had told him how she felt, and he knew she was adamant. I felt he was hoping that she would still show, but unfortunately, she didn't. Regardless, he enjoyed the day, and seemed like the happiest man alive.

That was the night we finally became intimate and consummated our marriage. It seemed to enhance my feelings for Karter, but they still hadn't reached my expectations. I didn't intentionally wait until we got married, but I believed, Karter did. Growing up, I wasn't introduced to religion. I had never gone to church, or heard anyone around me talk about God until I met Miss Val. No one I knew ever even prayed. I didn't know much about it, and I had no desire to entertain it, because as far as I was concerned, religion didn't exist, and God didn't exist.

Karter grew up in church, but recently he hadn't been as involved as he had been when he was younger. He did believe in God wholeheartedly, and I would often hear him pray, but that was as much religion that came through our house. When I told him that I didn't believe in God, he seemed extremely bothered by it, which let me know that his beliefs were very important to him. I honestly believed that our beliefs and non-beliefs regarding religion would be the end of us, but Karter still didn't give up on me.

We had never spoken of our religious beliefs until after we got married, which had probably been our first mistake, and once we did, I tried to avoid any more of those conversations. I explained to him that even if someone had tried to convince me at that time, including him, I could never believe that "God" could allow a child to go through the things that I had. With that being said, I preferred to just believe that we were put on this earth to fend for ourselves.

14 **"Do not be yoked together with unbelievers. For what do righteousness and wickedness have in common? Or what fellowship can light have with darkness?"**
– 2 Corinthians 6:14 NIV

He seemed shocked by my response, but he always told me that he wanted me to be honest with him, so I tried to do that to the best of my ability. There were times, however, that the truth just wasn't that simple.

Early on, I had expressed to Karter that I didn't want any children. My childhood had been so depressing that I didn't feel like I knew how to give a child a good life, and refused to bring a child into the world. Karter struggled with accepting my decision, but he had no choice. He tried to tell me to be more open-minded, and to realize that our life was a lot different than the life that I had. He wanted so badly to convince me that our child, or children would have a wonderful life because they would have wonderful parents. I couldn't argue that Karter would've been a wonderful dad, but I had no clue how to be a mother.

My way of thinking was different than most, and I blamed it on the life that I had previously lived. I was born into nothing and fought my way through life. I'd inadvertently found my way into the life I'd always dreamed of. On my way to getting there, I had adapted to every situation that I had been faced with, and never asked anyone for anything. As bad as my situation was, I'd tried to help whoever I could along the way. It was my turn. Sharing the life that I had worked so hard for with another human being didn't at all sound enticing to me. I was too selfish at that point in my life to be a mother, and I believed I had every right to be. I had earned the right to want what I had only for myself.

17 "You say, 'I am rich; I have acquired wealth and do not need a thing.' But you do not realize that you are wretched, pitiful, poor, blind and naked." – Revelations 3:17 NIV

After a couple of years of being married to Karter, I suddenly became ill. I began experiencing hot flashes where I would wake up drenched, severe headaches, and a terrible case of nausea. I had a feeling of what was going on, but didn't want Karter to know just yet, so I kept it to myself. While Karter was at work one morning, I went and picked up a pregnancy test from the pharmacy around the corner. When I got back to the house, I was so nervous, that I could barely get the test out of the box. I was hoping that I wasn't pregnant because I didn't want to have to learn how to love a child the way I had to learn how to love Karter. I was still working on that.

After I took the test, I waited. I left the bathroom and paced the floor, hoping that maybe I had just caught a virus. A million and one thoughts were going through my head. I was thinking of reasons why I couldn't have possibly been pregnant. Then, a thought would cross my mind negating my previous theories. I had been so adamant about not wanting kids, and had been so cautious that I couldn't stand to think that all of my efforts had been in vain.

I had quickly become mentally exhausted from the thoughts flooding my mind. I went back into the bathroom to check my results. As I held the test and sat on the floor with my back up against the tub, all I could feel was disappointment. There were many women who would've been thrilled to find out that they were carrying a life inside of them, but not me. I couldn't stand the thought of it. I screamed to the top of my lungs hoping that I would wake up from my horrible nightmare.

"Babe," Karter said, as he gently shook my body that was buried underneath the covers. He then pulled the covers from over my head and said, "Lena. What are you doing already in bed? The sun is still up."

Karter had just gotten off of work, and awakened me out of a deep sleep. I began to think maybe I'd just had a bad dream. I couldn't remember actually going to the store, or taking a pregnancy test.

"I'm just tired. I just need to rest," I whispered

"Ok. I won't bother you. I'll be downstairs. Just let me know if you need anything."

"Ok," I whispered.

Karter gave me a kiss on the forehead before I pulled the cover back over my head.

A few minutes later, Karter came back and said, "Baby, is this what I think it is?"

At that moment I realized it hadn't been a dream. I had been moping around the house all day making myself feel even worse than I had already been feeling. I was so distraught after seeing the result of the pregnancy test, I had forgotten it on the bathroom counter. I remembered that my life really had gone from great to miserable in a matter of minutes.

Karter sat next to me on the bed and snatched the covers from my head again. He was holding the pregnancy test in front of my face.

"Were you going to tell me?" he asked.

I wiped my face with the palms of my hands.

"I actually hadn't decided yet."

"What did you plan on doing? Getting rid of it without me knowing?"

"I don't know Karter! I don't know!" I shouted.

He stood up and said, "What do you mean you don't know? I thought we were better than that. That's what we're doing now?"

"I'm just so confused," I said, crying uncontrollably. "You just don't understand! I can't be a mother! I just want my life to stay like this. I won't love this baby!"

"Lena, answer a question for me."

I looked at Karter, waiting for him to ask the question, but I definitely wasn't expecting what he asked.

"Did you love me before we got married?"

I sat there wondering why he was asking me that question. It just seemed to come from out of the blue, but I decided to finally be honest about it.

"No," I said reluctantly.

"I knew that, but I willingly sacrificed my relationship with my own mother for a woman who I knew didn't love me. I had hope that you would one day love me, which, I believe now you do. The same goes for this baby. You think you won't or can't love it, just like you thought you couldn't love me, but I believe you can, and you will. Give this baby a chance like you gave me a chance."

"But I don't want to be a disappointment like my mom was to me."

"You are not your mother. This baby will have a good life. Just be happy with me, because I'm ecstatic! The woman of my dreams is having my baby, and I'm going to do whatever it takes to take care of the both of you. It doesn't get better than that."

I sat up in the bed with my knees to my chin. Karter wiped the tears from my eyes.

"Lena, it's not that bad. I'm here to help you, and I'm not going anywhere. Look around us. We have the perfect life for a perfect baby girl or boy. Let's do this, Baby."

I still didn't understand how I had ended up with Karter. No matter what, he was always there for me. Even if he didn't agree with me, or understand me, he still listened. He was always so gentle and patient, and always knew how to talk me off the ledge.

No other man could've been there for me the way Karter was. That's how I knew I had no choice except to learn how to love him. I knew I didn't love him exactly how he needed to be loved, but I loved him the best way I knew how, and he knew that. Eight months later, we welcomed, our beautiful baby girl, Nadia Lynn Robinson, into the world.

Nadia

Chapter Eleven

"Every time I come into this kitchen, there's a sink full of dishes!" my mom yelled, as she threw the dirty dishes down on the kitchen floor, shattering them into pieces. "Maybe if I just break them all, people around here will start listening."

My mom was having one of her episodes that had become more and more frequent over the years. I didn't quite understand it, but my dad always told me to never take it personal. She could be the nicest woman in the world one minute, and the next, she acted as if she was completely out of her mind. I was even embarrassed to have company over because I never knew who she would be, or suddenly become, within the course of the day.

When I thought about the earlier memories of my life, I felt joy in my heart. There was no denying that there was an enormous amount of love in my home. I could recall waking up early on Saturday mornings, watching Saturday morning cartoons with my dad, while my mom cooked a big breakfast just for the three of us. Breakfast normally consisted of blueberry pancakes, which my mom made from scratch. From the sweet aroma that would sweep through the house, you would've thought she was baking a cake. They were my absolute favorite. I once asked her who taught her how to make them, and she had shared with me that she worked in diner before I was even born, and that was their specialty. She was only a waitress at the diner, but had learned how to prepare the meals just like the chefs who worked in the kitchen. That was how she learned how to cook almost everything. Most women learn to cook from their mom, but my mom's mom had died before she was able to teach her much of anything. I didn't really know the details, but it seemed to be a conversation that was off limits, so I didn't ask any questions.

After breakfast, we would walk to the park, which was a couple of blocks down the road. They would each hold one of my hands, and count to three before quickly lifting me up off the ground, and slowly lowering me down. I would laugh hysterically from the butterflies that would flutter through my stomach, then tickle my heart, as I went up into the air.

I felt like those moments would last forever. I was too young to know much about love and relationships back then, but I wasn't too young to know that we were happy. My mom sometimes seemed a little down, but my dad would always do something silly to make her laugh, or come home with flowers to brighten her day. I figured that it may have had something to do with not having her mom around. Whatever it was, she seemed to sleep it away, and everything would just go back to normal. I had something exciting to look forward to each and every day with the two of them. I couldn't have imagined life to be any different, but one day, things just seemed to change without any warning.

The first time I noticed something just wasn't right was one evening when my dad and I had returned home from a college basketball game. Watching basketball was one of the things we enjoyed doing together the most. We walked into the house laughing at one of the corny jokes I had told. That was another thing we were known to do. We'd go back and forth telling jokes to see who would laugh the hardest. When we walked into the house, it looked like it had been ransacked. Sofa cushions and pillows had been thrown all over the family room, and shattered glass covered the floor. My dad quickly grabbed my hand, afraid that someone might've been in the house.

"Lena," my dad yelled, calling out for my mom, but she didn't answer.

As we walked further into the house, to the kitchen, we noticed that all of the drawers were pulled out, and the cabinets were open. There were sheets of paper all over the kitchen table, and the trash was poured out of the trash can onto the floor.

All of a sudden, my mom came out of nowhere with a knife in her hand, charging towards me and my dad. My dad quickly pushed me out of the way and grabbed my mom's hand, snatching the knife from her and throwing it down. He was then able to turn her around with her back facing him, and wrapped his strong arms around her in order to restrain her. She faced me, and the look in her eyes gave me chills. It was indescribable. She looked completely empty inside, and I could tell she didn't really understand what was going on.

As I watched in fear from the kitchen's entryway, my dad began calmly speaking to her, as she continuously tried to wiggle her way out of his grip.

"Lena, everything is ok. Just calm down so we can talk about it."

"What do you want to talk about Karter?! You want to talk about the woman you've been spending time with? I can't believe you even took our daughter to see her! Did the three of you enjoy the game?" my mom yelled.

My dad turned her around to face him and continued to restrain her by holding her arms at her sides.

"What are you talking about, Lena? Nadia and I went to the game alone. There is no other woman. Your daughter and I went to the game. Do you understand?" he said slowly, making sure she understood what he was saying.

"Stop lying to me! I found all of the hotel receipts, and phone numbers of different women. I even found receipts to restaurants that we've never been to together," she said, sounding as if she really believed what she was saying.

I knew my mom had to have been out of her mind, because never in her right mind would she had ever believed that my dad would cheat on her, especially with me hanging around. Everything that she was referring to was paperwork and receipts for my dad's job. He was a nuclear engineer and had to go on business trips from time to time. The receipts she found were from hotels that he had stayed at and restaurants where he had eaten while he was out of town. She had rummaged through everything in the house and made herself believe that my dad was hiding an affair from her.

My dad was finally able to lay her down while he ran her some bath water to help calm her down some more. My dad didn't feel the need to explain any of it to me, but it seemed as though he wasn't surprised by it one bit. Actually, he seemed as though he'd experienced it before, and was prepared.

After everything quieted down, and we all had turned in for the night, I got out of bed to go to the bathroom. As I crept past my parent's bedroom, I overheard my dad talking to my mom.

"It's getting bad, Lena. You could've killed me," he said.

"I just got a little confused, but I'll be ok. I promise. I'm sorry," she said, sounding remorseful.

"We need to at least get you on some medication before things get worse. I can't continue to walk into situations like that. I've been able to deal with it when it was just me, but we can't allow our daughter to be subjected to that. Nadia cannot see that again."

"Please don't try to make me take any medicine, Karter. I've been ok all this time."

"Have you really? Lena, you've been doing this for years, but when you start pulling out weapons, it's a serious problem. It's going to be harder and harder for me to protect you when I have to try to protect Nadia and myself at the same time, Baby."

"Karter, please. Just support me in this. I'll be ok."

My dad sat silently for a moment, seeming to not know what to do. He then said, "Ok, Lena. I'm here for you. I took a vow to love you and take care of you. That's what I'm going to do," he said before kissing her on the forehead.

I heard him walking towards the door, so I tiptoed and hid around the corner.

He then stepped out of the bedroom and shut the door behind him. He put his back up against the door and looked up to the ceiling with tears streaming down his face. I never thought I'd see the day that my dad would cry. He was never angry or sad, and that's the way I liked it. He was my Superman.

As I continued to watch my daddy in what had probably been his most vulnerable moment, he said in desperation, "God, please help my wife."

3 He heals the brokenhearted and binds up their wounds. – Psalms 147:3 NIV

The entire situation had caused me to be extremely fearful of my mom. I was only nine years old at that time and had no idea what the future of my family would look like. My mom was obviously sick, but I didn't know what type of illness would cause her to go crazy. Whatever medication my dad was talking about, I felt like she truly needed it, but I had faith in my dad. He always seemed to make things ok.

After that one episode, they continued, but thankfully, were never again violent. Most days, she was herself, but when she wasn't, she wasn't. There were days that she would run in the house saying that someone was following her, then there were days that she would come into my bedroom, and if it wasn't cleaned exactly the way she wanted it, she would tear it apart, ripping the covers off the bed and pulling everything out of the drawers and closet. I would get home from school, and before even being able to do my homework, I would have to put my room back together. She would act as if she didn't even remember doing it.

After going through it for a couple of years, my dad had finally decided to address it with me. He told me my mom was sick, but it wasn't the type of sickness like a cold or the flu, that you could take medicine for. He told me that the best type of medicine for the type of illness she was dealing with was a huge amount of love and support. He did tell me that if I ever saw my mom acting abnormal when he wasn't around, to go into my room, lock the door, and call him. Thankfully, nothing strange ever occurred while I was alone with her.

I loved my parents so much, and I wished everything could go back to normal. The majority of the recent memories that had been stored in my mind were memories that I didn't want to think about, so I tried to push them further and further into the back of my mind. I tried to keep all my earlier family memories to the forefront, along with the good ones that we'd recently created. I wasn't sure if I'd always have good new memories, but it wasn't looking good, so I enjoyed them while they lasted.

For my thirteenth birthday, my parents planned a big birthday bash for me in our backyard. My mom always liked to go all out for birthdays because no one did it for her growing up, so she would do all the planning, and my daddy would hand her however much money it would take to make sure everything was perfect. From the outside looking in, people would've said that we had a very traditional household. My mom stayed at home and took care of me and the house, and my dad worked, paid all the bills, and made sure me and my mom had everything we wanted and needed. My mom had always seemed very content with the way things were. She cooked and cleaned, and in return, lived a life of leisure.

As my mom finished decorating the backyard on the morning of my birthday, my dad quietly crept into my room while I slept.

"Nadia," he whispered, trying to wake me.

I had pretty long days between basketball practice, band rehearsals, games, and homework, so I slept pretty hard for a thirteen-year-old.

After my dad said my name, I rolled over so that my back faced him, and pulled the covers over my head.

He laughed, and said, "Ok. I guess you give me no choice."

He began tickling me, and I tried to ignore him and keep sleeping, but I was extremely ticklish and couldn't take it. He began singing the Stevie Wonder version of "Happy Birthday" as I laid there kicking, screaming, and laughing, all at the same time. He finally stopped tickling me and grabbed me, giving me a huge hug and kiss on the cheek.

"Happy birthday, Baby Girl," he said, smiling at me, and giving me a quick wink.

"Thank you, Daddy", I replied, cheesing, as I thought about the fact that I was now a teenager. I didn't know if anything about my life would change, although I could've thought of a couple of things that I wished could change. I was just excited that I would be able to say that I was thirteen.

When my daddy left my room, I could still smell the fragrance of his cologne. One thing about my daddy was that he always smelled so good. I would always smell him before he even walked into a room. Some people might've said he must've been wearing too much cologne, but it was the way I could count on finding him in a crowded room full of other dads.

Once I was awake, I couldn't wait to start the day. I jumped up out of bed, showered, and put on the outfit that my mom had bought me for this particular day during one of our shopping sprees that my daddy had sponsored. After getting dressed, I headed downstairs to see if my mom needed any help. I knew she would probably tell me no, because it seemed like when she kept her mind occupied, and stayed busy, she was in her happy place. The problem seemed to be when her mind was idle and began making things up on its own.

As I got towards the bottom of the stairway, I saw my mom cleaning the kitchen. She was so beautiful and seemed so peaceful. She wasn't smiling, but looking at her at that moment, I could tell she was smiling on the inside. When she heard me coming, she quickly looked up and her outward smile appeared.

"What are you doing awake so early? I thought you would be asleep for at least another hour," she said.

"Dad woke me up."

She grinned, and said, "Of course he did. I think he's more excited about your birthday than you are!"

"Where is dad?" I asked, as I looked around.

"He's getting ready to go pick up the cake. I don't think he left yet. Why don't you go find him? He might can use you help. It may be too heavy with all of those candles on it!"

We both laughed, and I ran to find my dad, so my mom could finish preparing the house for the guests.

I ran around the house, yelling my dad's name. He never replied, so I went looking around outside. The first thing I noticed were all of the vibrant decorations. Absolutely captivated by them, I began running my hands across the beautifully decorated tables, and balloons floating in the air. My mom had done a great job by herself, and I had become so distracted by her hard work that I had forgotten why I had gone outside, until I saw my dad's car pulling out of the driveway. I tried running to catch him before he pulled off. I waved my arms, as I ran, trying to get his attention. He saw me, but just waved, and kept going.

Disappointed, I went back into the house. My mom was no longer in the kitchen, so I went upstairs and knocked on her bedroom door.

"Mom, I tried to catch him, but he left without me."

"That's ok. He'll be right back", she yelled from the other side of the door. "I'll be out soon. I'm getting dressed."

While I waited for my mom to finish getting dressed, I sat in the family room in my dad's favorite recliner, watching TV until I finally heard her coming down the stairs.

"What are we going to do with that curly nest on your head?" she asked, smiling at me.

My hair was naturally curly, and extremely thick like my moms, but I just always brushed it into a ponytail, unless my mom decided to deal with it.

"This is fine," I said, running my fingers through my tangled ponytail, getting them caught between every strand.

She looked at me and shook her head. "Absolutely not! Turning thirteen deserves getting your hair straightened for the day!"

I didn't really care about having my hair straightened, especially knowing that it would revert back to normal as soon as the Texas humidity hit it. I was happy with just being able to have my family and friends there with me to celebrate my birthday. I knew it would make her happy, and she wasn't going to let up until I agreed, so I tried to act excited, and quickly jumped up and ran to the bathroom to get the hairspray and flatirons. I rummaged through the closet, making sure I had everything that my mom would need to make me as beautiful as she was. While I was collecting everything, I could hear my mom's voice, so I figured she must've been on the phone. With my hands full, and cords hanging down to my feet, I headed out of the bathroom, following my mom's voice.

Suddenly, I heard a loud shout. I dropped everything where I stood. I didn't know whether I should've run towards my mom, or away from her. I went with my gut and ran towards her voice. When I found her, she was sitting on the kitchen floor with tears streaming down her face, and the phone still to her ear.

"Noooooo! Noooooo! Stop lying to me!" she yelled, as she continued to cry.

I stood in the archway of the kitchen, and just from seeing my mom cry, my own tears suddenly began to flow. I didn't know what had happened, but I knew it had to have been bad. She covered her face and dropped the phone. I ran over to her, immediately dropping to my knees, and wrapped my arms around her neck. That was the day when all happy memories became only a distant memory.

Chapter Twelve

After my mom broke down, she tried to quickly pull herself together, and told me to put my shoes on because we had to go.

Concerned, I asked, "What happened? Why are you crying?"

Calmly, but voice still trembling, she replied, "Just do what I said."

As I put my shoes on, I asked, "How long are we going to be gone, and when is daddy coming back with the cake?"

My mom looked at me sternly with bloodshot eyes and yelled, "Nadia, stop with the questions and just do what I tell you to do!"

I didn't understand what was happening, but my mom's tone shocked me so much that I began shaking. I felt like running to my room, locking the door, and calling my dad, but something told me to just do what my mom was telling me to do. When we got into the car, I so badly wanted to ask her where we were going, but I was afraid. The only time I had seen my mom act so irrationally was when she was having one of her episodes. I was hoping this wasn't what that was because if it was, I had a very good reason to be afraid. I sat quietly in the passenger seat, with the seatbelt strapped tightly across my body, and my hands clasped together in my lap. I nervously twiddled my thumbs, feeling as if I was sitting at my desk on the first day of school.

The radio was on, but I could still hear my mom crying as she sped through the city. I felt like crying with her again, but tried to swallow the lump in my throat, and hold in my tears in fear that I would be yelled at again for doing something wrong. I held my head down and watched a tear roll off the tip of my nose onto my hand. I was so confused and didn't know what to do, so I did all that I could do. I remained quiet and waited.

I finally felt the car slowing down, so I slowly raised my head and looked out the window. I could see that we were in a parking lot full of cars.

"That was my parking space, idiot!" my mom yelled, as she honked her horn.

She finally made a sharp right turn into a parking space, and quickly put the car into park. Through the window, I could see the big, red, lit up sign on the building of the hospital that read "Emergency".

Without looking at me, my mom said, "Come on. Let's go."

We both got out of the car, and she aggressively slammed her door. We walked briskly through the parking lot to the sliding doors at the front of the building. There was a desk ahead with two women sitting there. Before we could even get there, one of the ladies greeted us.

"Hi. How can I help you?" she asked.

My mom waited until we approached the desk to start talking.

"I'm looking for my husband, Karter Robinson," my mom said in a low tone, leaning over the desk into the woman's space, as if she was telling a secret.

The woman's expression completely changed after my mom told her why she was there. Her smiling eyes now looked sad. Now that I knew my dad was at the hospital, I became even more worried. I wondered if he had been in a car accident, or maybe he had fallen while he was picking up the cake.

"What's your name, Ma'am?" the woman asked, in the middle of my thoughts.

My mom, sounding irritated, said, "My name is Lena . . . Lena Robinson! What does that even matter when I'm just asking you to see my husband?

"Well, Ma'am, we can't just let anyone . . .

Before the lady could finish her sentence, my mom interrupted her.

"I'm not just anyone! I told you I'm his wife, so where is my husband, lady?"

Although the woman looked like she wanted to say something else, she looked at me, then back at my mom, and said, "Let me get the doctor."

As we waited for the woman to return with the doctor, my mom paced the floor, constantly saying, "Oh God! Why!"

She kept looking up at the ceiling as if she was waiting for God to answer her. I stood with my back up against the wall, and would look up whenever she did so that I wouldn't miss it if God did answer her. Even though we never went to church, I did know who God was. My dad taught me what I guess you could call "The Basics", but I had never heard the word "God" come out of my mom's mouth. My dad would pray before meals, and when I would do something wrong, like tell a lie, he would tell me that God wouldn't like that. He told me if the Bible said not to do something, I was never to do it under any circumstances. If my mom was around during any of his Godly lectures, she would just sigh and walk out of the room. I had a hard time understanding any of what my dad would try to teach me because I had never even seen a Bible in our house. It was hard for me to believe something that I never saw. Even when he would tell me that God wouldn't like it if I had done something bad, to me, it kind of felt like when parents would tell their kids that if they weren't good, Santa wouldn't bring them anything for Christmas. I had found out that Santa wasn't real when I was around eight, and I wondered if there would ever be a day that someone would tell me that God wasn't real. My thoughts on that were changing as I saw my mom standing there talking to God, and asking for Him to respond. I thought, *Maybe God is real . . .*

The doctor finally arrived. He was a tall, thin, white man with white hair. The woman who had gone to get him came out walking next to him and pointed towards my mom. When he spoke, he had a very deep voice that carried throughout the entire room.

He walked up to my mom and said, "Hello, Mrs. Robinson. I'm Dr. Galloway," he said, as he held out his hand for my mom to shake.

She had calmed down a little bit, so she reached out and shook his hand.

He continued, "The receptionist filled me in, telling me that you're the wife of Karter Robinson."

My mom replied, "Yes, I am."

"Ok, Mrs. Robinson. Let's go to the back so we can talk in private."

They began walking towards the double swinging doors and I followed behind them. My mom looked back to make sure I was close behind.

The doctor then stopped, and turned around, not initially realizing that my mom wasn't alone.

Looking down at me, he said, "And who do we have here?"

"Nadia," I said, smiling, but not really sure if it was ok to smile, so I quickly deviated back to my previous, sad disposition.

"Nice to meet you, Nadia. I'm Dr. Galloway."

I nodded my head as we continued to walk.

The doctor finally stopped walking and opened a door that had his name on it. He turned on the light and gestured for us to go in.

"Have a seat Mrs. Robinson, and Miss Nadia."

We sat at his desk, and he sat directly across from us. His face was very serious, and it looked like he was trying to gather his words. My mom was growing more and more impatient.

"Can everyone please stop looking at me like I'm stupid and tell me what's going on with my husband? Can we take him home?"

Dr. Galloway deeply inhaled, then exhaled.

"Mrs. Robinson, I'm so sorry. . ."

Before he could finish, my mom began screaming. I jumped up out of my chair and went and held her.

"Please, Mrs. Robinson. We have to get through this part. I know it's hard not knowing, but I have to give you the information that I currently have so that you can make some decisions."

He grabbed some Kleenex and handed them to my mom. She closed her eyes and took a few deep breaths.

"Ok. I'm sorry, but I'm just so overwhelmed."

"Understandable," Dr. Galloway replied. He continued, "Your husband had a brain aneurism that has ruptured.

My mom interrupted before he could finish.

"I was told he was unconscious when they called me. Please just tell me he's conscious right now, and he'll be ok!"

"I would not be doing my job, or doing you any favors if I just told you what you'd like to hear, Ma'am. That would be of a great disservice to you. As much as I wish that I could tell you that, unfortunately, I can't, and again, I'm sorry."

My mom rocked back and forth in her seat and nodded her head. "I understand," she replied.

I was not only worried about my dad at that point. I was also extremely worried about my mom. This was a lot for her to handle, especially with her condition. She was liable to snap at any moment, and I was very fearful of that happening.

"When he got here, he was unconscious. We quickly assessed the problem and got him into surgery to attempt to repair the aneurysm and stop the bleeding. He's with the best neurosurgery team that we have. Let me assure you he is in very good hands."

Dr. Galloway continued with describing what an aneurysm was and how the surgeon would attempt to repair it. While listening to all of the big medical terms the doctor was using, I became lost in my own little world, imagining my dad healthy again. I just wanted for him to walk into that room so I could jump up and give him a big hug and see my mom smile. He was so big and strong that I would've never imagined that one day I would be at a hospital waiting to see if he was ok. I couldn't remember my dad ever even having a cold. He was always well and taking care of someone else.

After the doctor finished giving my mom even more information to digest, she looked very confused, and could barely get her words out.

"But how? He just went to pick up the cake," she mumbled, as she shook her head. "How did that result in all of this?"

"It happened at the bakery," Dr. Galloway said. "The clerk told the EMT transporters that one minute he was fine, waiting for her to bring the cake from the cooler, and when she returned, she knew something wasn't right. He put his hands to his head and told her he suddenly had a headache. She knew it wasn't just a headache because he looked like he was in excruciating pain, and his speech was very slurred, which are very common symptoms of an aneurysm. She asked him if he needed to sit down for a moment, but before he could sit, he passed out onto the floor. She immediately called 911."

I began crying uncontrollably. My mom grabbed me, and tried to comfort me, but she couldn't even comfort herself.

"Dad's here all because he went to get my stupid cake. He would be ok if I would have been with him, or if he had been home with us. I didn't even need a stupid party!" I sobbed.

"Nooo!" Dr. Galloway, replied. "This is not your fault, Nadia. Don't you ever think that. Your dad was already a little sick and didn't know it. Sometimes that happens."

I wanted to believe him, and I tried my best to stop crying.

"So, what do we do now?" my mom asked, as she continued to hold me.

"Your husband will be in a medically-induced coma after surgery, and unfortunately, we'll have to wait to see how his body handles everything. Under normal circumstances, we would have the next of kin to let us know whether or not they'd like us to resuscitate before the patient goes into surgery, but since you

weren't here when he went into surgery, we now need to know
right away. It's up to you, being his wife, whether or not you'd like
a "Do Not Resuscitate" order. I do have to explain that if you do
decide that you want us to resuscitate, your husband could
possibly be in a vegetative state or non-induced coma, and you
would then have to make another decision as to whether or not
we should remove life support."

My mom looked even more overwhelmed than before. She
looked as though she just wanted to run away from it all, but she
tried to remain as strong as possible and push through. I just
watched as she nodded her head each time the doctor gave her
another hard pill to swallow.

Dr. Galloway pulled a form out of one of his drawers.

"I just need for you to fill this out either way so that your
decision is stated on an official document. Let me know if you
need to consult with anyone else. If so, you would need to do that
quickly in order for us to follow your orders."

Sadly, my mom said, "There's no one else. It's just us."

And that was the truth. It was just the three of us. I didn't
have any living grandparents. The only one that was living when I
was born was my dad's mom, but she never came around. My dad
had received a call a few years prior telling him that she had died.
He took care of all of the funeral arrangements and attended the
funeral while my mom and I stayed home. My dad's relationship
with his mom was another subject that was off limits in our
house, just as the subject of my mom's mother was.

The doctor placed the form and an ink pen on the desk in
front of my mom. I didn't know what an aneurism or a "Do Not
Resuscitate order" were, but whatever they both were, it
sounded like my mom was in control of how things might've
ended for my dad. She picked up the pen and took a deep breath
before checking one of the boxes and signing her name on the
signature line. She then quickly slid the paper across the desk to
the doctor. After picking up the document and reviewing it, he
looked up at my mom and nodded. She responded by nodding in
return.

Chapter Thirteen

Six hours had passed, and my mom and I were still sitting in the hospital's waiting room watching re-runs of "Good Times." We needed something to make us laugh, and "Good Times" would normally do the job, but the episode when James Evans was killed in a car accident happened to come on. That was definitely bad timing, and there was absolutely no laughter in the room. My mom grabbed the remote from the coffee table and flipped through the channels, trying to find something more appealing to watch. For the first couple of hours of sitting there, I watched my mom make phone calls using the waiting room's phone to call the parents of all of my friends who were supposed to come to my party. I could tell she was getting irritated by all of the questions many of them were asking, and I was just wishing that they would stop it. I already knew my mom was on edge, and I could tell if anyone said the wrong thing, she was going to lose it. I didn't have my dad there to help deescalate the situation if she did get out of control, and I didn't feel as though I was capable of helping her.

After my mom finished making calls, she stood up, walking back and forth from the window to the sofa. She was looking for anything to distract her from thinking about the reality of what was happening. The doctor had told us it would be between three and five hours before we would hear anything. If they ran into complications, it would be longer. Still, six hours later, no one had come to give us any further information.

I must've fallen asleep watching television, right along with my mom. I heard a nearby voice say, "Mrs. Robinson."

I opened my eyes as I lifted my head from my mom's lap. A very pretty, petite black woman wearing burgundy scrubs, and a stethoscope around her neck was standing in front of us.

My mom immediately rose to her feet, towering over the woman.

"Yes! How is he?" my mom asked anxiously.

"Hi, Mrs. Robinson. I'm Grace. I'm one of the surgical nurses that was in the operating room with your husband. The surgery went as well as can be expected. He is in a medically induced coma at this time, which the doctor said he already explained to you. We do also have him on a ventilator because he does seem to need some help breathing. He'll be placed in ICU once he comes out of the recovery room within the next hour.

"So, when will he be out of the coma?"

"I wish I could answer that question for you. It just all depends on how quickly his brain heals. The doctor will be keeping a close eye on him, which is why he'll be in ICU. If we see the brain isn't healing as quickly as we would like, we'll keep him in the coma until we feel it's safe to stop sedating him. At this point, we still don't know what condition he'll be in once the coma is lifted. It all depends on how much brain activity he has."

"So, you don't even know if his brain is still even functioning?" my mom asked, sounding frustrated.

My heart began pounding so hard, it was painful. I could feel the lump in my throat returning, which meant I would soon have to try to hold back my tears. I was smart enough to know that our brains controlled almost everything, so if my dad's brain didn't have any activity, I knew there would be no hope for him. He was the smartest man I knew. I didn't just feel that way because he was my dad, but because he was able to do anything anyone asked him to do, and if someone had a question, he always had an answer.

"We're hoping for the best, Mrs. Robinson. I'll let you know when you can go in to see him."

My mom stood there speechless as the nurse waited to see if she had any other questions.

She gave my mom a moment to digest the information that she'd just given her, then grabbed her hand and said, "I don't know what your beliefs are, but I do know that right now, the best thing you can do for your husband is to pray for him. Have faith and believe that God can, and will heal him. I don't mean to get super spiritual on you, but God is our real doctor, and he can work miracles. Working here, I have seen many people come back from a lot worse."

My mom still didn't say anything, and the nurse walked away looking defeated. I didn't think my mom had heard a word that the nurse had said beyond the point of her saying that they were hoping for the best, or it might've been that she just wasn't interested in anything else she had said. I had heard everything, and what I heard had aroused a tremendous amount of curiosity within me about God and how he managed to work all these miracles. I sat back down on the sofa and watched my mom just stand there, looking as though she was about to have a breakdown. I could tell that she didn't have much left in her, and her hope was hanging on by a single thread.

3 "You will keep in perfect peace those whose minds are steadfast, because they trust in you. 4 Trust in the Lord forever, for the Lord, the Lord himself, is the Rock eternal." – Isaiah 26:3-4 NIV

As we had another long session of just sitting and waiting, my stomach began to growl. We had been at the hospital all day and hadn't eaten a thing. I looked over at the vending machine and stared at all of the candy bars, chips, and cookies, trying to decide which one I wanted even though I didn't have money to buy anything. I didn't have the courage to ask my mom for money, so I just sat there hoping that she would become as hungry as I was and buy us both something. In the meantime, I tried to think positive thoughts that didn't involve food in order to keep my mind off of my hunger.

My imagination never failed to take me to happy places when I needed it most. I closed my eyes and almost instantly imagined my daddy coming into the house with my birthday cake. My mom was just finishing up my hair, which hung down over my shoulders, down to my tiny waist.

"Did a pretty little teenage girl order a birthday cake? I think her name is Nadia!" my dad yelled from the kitchen.

I jumped up out of the wooden barstool my mom always used when she did my hair, and ran to greet my dad. When I saw him, he immediately opened his arms. He was my human teddy bear, and was always prepared to give me a giant hug. This was no different. I smiled with my eyes closed, as I took in the scent of his cologne.

"Do you think she needs something to eat?" I heard the voice of an unfamiliar man ask, interrupting my happy thoughts.

I opened my eyes and saw a dark complected, bearded man sitting across from me and my mom. I looked around the rest of the room and didn't see anyone else, so I assumed he was there alone. I didn't know how long I had been lost in my thoughts, so I wasn't sure how long he'd been there.

"Yeah, she might be hungry. We've been here all day. I just don't want to miss the nurse or doctor coming in to get us," my mom replied to the man who seemed concerned about me.

"Yeah, I know what you mean. Waiting is always hard. You don't want to do anything until you get answers."

My mom glanced down at the man's hand, then asked, "Are you waiting on your wife to come out of surgery?"

The man looked down and smiled. He began twirling the ring that he had on his ring finger that indicated to my mom that he was married, and said, "No. I'm not married."

"Engaged?" my mom asked curiously?

"Actually, divorced. I just never took my ring off. It wasn't my decision."

"I'm sorry. How long have you been divorced?"

By this time, I had turned all the way around in my seat to face my mom. I hadn't heard her talk to anyone so sweetly, and in such a calm tone since we'd been there, and now she seemed so caring as she spoke to this complete stranger. The more that I was around adults, the less I seemed to understand them.

"It's been almost two years," he replied.

"Wow. You must really love her to still be wearing your ring."

"Of course, I do. She was my wife. I'll always love her, and like I said, I'm not the one who wanted the divorce," he said, sounding as if he was getting irritated by the questions being asked.

My mom took notice of his tone and backed down. "Sorry. I'm just trying to keep my mind off of everything that's going on. It feels kind of good to talk."

The man began stroking his bearded chin, and said, "No, I'm sorry. It's just a sensitive subject sometimes, so to get off of that subject, I'm here to support my lifelong friend. He doesn't have any family. I'm really the only person that he has around in his life who he can trust. He had a heart murmur and had to have surgery to have a valve repaired. What about you?"

My mom just sat there with a blank look on her face. He waved his hand in front of her to see if he had her attention, and she finally snapped out of it.

"I'm so sorry. You have to excuse me. I'm not all the way here. What did you ask me?"

"No need to apologize. Who are you here to see about?"

"My husband," she said, with hesitation. "I'm not sure how he's doing. He has a ruptured aneurysm. He and my baby girl are all I have," she said grabbing and holding my hand.

She looked like she was about to cry again. I didn't realize how tall the man was until he stood up and went over to the coffee table to grab some Kleenex. He looked like some of the basketball players I would see on television when I would watch NBA games with my dad.

He walked back over and handed my mom the tissue.

She looked up at him and said, "Thank you . . ."

"Darryl", he said, ending her sentence.

"Thank you, Darryl. I guess I should've asked your name before getting all in your business."

"That might've been nice!" he said, laughing. "Now what's your name?"

"Lena," she replied as she wiped her eyes.

Darryl looked at me with a smile, and said, "And what about you, little lady?"

I opened my mouth to respond, but before I could, my mom said, "Nadia. She's my one and only."

She was always very protective of me and always warned me not to talk to strangers as if I was five years old and didn't know any better. While she continued to have small talk, my stomach continued to rumble as if it was also a part of the conversation. I sat quietly, feeling a little more at ease. Even though I was starving, I felt better because my mom seemed a lot calmer, which took a lot of pressure off of me. I was thankful that Darryl had come in when he did. He had been like a breath of fresh air to the both of us.

As they were talking, the nurse came back in.

"Mrs. Robinson, you can come see your husband now."

I quickly jumped out of my seat in excitement. My mom stood up and looked around, making sure she had grabbed everything. She told Darryl it was nice meeting him, and thanked him for the talk.

"Thank you, ladies. Good luck with everything," he said as he smiled and waved goodbye.

We followed behind the nurse as she led the way so that we could finally see my dad. I couldn't wait. I had hopes that he would be good as new. I knew he'd just had surgery on his brain, but I didn't quite understand just how serious it was. I had tried to comprehend all of the information that the doctor and the nurse had given my mom, just in case she missed anything, but I only fully grasped the information that I could make at least a little sense of, and out of that, I had created the most positive scenario in my head as I could. I refused to believe there was any possibility that my dad would never be the same.

We walked down a long hallway with several rooms. Some of the doors were open, and some were closed. I could see some of the patients with several people in their rooms talking and laughing, then there were people in their rooms, alone, watching television. I felt sad for them. They were sick and had no family or friends to see about them. I imagined my dad to be feeling that same way at the moment, and that made me even more sad and anxious to see him.

The nurse finally stopped in front of room 2115.

The door was closed, and before opening it, she turned around and said, "Before going in, I just want to prepare you for what you'll see. A lot of people become upset when they see their loved ones this way because they're not expecting it. He does have a lot of equipment attached to him, but it's necessary for us to provide him with the best care possible. Please just keep that in mind when you go in."

I grabbed my mom's hand to try to help console her. I could feel her palms begin to sweat, and as the nurse began to open the door, she squeezed my hand tighter and tighter. As we slowly entered the room, we could hear the beeping of the heart monitor and the whooshing sound of the ventilator that was helping my dad breathe. When we were in plain sight of the hospital bed in which my dad's still body lied, my mom stood over him and slowly put her hands up to her mouth in disbelief. Her body trembled, but she didn't make a sound. The nurse stood on the other side of the bed holding her clipboard in one hand, and fiddling with all of the cords and tubes that were connected with the other. She looked as though she wasn't sure of what to say, or if it was the right time to say anything at all.

I waited for my dad to open his eyes, but he didn't. I wondered if he would if he heard my voice. I wanted to call his name, but I had that stupid lump in my throat again that made me feel like I was going to cry if I opened my mouth. My dad's head was wrapped in bandages. The ventilator was next to his bed with tubes coming out of it, going into his nose and mouth. He looked so uncomfortable, but I tried to believe that it looked worse than what it actually was, and that he'd be ok.

While my mom just stared, I stood closer to the bed, and put my hand on top of the hand of the man who I called my superhero. His hands were perfect. I had given him a manicure the day before, while he slept in his favorite recliner after a long day of work. I could still see the glossy finish from the clear nail polish I had applied. I rubbed his hand, and it was warm.

"Daddy," I whispered. "Please wake up. I know you can hear me."

I didn't really know if he could hear me or not, but I was believing what I wanted to believe. That was the only option I had. My mom put her hand on top of ours. A tear rolled down my face after my daddy didn't move, even after I had spoken to him.

"Keep talking to him," the nurse said. "I believe he can hear you, too."

I looked at her, and she smiled at me. I smiled back, and she then excused herself and went into the bathroom.

"Babe, please be ok. We love you, and miss you already. Please just fight and get through this so we can go back to being a happy family," my mom said as her voice began to sound hoarse. "You know I can't do this without you. I need you. We need you."

I suddenly heard a voice coming from the bathroom. I thought maybe the nurse had went in there and taken a call, but when I listened closely to her words, I knew that wasn't at all what she went to do.

"Father, I come boldly to your throne today and ask that you do your will in this family's life. Please provide them with the support that they'll need to get through this tragic event. They won't be able to get through this without you, so please remain in their presence . . . Give them faith that you are working things out for their good, and give them peace in their hearts that passes all understanding. This comes as no surprise to you, Lord, and you make no mistakes. You say in your word, that weeping may endure for a night, but joy comes in the morning. I've seen you hold true to this so many times before, and you always keep your word. I trust and believe in your word, today, Lord, and with that I know your will is done. Thank you, Father. Amen."

When Nurse Grace came out of the bathroom, I ran and wrapped my arms around her.

"Thank you for talking to God for us."

"You are so welcome. You can talk to him, too."

I raised my eyebrows and said, "Do you think he'll listen?"

She smiled at me reassuringly, and said, "God listens to everyone!"

My mom walked over and grabbed me.

"Please don't give my daughter false hope. If God listened, my husband wouldn't be lying be lying in this hospital bed right now. He would be home with us!"

I could tell Nurse Grace was completely shocked by the way my mom had reacted, but that didn't stop her from saying what she felt she needed to say.

"I understand how something like this can cause you to lose faith, but that's exactly what Satan wants you to do! When you lose your faith, he has room to control you. Don't allow that, please."

"Look, I know you're coming from a place that you feel is good, but I'm a realist. If it looks like a duck, swims like a duck, and quacks like a duck, then it's a duck, so when something doesn't look good, it's not! Look at my husband right now! Does he look good?"

"Mrs. Robinson . . ."

"Exactly! No, he doesn't! Just leave! We'll be fine."

My mom cut her eyes at Nurse Grace as she walked towards the door. I felt bad for her. She hadn't done anything wrong in my eyes, but my mom was so angry. I just couldn't understand it.

Nurse Grace opened the door to leave the room, but before leaving, she said, "I'll be at the nurse's station. Please let me know if you need anything, and I'm so sorry for overstepping."

My mom turned her back on Nurse Grace, but I kept my eyes on her. There was just something about her that made me feel good inside. She brought a different type of light to the room. When she caught me staring at her, she waved and gave me a slight grin before walking out and shutting the door behind her. After she left, it felt like the entire room went dark, and my temporary feeling of comfort and tranquility left with her.

Chapter Fourteen

After my mom could no longer stand looking at my daddy in that condition, she decided that we should go home and get some rest. Nurse Grace never came back, but a different nurse did stop by a few times to make sure everything was ok.

As I still stood by my daddy's bedside, she said, "Come on, Nadia. Let's go home."

She walked towards the door, and I quietly said, "Goodnight, Daddy," and kissed him on the hand.

When I turned around, my mom was standing in the doorway, watching me. She cleared her throat and took a deep breath as she took one last look at my dad. As soon as we stepped outside the hospital doors, the strong evening wind seemed to carry us through the parking lot, and the humidity immediately saturated my skin. We had been inside the hospital for so long, my mom couldn't remember where she had parked the car. She asked me if I remembered, and of course, I didn't. All I could remember was her acting like a maniac as she was trying to find a parking space while I sat in the passenger seat afraid to say a word.

We aimlessly walked through the parking lot for a couple of minutes, until someone in a parked car began to shine their bright lights on us. My mom turned around and looked towards the parked car, squinting her eyes. The car then began to slowly move towards us.

"It's probably just parking lot security trying to make sure we're ok," she said, trying to reassure us both.

When the car finally reached us, we still couldn't see who was inside because the windows were so dark. The passenger side window began to lower, and I then saw that it was Darryl from the hospital waiting room.

"Darryl!" my mom said, sounding shocked to see him.

"Spence," he replied.

She looked confused, and asked, "Who is Spence?"

"Me. My name is Darryl Spencer. All my friends call my Spence, and since I've run into you twice in one day, I now consider you a friend, so call me Spence."

Darryl, Spence, or whatever his name was seemed to be very charming. He certainly seemed to be the only person to get my mom to crack any type of smile with everything that was going on.

"Ok . . . Spence," she said with a small grin. "What are you still doing here, and why are you just sitting out here in the parking lot?"

"I was about to leave, but while I was finishing up returning some calls that I'd missed, I happened to see two beautiful ladies who looked like they were lost."

My mom, holding a handful of her hair to keep it from blowing wildly in the wind, looked as if she might've been blushing.

"Yeah, just a little lost. I can't find my car," she replied.

"Hop in. I can drive you around until we find it."

My mom thought about it for a second, then said, "No, we're ok. It has to be nearby."

Spence quickly opened his door and got out of the car. "Come on. It's too dark . . .," he paused, as he caught his baseball cap from flying away. "And too windy!" he continued.

He opened the front passenger and back door, then gestured for us to get in. We both stared at him for a moment, then looked at each other.

"I promise I don't bite," he said.

My mom then nodded at me, letting me know it was ok, so I got in.

As he drove around the parking lot, and my mom and I both looked out the window in search of our red Thunderbird, Spence asked how my dad was doing. My mom just told him as best as to be expected, but didn't go into detail.

"Did you two ever get a meal?"

As soon as there was the mention of food, my stomach growled loudly. It was so loud, they heard it from the front seat.

"I guess that answers my question," Spence said. "Let me take the two of you out to dinner."

"Oh no. That's not a good idea. We'll get something on the way home," my mom said.

"She's obviously hungry, so just let me do that for you. I know you've had a long day."

My mom became defensive, and said, "Look, I'm not neglecting my child. Like you said, it's been a long day. Neither of us have eaten, but I'm fully capable of handling it."

"I didn't mean it like that. I was just trying to help. I apologize if I offended you."

Without addressing his apology, my mom pointed and said, "There's my car straight ahead."

Spence pulled up next to our car, looking disappointed. His charming smile had completely disappeared.

Before getting out the car, my mom looked at him and said, "Thanks for your help."

She then slammed the door and opened my door for me. Before we began to walk away, I heard the annoying sound of Spence's squeaky car door opening.

"Hey, you think we can keep in touch, just so I can check on you from time to time?"

He reached into his car, and said, "Here. I have a pen and paper so you can write your number down."

"I don't think so, Spence. We'll be fine, and I don't need anyone checking on me."

He quickly began writing on the paper. When he finished, he ran over to my mom and said, "Well, at least take my number, just in case you ever need anything. Even if just someone to talk to."

He held the piece of paper in front of her and stood there looking pitiful, as if he was at her mercy. He had taken his hat off, and the parking lot lights shined upon his bald head, revealing the beads of sweat that were appearing one by one. She just stared at him for a moment. It felt like a dramatic scene from a movie, and the audience was waiting with anticipation to see what she was going to do next. At that moment, she cut her eyes at him, and snatched the small piece of paper from his hand. She then proceeded to walk away towards our car. I followed close behind.

"Ok. Talk to you later," Spence said.

13 **"No temptation has overtaken you except what is common to mankind. And God is faithful; he will not let you be tempted beyond what you can bear. But when you are tempted, he will also provide a way out so that you can endure it." – 1 Corinthians 10:13 NIV**

"Temptation usually comes in through a door that has deliberately been left open."
- Arnold Glasow

Chapter Fifteen

The next few weeks consisted of the same routine, day in and day out. I would wake up, eat breakfast, go to school, go to basketball practice, visit my dad, and go home to eat dinner at the dinner table, while staring at my daddy's empty chair. Nothing was the same. Everything about my days seemed empty. My mom rarely ever smiled, and when she did, it no longer seemed genuine. It was like she only did it because she felt like it was the right thing to do. I smiled because sometimes it just made me feel better. Even though I knew my mom's smiles weren't genuine, I preferred that over having to deal with her not being in her right mind. Considering everything she was going through, her mental state had surprisingly seemed to be under control. Miss Val, the woman who'd given her a job at the diner where she learned to cook those delicious blueberry pancakes, would stop by whenever she had time. She was more like a mother to her than anything else, and she always seemed to temporarily get my mom in good spirits. She lived pretty far, and she was older, so she couldn't come as much as she would've liked to. I knew that

Miss Val was also aware of my mom's condition after overhearing her ask my mom had she been taking her medication. My mom, of course, lied to her, and told her, yes, and Miss Val didn't question her any further. I had been tempted to tell Miss Val the truth, but I knew that it would've upset my mom, and I was just trying to keep the peace.

The doctors weren't telling us anything different than what they'd initially told us after my dad was out of surgery. The only thing that had changed was that they were able to take him off of the ventilator, so he was able to breathe on his own. His brain was still in the process of healing, and he remained in an induced coma. I talked to him every day, telling him how my day was, since he was unable to ask me, as he normally would when he got home from work every day. I imagined him looking at me, smiling, as I told him about how I aced a test, or laughing as I told him one of my corny jokes that one of my friends had told me. Seeing and talking to my dad always made my day complete, even if he couldn't talk back to me. Like Nurse Grace had said, I knew he could still hear me.

Ever since the day that my mom had had the altercation with Nurse Grace, we hadn't seen her. My dad had been moved from the general ICU section of the hospital to the neuroscience intensive care unit where they could be sure to keep a very close eye on him after seeing that the aneurysm wasn't healing as they had hoped. There was an entirely different team of nurses in that area. They were all very nice, but I did miss Nurse Grace, and looked around for her each time we were in the hospital. Sometimes I would ask my mom if I could go to the cafeteria or vending machine to get a snack in hopes that I would run into her.

Our house was always so quiet. There wasn't much talking between me and my mom, and the most talking I would hear her doing was when she was on the telephone trying to take care of the business that my dad would've normally handled. I would often ask to go spend time with my friends on the weekends just so that I could feel some type of sense of normalcy.

My best friend's name was Ava, and we used to call each other sisters, even though everyone knew we really weren't since they could clearly see the color of our skin. I was one of only four Black kids at our elementary school, and when I first began attending, the kids were rude and they didn't go out of their way to talk to me. I felt alone and didn't look forward to much when I went to school, like most kids at that age who were excited to make new friends. I remembered the day in second grade very clearly when that had changed for me.

The class was completely quiet as we sat at our desks completing an assignment that the teacher had given. There was a knock on the classroom door. When the teacher walked over and opened it, the principal was standing on the other side with a little girl who had curly, sandy brown hair and blue eyes. My teacher smiled as she spoke with the principal, and gestured for the little girl to go inside. As she was walking in, she glanced over at me and smiled. I could never forget that smile because her two front teeth were missing, and even though her smile was "broken", it had been the most genuine, perfect smile that I had ever gotten from anyone in that entire building.

After waving goodbye to the principal, the teacher shut the door behind her and said, "Class, put your pencils down for a moment. I have an announcement."

We all put down our pencils and looked towards the front of the classroom.

"This is our new student, Ava Kelly," our teacher, Mrs. Johansson said. "She's new to Texas, coming all the way from Georgia, so let's be sure to make her feel welcome! She's a long way from home."

Mrs. Johansson looked around the classroom for an empty seat where Ava could sit. She looked right past the empty seat next to me and sat her next to a girl named Stephanie Alexander. Everyone loved Stephanie, but she always looked at me like I was an alien. Somewhat how everyone else looked at me, but worse. I was disappointed because I had hopes that I could finally make a friend, but I had survived that long without, so I knew I'd still be fine.

Stephanie, and everyone else sitting in her area, immediately began drowning Ava's ears with conversation, trying to learn more about her after she sat down. I just sat there, staring from the other side of the classroom, hoping she'd look my way so that I could at least give her a friendly wave.

"Ok class. Settle down. I know you're excited to get a new classmate, but we need to stay on task. You'll have lunch and recess to talk all you want."

The room became quiet as everyone picked their pencils back up and continued working. Ava got herself settled in at her desk, then Mrs. Johansson asked her to come up to her desk, which she called "her office", so that she could go over the classroom rules and assignment with her.

The morning quickly passed, and it was soon time for lunch. The lunch bell rang, and we all stood up and got in line. I was always near the back of the line because everyone else walked quickly so that they could stand in line near their friends. I didn't have any friends, so I wasn't in any hurry to be near anyone in specific. Since it was Ava's first day, she was in the front of the line so that she could be near the teacher to help guide her.

We got to the cafeteria and stood in line with our trays, waiting to be served. Once I got my food, I walked towards the tables that were reserved for my class and saw that everyone was sitting around Ava, doing more talking than eating. I went and sat in my usual spot at the end of one of the tables by myself. When I finished eating, I went outside for recess and played on the jungle gym. I saw the other kids coming out one by one, playing on the swings and slide. As I swung from the bars of the multi-colored jungle gym, I suddenly heard a sweet, country voice behind me.

"Hey, you wanna get on the seesaw with me?"

I jumped down from the bars and turned around. Directly behind me stood Ava, smiling from ear to ear.

Smiling back, I said, "Sure!"

"What's your name?" she asked.

"Nadia," I replied.

Without saying anything else, she grabbed my hand, and we both began running towards the seesaw. As soon as we got there, Stephanie, out of nowhere, quickly jumped onto one of the seats.

Stephanie looked at me, frowning, then said, "Come on Ava. Get on the other end!" as she tossed her fine blonde hair over her shoulder.

Ava said, "No thanks. We'll just get on the swings."

We began walking away, and heard Stephanie say, "Nigger lover!"

Ava stopped in her tracks, turned around, and charged towards Stephanie. She yanked her off of the seesaw and threw her to the ground. I ran over wanting to help Ava, but she didn't look like she needed my help at all. Hair was flying all over the place as Ava flung Stephanie from one end of the playground to the other as she tried to escape. Everyone else finally took notice of what was going on, and the recess aid ran over and broke up the fight. Ava ended up getting suspended from school for defending me after only her first day. The principal asked me what happened, and I told her what Stephanie had said, but it didn't matter. All that mattered to her was that Ava had come in and disrupted what the entire school felt was an atmosphere of unity and respect. They didn't realize, or just didn't want to admit to the fact that Ava, who was only seven years old, was attempting to fight for unity and equality the best way she felt she could. From that point on, Ava and I had been inseparable, and I never again felt the rejection that I had felt every day when I went to school. Ava made me feel just as important as everyone else.

15 "If the world hates you, keep in mind that it hated me first." – John 15:18 NIV

Later on, I found out that when Ava lived in Georgia, she went to a school where she had been the only Caucasian student to attend. She didn't see color, and was always friendly to everyone. Her parents had taught her about the "N" word at a young age, and how racist, disrespectful, and inappropriate the word was, so when Stephanie said it, it infuriated Ava. She couldn't understand how people could treat others so badly just because of the color of their skin. With that being said, when Ava's parents found out why the fight occurred, they were upset that she had resorted to violence, but were proud that she had stood up for what was right. Everyone else at school made sure that she knew they weren't happy about what she had done, but she didn't care. She kept a smile on her face no matter what.

"Are you going to see your dad, today?" Ava asked one day as we walked out of the gym after basketball practice.

We had joined the basketball team together. I would've never joined if it hadn't been for her. I didn't have any interest in being a part of any teams before she had come to our school. She was on the basketball team at her school in Georgia, and she was very good at it. When the school announced that tryouts would be in a few weeks, she asked me to try out with her. I told her I didn't know how to play basketball, so I began going to her house every day after school, and she would teach me on the basketball court that her parents had set up for her in the backyard. By the time it was time to try out, I was almost as good as Ava. That was when I became interested in sports and began watching them with my dad.

"Yeah, I'm going to see him today. I just wish he would get better. I want everything to go back to normal," I replied to Ava, with my head hanging low.

Ava grabbed my hand, and said, "I pray for him every night before I go to bed. Everything will be all right."

I looked up at Ava and said, "You pray for my dad?"

"Of course, I do! Why wouldn't I? You're my best friend."

We then heard a horn blow as we approached the front of the school where all of the parents were parked to pick up their kids. I looked for my mom's car in her usual spot, but someone else's car was sitting there.

"Ava! Nadia!" we heard Ava's mom yelling out of her car window. She stuck her hand out the window and gestured for us to come to the car.

We began racing, and when we got to the car, I looked at Ava's mom with a puzzled look.

"You'll be riding with us today, Nadia. Your mom called me and said she had to go to the hospital right away."

My heart sank. "Is my dad ok?", I asked.

"Come on. Get in. I'm sure everything is fine."

Before getting in, I looked at Ava, who had already climbed into the backseat, as if she was going to give me some information that her mom had left out. She said nothing, so I climbed in next to her. I was extremely worried. My mom never went to the hospital without me. I could only think negative thoughts.

"Are you taking me to the hospital?" I asked Ava's mom from the backseat.

"No, Honey. Your mom told me to take you home with us and she'll pick you up later."

I held my head down for the rest of the ride to Ava's house. I could see Ava staring at me out of the corner of my eye. I knew she wanted to help, but I didn't feel like anything was going to help me feel better except to see my dad awake, sitting up in his bed, smiling.

Ava's mom, Mrs. Kelly, pulled into their circular driveway, and Ava and I grabbed our bookbags off the floor and got out. I walked slowly behind them, dragging my bookbag, as we walked towards the front door. Ava looked back, then reached out for my hand. I didn't reach back out, so she grabbed it. She then took my bookbag out of my hand, and carried both mine and hers.

When we got upstairs to Ava's room, I sat on Ava's bed without saying a word. Ava stood in front of me and said, "You wanna pray about it?"

I looked at her, and in shame, said. "I don't know how."

"You don't know how to pray?" she asked in shock.

"No. No one ever taught me. I've never even been to church."

"Come here. Let me show you something," Ava said, as she walked towards her mirrored closet door.

She opened the door, and there were pieces of paper taped to the walls. Each one had a quote written on it.

"Why do you have these taped to your walls?" I curiously asked Ava.

"These are all Bible verses that I learned in Sunday school. When I feel really down and want to be by myself, I come in here and close the door to pray. It helps me feel better."

6 "But when you pray, go into your most private room, close the door and pray to your Father who is in secret, and you Father who sees [what is done] in secret will reward you." – Matthew 6:6 AMP

Since I'd known Ava, I had never seen her sad. She always seemed so happy and ready to help whoever she could, so it surprised me to hear her say that she prayed when she was sad. Maybe that was precisely the reason I'd never seen her cry or be sad, and I began to think maybe prayer was the answer to my happiness, but how could I possibly be happy when my dad was lying in a hospital bed? It just didn't make sense. None of it.

"You just sit in here by yourself?"

"Not really. God is in here with me listening to everything I say."

"How do you know he's listening? Can you see him?"

"I just know!" Ava replied, sounding like she was getting a little irritated with my questions.

I wasn't trying to upset her. I just didn't understand anything that she was talking about. It was very apparent that Ava and I had been raised very differently, but I was curious to learn some of the things that she knew.

"I remember when my grandma got sick and was in the hospital. I prayed for her every single day. That's when I set up this little space for myself because it was a place where I could pray, and cry if I needed to. I loved my grandma so much and hated seeing her in so much pain. I prayed that she wouldn't hurt anymore and be able to smile again."

I remembered when Ava's grandma had been sick a couple of years before, and she ended up dying, so I didn't understand how Ava's prayers helped the situation.

"So, did God help your grandma?" I asked, anxiously waiting to hear what Ava's answer would be.

To my surprise, Ava replied, "Yes."

"Didn't your grandma die?" I said, ready to dispute her claims.

"Yeah, but she's no longer in pain, and I'm sure she's smiling down on us. I was sad when she died, but my mom helped me understand that she was in a better place."

I understood what Ava was saying, but I wanted my dad to be with me. I thought, *What if I pray that my daddy gets better and God feels like the only way he can be better is if he goes to Heaven?*

That wasn't what I wanted. I learned later in life that it wasn't at all about what I wanted, but what God wanted for our lives. The way in which I thought as a kid was very selfish, but, I, of course, didn't realize that. We may think that something should go one way, but God sometimes has a different plan.

Ava told me to kneel beside her in her "prayer room" so that we could pray together. I really wasn't up to it, but I did it anyway because I knew she wouldn't stop asking. She was very persistent.

"Now put your hands like this," she ordered, as she placed the palms of her hands together in front of her face.

I followed her lead, even though I still didn't see the purpose.

"Now close your eyes and pray."

"I told you I don't know how. What do I say?" I asked.

"Say whatever you feel. Whatever you want to tell God, say it."

I still didn't feel comfortable with the whole thing, especially with Ava sitting there watching and listening.

"You don't have to pray out loud. You know how we read silently?"

"Yeah," I replied.

"You can pray silently, too. God will still hear you. Let's do it together."

Ava and I knelt quietly, with our eyes closed, and the palms of our hands together in the shape of a lotus. I remembered asking God to heal my daddy's aneurysm so that he could wake up. I wanted to see his eyes open. I wanted to see him smile. I didn't know what Ava was praying, but when I opened my eyes, she still had her eyes closed. I could tell that she took prayer very seriously, so I didn't move. I didn't want to interrupt her because it really seemed like God listened to, and favored her.

When she finally finished, she opened her eyes, looked at me, and said, "Amen."

I didn't know if I was supposed to feel any differently, but I didn't. I felt like I'd had a conversation with myself in my head, but I had made Ava happy.

Just when we were about to start our homework, Ava's mom called us from downstairs.

"Nadia, your mom is here."

I hurriedly put all my things back into my bookbag and threw it on my shoulder as I ran out of Ava's room. As I ran down the stairs, I saw my mom standing at the bottom of the staircase talking to Ava's mom. When I reached the bottom, I immediately gave her a hug.

"Thank you for bringing her home with you, Sharon. I don't know what I'd do without you," my mom said to Mrs. Kelly.

"No problem at all," she replied as we walked out the door.

"See you tomorrow, Nadia," Ava said from the staircase.

I turned around and waved goodbye.

Before even getting into the car, I asked, "Did you already go see Dad?"

"Yes, Nadia, I did," she said, looking at me hopelessly.

After we both got into the car, I asked, "Is he better?" hoping that was the reason she had to go to the hospital early, leaving me behind.

It took a moment for my mom to respond, but when she did, it wasn't anything I wanted to hear.

"Your dad developed an infection of the brain."

My brain began churning, and as silly as it may sound, I immediately recalled my mom always telling me to use an antibiotic cream on my wounds so that they wouldn't get infected.

To me, it only made sense when I asked, "Well, can they just use an antibiotic cream for it?"

"I wish it was that simple, Baby. The doctor is putting medicine into his IV to try and get rid of it."

I had learned what an IV was, and some of the other equipment in the room with my dad just from being at the hospital so much. I was intrigued by it all and I would ask the nurses a million and one questions each time they would walk into the room. I think I asked more questions than my mom.

"Can we go see him?"

"Nadia, I just came from the hospital. You're not going to see anything different from what I just saw, which is your dad lying in the same position that he's in every day when we go see him. I think it'll be good for you to just take a break from seeing that today."

I could feel my eyes welling up with tears. I didn't want to take a break. I wanted to see my dad every day. I would've sat there all day, every day if I could have. I couldn't believe she had said that. She made me feel like she was telling me to give up on him, and that wasn't something I was willing to do.

"Mom, please!" I begged. "I need to see him."

My mom continued to drive and didn't reply to my whining. I was desperate and had to think of something fast to plead my case as to why I needed to see him.

"I need to talk to him. He needs to hear my voice."

"He cannot hear you!" my mom yelled, as she slammed on the brakes at a stop sign she'd almost run.

"He can hear me!" I yelled back, with tears running down my face. I had never yelled at my mom, but she just wasn't hearing me. I needed to see my dad and I wasn't willing to take no for an answer.

My mom put the car into park as we remained sitting at the stop sign. She looked at me as a thick vein protruded down the middle of her forehead. I was terrified. Cars began pulling up behind us honking their horns. She just continued to stare at me, ignoring whatever else was going on around us.

"You will never raise your voice at me again! Do you understand me?" she said, clearly enunciating every single letter and syllable that came from her mouth.

I nodded my head.

"Do you understand me?!" she yelled.

"Yes," I said, in a shaky voice, trying to keep from crying.

Cars were going around us as our car sat at the stop sign. My mom put the car back into drive. I sat in shock, with a whirlwind of emotions going through my mind. I felt angry, sad, frustrated, disgusted, lonely, and most of all, hurt. During the ride home, I closed my eyes trying to understand why my mom was acting that way. She knew how important it was for me to see my dad, and she was choosing to deprive me of it.

I finally felt the car come to a complete stop. I opened my eyes, and upon looking out of the window, my eyes lit up at the sight of the hospital. I guessed my mom had thought about it on the way home and realized this was something that I needed.

Before opening her car door, she looked over at me.

"Thank you," I said appreciatively.

I appreciated this visit more than any other time we'd visited. I assumed it was because this one had almost been taken away from me. It's true what they say about taking things for granted. I had never imagined not visiting my daddy every day. It had become routine. The thing about something becoming routine is that you assume it can't be changed or taken away.

I felt so much excitement the entire way to my dad's room, but when I walked in, everything was exactly the same, as my mom had said it would be. I had hoped that some type of miracle had occurred, and there would be a change, but at that point, I was just happy to see him. I ran down my entire day to him, as I always did. I left out the part about Ava showing me how to pray because my mom was sitting in the chair in the corner of the room listening, and I knew how that type of talk made her react.

As I went on and on, I began to notice something happening. His mouth began to turn up. I leaned in closer to make sure I wasn't just imagining things.

"Daddy?" I whispered.

His eyes were still closed, but I could see them moving underneath his eyelids. It looked like he was trying to force them open, but couldn't quite get them there. He then made a moaning sound.

My mom quickly jumped up and ran over to the bed, "Karter? Can you hear me?" She began rubbing his arm, and began yelling, "Nurse! He's waking up."

No one came, so she ran out of the room to get someone.

"Daddy. I'm here. Please open your eyes."

As soon as I said that, it seemed as though he began trying even harder to get his eyes to open. Suddenly, one eye popped opened, then the other slowly opened up. I leaned in even closer to make sure he could see me. I smiled, then his mouth turned up even more than it had before.

My mom ran back in with the nurse, and my daddy wouldn't take his eyes off of me. It seemed like he didn't even realize anyone else was in the room. It was just me and him.

"Mr. Robinson, can you hear me?" the nurse asked my dad.

His eyes remained fixated on me, and he continued to smile.

"Please stand back," the nurse said to me with authority as she got closer to my dad and pulled something out of her pocket. It was a penlight in which she shined into my dad's eyes. His eyes still did not move. She then rolled the blood pressure monitor close to the bed and began taking his blood pressure.

"What's going on?" my mom asked, sounding helpless.

"I'm trying to find out, Ma'am. I have to first take his vitals."

After she took my daddy's blood pressure, with urgency, she said, "I have to get the doctor."

A few minutes after the nurse left the room, a doctor and other nurses entered. They rushed us out and shut the door. It seemed like we stood outside of that room for hours, but it was only maybe fifteen minutes later when someone opened the door.

"Mrs. Robinson," one of the nurses said, as she stuck her head out the door.

"Yes."

"You can come in. The doctor would like to talk to you."

When we walked into the room, the doctor was standing over my dad. His eyes were still open, but didn't seem as if they had moved. The smile was completely gone.

"Hi, Mrs. Robinson. I just wanted to give you an update on your husband's status. He came out of the induced coma due to the medication we're treating him with for the infection. He doesn't have much brain activity and is currently in a vegetative state."

"But he looked at me and smiled," I interrupted.

The doctor looked at me, then at my mom before saying, "Patients in this state may smile, open their eyes, shed a tear, or even moan, but they are not aware of what's going on. Your husband's brain is around ninety-five percent healed. He should definitely have more brain activity than what he has at this time."

"What does that mean?" my mom asked, sounding panicked.

"It means, unfortunately, I can't promise that he'll come out of this even if we do get the infection under control. We'll continue to monitor his brain activity and vitals, and hope for the best."

I could see my mom beginning to lose her composure, then it began.

"I'm so tired of people telling me to hope for the best!" she said, as she picked up the chair and threw it against the wall. "How am I supposed to do that when all you people ever do is give me bad news and send me home to take care of our child by myself?" She then snatched the telephone, ripping the cord out and throwing it to the floor. "What does he need this for? It's not like he can call me! I just want to scream!" my mom yelled.

"Ma'am please calm down," one of the nurses said as she fearfully stood in the corner. "You do not want them to have to call security to restrain you.

I was just as afraid as everyone else that was in the room. I knew what my mom was capable of when she got like that, and it was never good. This was a time when I needed my daddy to step in.

After the nurse asked her to calm down, she looked around at everyone in the room, realizing what had happened.

Seeing that she was starting to calm down, the doctor said, "I'm sorry. I wish I could deliver better news." He then walked out with the rest of his team behind him.

I didn't like the things that I had heard the doctor say, especially when he insinuated that my dad wasn't aware that I was there. I knew that my dad had responded to my voice. He smiled because he heard me, and he opened his eyes because he wanted to see me. No one could've ever taken that away from me. What had given me even more reassurance was the fact that I received exactly what I had prayed for in Ava's closet. God really had heard and listened to me. I was still sad, but I no longer felt like I was alone, and I knew there was someone I could always talk to about anything.

My mom continued to cry, pacing the floor, and repeating over and over again, "I can't believe this! Why is this happening to me?"

I wanted to share my experience with her, but I knew she wouldn't understand. I chose to not allow her to take something so valuable away from me. My faith. While she continued to have her pity party, I stood over my dad and held his hand. I gave him a kiss on the cheek and whispered into his ear, "I love you, Daddy."

Chapter Sixteen

The next morning, I woke up extra early for school. There was one extra thing on my agenda to do before going to school, so I made sure that I had plenty of time to do it. I was surprised to hear my mom's voice, especially with it being so early. I didn't want her to know that I was already awake, so I quietly crept to my door, opened it, and stuck my ear out, trying to hear what my mom was talking about. It was odd for her to be on the phone so early, so I was wondering if something had happened overnight at the hospital.

"I'm so glad that I have you to talk to. I don't know what I would do without your conversation. You've just been so supportive, and I truly appreciate you," she said to the person on the other end.

I had no idea who my mom could've been talking to. She had a few friends, including Miss Val, but she rarely ever talked to them on the phone. As a matter of fact, she never really talked on the phone at all, so I would've never imagined her talking at five in the morning. I continued to listen, trying to see if I could figure out who the person was on the other end. As she began to laugh like I hadn't heard her laugh in a long time, it didn't even matter anymore. I was just thankful for whoever it was she was talking to. It was nice to hear laughter in the house again.

I then quietly closed my bedroom door and walked over to my closet. I opened the door, looked into the darkness, and took a deep breath. I wondered if I should've left the light off or turned it on. I wasn't sure if God would be able to see me in the dark, so I pulled the string hanging from the ceiling so he could see that it was me talking to him. I shut the door behind me, and stared at the bare white walls. I didn't have anything special taped to them like Ava, and I really didn't understand what the purpose was for her having Bible scriptures taped to the walls. I just hoped God would listen to me the way that he did at Ava's house.

I got down on my knees, put my palms together, and closed my eyes like Ava had taught me. At first, I felt weird. My first thought was to pray silently, but I felt the need to do more, so I began to pray aloud.

"Hi, God. It's me again. Thank you for listening to me yesterday. My dad opened his eyes and smiled at me, just like I told you I wanted him to. The doctor didn't tell us any good news about him, and it doesn't sound like he's going to get better, but Nurse Grace told my mom that you're our true doctor, so can you please help my dad? I don't like seeing him like that. He's such a good father to me, and husband to my mom, and he tries to help everyone, so I really don't understand why this is happening to him, but if he did something bad that I don't know about, can you please forgive him? He can't say he's sorry right now, so I'm saying sorry for him. I know he would say it if he could . . ."

"I thought I heard talking in here! What are you doing?" my mom yelled, after opening my closet door, interrupting my conversation with God.

I quickly got off of my knees and sat on the floor with my back up against the wall. My mom had startled me to the point that my heart felt like it was about to jump out of my chest.

"I said what are you doing?" she repeated, sounding angrier than the first time.

"I was praying," I stuttered knowing she knew exactly what I was doing, but wanted to hear me say it.

My mom put her hands on her hips and said, "Praying? Praying to who?"

I had begun to calm down, so I stood up, and said, "To God."

My mom shook her head and put her hand on my shoulder. She then looked into my eyes and said, "Baby, don't you think if there was really a god who really cared your daddy wouldn't be in a hospital bed right now? We don't have anyone to help us. All we have is each other, so we have to stick together. Where are you getting this nonsense from anyway? Are you believing what that crazy nurse was trying to feed us?"

I nodded my head. I didn't want my mom to know that Ava was the one had been talking to me about God because I was afraid that she wouldn't let me see her anymore if she did. I already didn't have my dad to talk to. I couldn't lose my best friend, too.

"Listen, Nadia. We're going to get through this, but closing yourself up in closet talking to a wall isn't going to help. You understand?"

Again, I nodded my head, in agreement with my mom. I loved her, just as much as I loved my dad, but I had seen something miraculous happen. I prayed and something had actually happened. Nothing, up to that point, that my mom had said or done had helped the situation one bit. With that being said, I had to believe in what worked, and from what I'd seen, that was prayer.

After my mom left my room, I placed the palms of my hands back together again, closed my eyes, and said, "Amen," to complete my prayer, since I wasn't sure whether or not it was a requirement. I wanted to make sure it was done right.

At exactly one o' clock in the afternoon on that same day, forty-three days after my thirteenth birthday, I believe that the prayer that I had prayed that morning freed my dad from his pain and suffering. While I was at school, the doctor called my mom and told her that the infection had become so severe that it was spreading throughout his body, and his organs were shutting down. He wasn't even able to breathe on his own any longer, so he was placed back on a ventilator until my mom got to the hospital. She didn't even wait for me to get out of school to take him off life support. She had them to pull the plug shortly after she got there.

"Your father died today," she said in dry, unaffected tone, as soon as I jumped in the passenger seat after standing in front of the school waiting for her to arrive.

At first, I didn't react. I couldn't believe that it was true due to her extremely cold demeanor. I sat there trying to process what she had said, but I couldn't process it because the other part of my brain was waiting on her to say that she was just kidding. It didn't make any sense for her to joke about something like that. In fact, that would've been a pretty cruel joke and I knew that, but it just seemed so unreal.

My heart felt like it was in the pit of my stomach the rest of the way home. I thought about what I had prayed just hours before, and now my dad was gone. Did I want my dad to die? Of course not, but like Ava had said about her grandmother, he was in a better place.

I felt like I no longer knew the woman that my mom was becoming, and I knew it would now just get worse because it was official that my dad would never again be around to help her. I didn't know if I should've believed that she just didn't care, or if it was just a part of her illness. I knew she had loved my dad. There was no denying that when anyone saw them together. They made everyone smile just by seeing them enjoy each other. From the time my dad went into the hospital up until that moment, it seemed like my mom's entire soul had been poisoned. I honestly believed that each visit to that hospital killed her more and more. She became so cold, and her heart hardened.

When we walked into the house, it seemed different from the other days since my dad had been in the hospital. Before, I had hope that he would walk through those doors again. Now, it felt strange to know that he would never again step foot into the home that the three of us shared together. I would never hug him again. He would no longer be able to help me with my homework. We would never watch basketball again. He would never be at anymore of my basketball games to cheer me on. I would never again hear his goofy laugh. I would've never imagined that my twelfth birthday would've been the last one he would've celebrated with me. My birthday would never be the same. I felt so many emotions, but I had no idea how to manage them all.

I wanted my mom to hold me and tell me everything would be ok. I wanted her to tell me how much my dad loved us both, but he'd want us to remember the good times, and to keep living and continue making him proud. I just wanted her to act like my mom. She had said that all we had was each other, but she hadn't been there for me emotionally, and hadn't allowed me to try to be there for her. I hadn't realize the cons of not having any siblings until that day. Being the only child could get lonely, and that was probably why Ava and I had grown so close so quickly. Being the only child was one of the things we had in common.

My mom hadn't said one word to me since she'd told me my dad had died. As soon as we walked into our dark, quiet home, she went straight to the refrigerator and pulled out one of her many bottles of wine. Lately, it didn't matter what the occasion was, or if there was an occasion at all, she always had a bottle of wine ready.

Without turning on any lights, I watched her pour a glass of wine and very casually walk upstairs to her room with the glass in one hand, and the bottle in the other, and shut the door. I stood in the darkness, not knowing what to do next. I was hurting badly. I just wanted someone to talk to. Anyone. I thought about picking up the telephone to call Ava, but I knew I would probably do nothing but cry. I did the next best thing I could think of doing. I went into the family room and stared at my daddy's empty recliner. I closed my eyes for a moment, envisioning him sitting there watching television. I opened my eyes back up, disappointed that the chair was still empty. I slowly walked over to it and climbed in, sinking my face into the cushions. I immediately found his scent, which made me feel closer to him.

"God, please help," I said, right before falling asleep in what felt like my daddy's arms.

Chapter Seventeen

From my seat at the front of the funeral home's chapel, I watched everyone walk in. I tried to avoid facing forward because I couldn't stand the view ahead. It was my dad's cold, lifeless body, lying there alone, in a casket. My mom walked around, greeting all of her and my dad's friends, and the few distant relatives that the both of them had. She wore a black belted dress, and high heels. Her jet-black hair was pulled back into a bun, and she wore a chic, black, mesh veil which made it quite evident that she was the widow of the deceased. Her bright red lipstick stood out from her mocha skin and elevated her beauty to another level. She was beautiful on the outside, but only I knew that she was a complete mess on the inside, just as I was.

Everyone who entered the chapel gave her a hug and whispered, what I assumed to be words of encouragement, into her ear. They would only notice me after walking away from the casket from paying their last respects to my dad. By the end of the service, I knew I'd probably have around fifty different shades of lipstick on my cheeks and forehead.

Ava, her mom, and her dad also dropped by to pay their respects. Ever since the day Ava and I had become friends, my dad and her dad had also become pretty close. They all gave me a big hug, and her mom told me to let them know if my mom and I needed anything. My mom had missed them walking in the door, so when she noticed them talking to me, she came over.

As she hugged Mrs. Kelly, in a soft voice, I heard her say, "Thank you so much for all that you've done to help with the services. I had no idea there was no life insurance. I left all of that for Karter to handle."

"Don't you worry about that. We're here to help a friend in a time of need."

After hearing what my mom said about the life insurance, I couldn't believe that my dad would've left us in a bad situation. It wasn't like him. I knew that he was very responsible, and always took care of us, but I also knew that no one was perfect, no matter how perfect they seemed, so maybe he'd just dropped the ball.

At that moment, a very loud and obnoxious woman came out of nowhere, grabbing my mom's arm. I had never seen the woman before. She resembled my mom, but I could tell she wasn't quite as reserved, especially during the current circumstances.

"Hey, my favorite cousin! I am so sorry about Karson. I didn't get to know him very well, although I tried, but he had you living well. You got with him and forgot all about the rest of your family!"

"Karter . . ." my mom said.

The woman frowned and tilted her head in confusion.

"My husband's name is Karter, and you, of all people should know that."

"Oh. I'm sorry, girl! It's been so long since you swiped him up from right up underneath my nose, but I can't blame you. He was a fine man!" she said, smiling, and putting her hand up to give my mom a high five.

Ava and her parents stood back, watching in disbelief, as I watched in embarrassment. After hearing that she was my mom's cousin, I saw exactly why we didn't go around family.

My mom's uncompassionate cousin continued, "So what happened to him, because you know how rumors get started, so I just want to get the facts straight from you so I can set everyone else straight."

My mom's arms hung to her side, and I saw both of her hands slowly begin to ball up in a fist.

I jumped up and grabbed one of her hands and asked, "When can we go?"

"Awww! Is that you and Karson's baby girl? She looks just like her daddy! Hey, little cuz! I'm Cousin Lily. We'll have to get together one day. I have some stories to tell you about your momma!"

As Cousin Lily continued to talk, I began pulling my mom away from her before she did something she might've regretted later.

As I snatched her away, my mom yelled, "Karter! His name is Karter!"

Everyone in the chapel became quiet, and all eyes were focused on me and my mom. She snatched the veil off of her head and threw it down. She then burst into tears and fell to the ground. The crowd began hovering over her, trying to see if she was ok. The funeral home directors came in, clearing everyone out of the way.

"What's going on here?" the shorter, light complected woman with freckles asked, as she looked around at everyone.

"I was telling her how sorry I was for her loss and she just lost it! I'm not surprised though. She was always a little crazy. She could never control her temper."

"Please get her out of here!" my mom yelled.

"I'm sorry ma'am. You have to go," the male funeral director said, as he motioned her towards the door, and escorted her out.

She continued to talk badly about my mom the entire way out. In the midst of all the commotion, Miss Val suddenly appeared, and knelt down next to my mom.

"Breathe, Lena. You got this. In and out . . .," she coached my mom's breathing, trying to help calm her down.

I had seen my dad calm her down the same way, and I realized that I would now probably have to accept that responsibility unless Miss Val would agree to live with us, and I didn't see that happening. After Miss Val had calmed her down, and the spectators were still taking notes on what they could go home and gossip about, we helped her up off the floor. Miss Val hugged her, while gently caressing her back. She then turned around and hugged me.

"God will get you through this, Nadia. He's the only one who can," she whispered in my ear.

After she released me, I looked at her, helplessly.

"What's wrong, Nadia?" she asked, with concern in her eyes.

I looked around making sure my mom was no longer around and I spotted her sitting next to Ava's mom. While the coast was clear, I desperately said, "I don't know how to help her."

"Oh, Nadia. It will be ok. Your dad would call me from time to time just to talk. Your mom is a beautiful person, but she's been through a lot and has some issues. She refuses to take medication to help her, so I just continue to pray that she'll do what she needs to do and get the help that she needs. Especially after this. I don't want you to carry this burden."

As she spoke, she pulled a pen and a gum wrapper out of her purse and began writing.

"Here. If you ever need me, just call. No matter what it is. Don't worry, Baby."

It made me feel better knowing that Miss Val knew exactly what I was going through. I never knew my dad talked to her about things, but I was glad that he had. I felt that I still had some type of security in my life.

"Thank you," I said to Miss Val, as I gave her another hug.

After our conversation, I saw my mom had gotten up, and she was standing in the aisle talking to someone. When I looked closer, I realized that it was Spence, from the hospital. Miss Val and I looked at each other, and I quickly walked over, wondering why he was there, and how he even knew anything about my dad passing.

I stood next to my mom, trying to closer analyze the situation.

"Hey, Nadia. I'm so sorry about your dad," Spence said.

"Thank you," I replied.

"You remember Spence, don't you?" my mom asked.

"Yeah."

Both, my mom and Spence began to look uncomfortable, and looked at each other as if they were looking for the other to say something to make it less uncomfortable.

"Nadia, I know losing your dad is hard, and I know from experience that not having one around is rough, so I just want you to know I'm a dad myself, and I'm here to be a father figure to you whenever you need it."

"She won't be needing that," Miss Val said sternly, as she walked up behind me.

My mom looked stunned, not realizing that Miss Val was nearby, watching everything that was happening.

"Who are you, anyway?" Miss Val asked, folding her arms.

Right when Spence was about to respond, my mom said, "Spence is a friend of mine. I met him in the hospital when Karter was first admitted. He's a financial consultant, and has been helping me get through everything the best way I can. You know there was no life insurance policy, so he's been helping me figure out how I'm going to manage to survive."

"I see. Well, my doors are always open for you to come work back at the diner. Don't get yourself caught up in something that you shouldn't be involved in." Miss Val said, as she looked Spence up and down and walked away.

My mom rolled her eyes, and then continued her conversation with Spence. "Sorry about that," she apologized.

I was sad to say my final goodbyes to my dad, but I was happy when the day was over. All of it was just too much for me, and since I couldn't have my daddy back, I just wanted to get started trying to figure out how I was going to live without him. He was the first man I ever loved, and I knew that my previous life would now be a distant memory.

Chapter Eighteen

Every day seemed excruciatingly long. Everything I did felt like I was going in slow motion. I had tried to go back to my normal life, but nothing about it felt normal. Basketball wasn't even the same anymore, so I quit the team. All I ever seemed to want to do was sleep so that I could hope that when I woke up, everything that had happened over the past few months had been a bad dream. I had isolated myself from everyone outside of school, even Ava. She would try to call me, or come over to the house, but I would always lie and tell her that my mom and I had plans. Truth was, my mom and I never had plans, and she didn't seem to have a problem with it. She had started getting out more often, but never asked me if I wanted to join her. After school, I stayed closed up in my room every day until it was time to eat. That was when my mom and I would have our one conversation for the day in which we would only speak maybe a total of fifty words to one another. I tried to pray all the time, but I never knew what to ask for in prayer. I didn't know how things could be better. Those were the days that I felt like I needed Ava. Since I didn't know what to say, I said my short, simple prayer that I would pray whenever I was at a loss for words. They were three short words, but I didn't have anything else. Those words were, "God, please help."

Just when I thought things couldn't possibly get worse, the unthinkable happened.

"Nadia! Come eat," my mom yelled from downstairs.

In my sweats and t-shirt, which had recently become my everyday attire, I dragged my feet down the stairs. When I got to the kitchen, my mouth almost hit the floor. Spence was sitting in my daddy's chair at the kitchen table.

"Hey, Nadia!" he said.

My breathing began to escalate as I looked over at my mom, who was obviously fixing a plate for Spence.

"Don't be rude, Nadia. Say hello!" she said, smiling as if nothing was wrong.

"Get up!" I said angrily.

Spence looked at me with intensity in his eyes.

"Do you talk to adults like that?" He then looked at my mom and said, "Lena, is this how you train your child to talk to adults?"

"Nadia, you need to apologize," my mom said.

"No! He needs to get out of my daddy's seat!"

My mom put Spence's plate on the table in front of him.

"Thank you, Babe," he said to her, but grinning at me, attempting to get under my skin.

She then walked over to me and said, "Your daddy is no longer here, so that seat is no longer his. If Spence wants to sit there, he is welcomed to do so!"

I was so infuriated that evening that I didn't even eat. I ran upstairs and slammed the door. I began piecing things together in my mind. The phone conversations full of laughter that my mom had before my dad was even gone, Spence showing up at my daddy's funeral, my mom's sudden outings without me, and tonight, a sudden unwelcomed visitor sitting in my daddy's seat at the table. My mom had been seeing Spence for no telling how long, and then just decided to introduce the relationship to me during dinner, only months after my dad died.

Things only went downhill from there. Spence began coming by several nights a week to eat dinner and hang out with my mom. Unfortunately, if I wanted to eat, I had to tolerate him and the entire situation. As I would sit at the table with them, trying to quickly finish my meal so that I could remove myself from their presence, Spence would talk about his two sons who were a little older than me. I assumed they were kids of the ex-wife who he had never gotten over, and said he'd always love. Did my mom not even think about that, or was she even thinking at all? It seemed as if this man had put a spell on her, or maybe he had been giving her money. I'd noticed that my mom always had money to do things, and didn't seem like she was struggling paying the bills. I couldn't understand how she was doing that without working. She didn't even have money to pay for a funeral.

Many of my questions were answered one day when I unintentionally heard a conversation between Spence and my mom when they thought I was closed up in my room, as I usually was. On my way to the bathroom, I stopped on the catwalk and noticed Spence and my mom below, sitting in the family room. Lately, there had been nothing abnormal about that, but what made me stop was that Spence had decided to sit in my dad's recliner, which he never did. They were talking, so instead of confronting them about my daddy's recliner, I decided to listen.

"Did you think any more about the investment account I mentioned to you for the money from the life insurance policy?" Spence asked.

"I don't think I want to invest that money. I think I'll just keep it stashed away," she replied.

"A million dollars is a lot of money to just be stashing away. You should really let me invest it for you. You know that's my expertise."

At first, I was confused, but the more and more I listened, I realized that my mom had made everyone believe that she didn't have any money to pay for the funeral, and let Ava's parents pay for it, when she had a one-million-dollar policy. Now, it seemed that Spence was trying to get his hands on it.

The conversation became even more interesting when they began talking about living arrangements.

"I think I'll be able to make a better decision about the money after we get the house. I'm so excited."

"The boys and I are, too. I'll be glad when you get out of this house. Every time I'm here, it feels like he's watching us."

"You're so silly," my mom laughed.

My mom and Spence had an entire plan to move in together and leave our home. Our home was the only home I knew. It had been the home where all of my memories existed. She was snatching away everything that I had left of my dad, one by one. The woman that I was living with was not the same woman that gave birth to me, and no one could convince me otherwise. Everything from that point on moved so quickly. Within one month's time, my mom sold our house and bought a new house that was in a totally different neighborhood, and sadly for me, in a different school district. It wasn't far from the hospital where I had spent all of my final moments with my daddy. I felt like I was forced to leave my entire life behind, including my best friend, Ava.

Chapter Nineteen

The day we moved into our new home, was the day that I met Spence's sons, William and Josiah. When my mom and I pulled up to the house, the moving truck was already sitting outside. From the outside, the house looked like something that I thought I would only see on TV. Never in a million years could I had ever imagined that I would ever live in a home like that.

"So, what do you think?" my mom asked before we got out of the car.

My first thought was why was she asking me what I thought when it hadn't seemed to matter what I thought about anything else lately. It certainly didn't matter when she decided to throw my dad's recliner out in the dumpster, and told me we just didn't have the space. By looking at the house right in front of me, we had plenty of space. I would've put it in my bedroom if I had to.

"It's nice," I said, nonchalantly.

She looked at me as if she was disappointed, and said, "Come on. Let me show you around."

As we walked into the house, Spence was coming down the spiral staircase.

"There's my girl!" he said, referring to my mom, of course. I could tell that he wasn't very fond of me, and the feelings were mutual.

"Where are the boys?" my mom asked.

"They should be right behind me. I was just getting them set up in their rooms."

I then saw two boys coming down the stairs. They looked almost exactly alike, but one was just a little taller, and dark complected like Spence. The other had a caramel complexion like me, and wore big, thick glasses.

"Hey, boys!" my mom said excitedly.

"Hey Mama Lena", the shorter boy said. The other one, who I assumed to be the oldest of the two, just nodded.

Mama Lena? I thought to myself. I must've really been out of the loop because they seemed very familiar with my mom.

"This is my daughter, Nadia. Nadia, this is Josiah, Spence's youngest son," she said.

Josiah stuck out his hand for me to shake, and said, "You can call me Joey."

"What's this handshaking all about?" Spence said. "We're all family. It's ok to hug each other!" he continued as he forced a group hug between him, myself, and Joey.

Spence's other son didn't seem very friendly. He stood there expressionless, which made me wonder if he felt the same way about this situation that I did.

"This is my eldest son, William," Spence said. "He looks mean, but he's just a big pushover."

"Yes, he is!" my mom agreed.

William's expression completely changed, revealing a welcoming smile. It was a little disturbing.

"Nice to meet you, Nadia," he said.

I tried to convince myself that maybe things wouldn't be too bad. I had to make the most of the situation because it wasn't like I had many other options.

My mom and Spence took me on a tour around the house. The boys followed along, even though they seemed to know their way around pretty well. I seemed to be the only outcast. When we got to the second floor, there were three bedrooms, and they had all been claimed.

My mom looked at Spence and said, "Didn't we agree that one of these rooms would be Nadia's?"

"Yeah, but I felt it would be better if the boys are down here with us, and Nadia have her privacy up there," he said, as he pointed to the narrow staircase heading up to what looked to be an attic.

"And the walls are soundproof, so she can play her music as loud as she wants."

"She's only thirteen. I don't feel comfortable with her being up there by herself. Will is nineteen, and that was the reason we said that he could have that room. Nadia doesn't play loud music. Will, on the other hand, does."

"I can take that room," Will interrupted.

"No. You're good. Nadia will be fine, won't you Nadia?" Spence asked.

"Yeah, that's fine."

My mom looked at Spence like she wanted to say something, but just led me up the stairs. It was a very private area, and I would at least have my own bathroom. It was like a master suite, but there was no closet, and no windows. There was only a clothes rack for me to hang my clothes.

"You sure this is ok?" my mom asked again, trying to sound as if she was really concerned.

Before I could answer, Spence said, "We're not about to keep talking about this. This is the way it's about to be, so let's move on.

I had never really seen my mom succumb to anyone, not even my dad, and I was just hoping she wasn't holding everything in, because if she was, I knew that she would eventually snap. Her moods had seemed stable lately, but I knew from experience that that could've changed in a matter of seconds. I wondered if

Spence had any idea about her condition. If not, he'd be in for a rude awakening, and might've just found himself looking for another place to live. That was assuming that my mom had paid for the house with the life insurance money.

I got along pretty well with Will and Joey. Joey was sixteen, so we were closer in age and had more in common. I had once asked about his mom and he said that he didn't know where she lived. He and Will would talk to her on the phone, but she refused to let their dad find out where she was. It sounded like she was in hiding, but I couldn't get Joey to go into detail about it. Whenever I would start asking too many questions, he would change the subject.

When I watched my mom and Spence together, they seemed happy, but I could also tell that Spence was very controlling and manipulative. If my mom had an opinion about something, he had a different opinion, or if she wanted something one way, he wanted it a different way, and It was either his way or no way. Amongst all of the many other things that had changed about my mom and her behavior, I had also begun noticing that whenever I saw an argument about to erupt between my mom and Spence, she would go into the bathroom and be in there for a while. I knew she was probably in there calming herself down, but I knew that one day it wouldn't be that simple.

Soon, there weren't only arguments. Spence began to be not only emotionally, but also physically abusive to my mom. That's when it dawned on me why Joey and Will's mom probably got as far away from him as possible. I could tell Will and Joey had been around that kind of thing all of their lives because they just acted as if it was normal. When I would hear the arguments begin to escalate, I would go up to my room and close the door. I had tried to defend my mom once and learned my lesson. She had ended up turning on me as if I was the one abusing her. When I was in my room, I was in my own world. I couldn't hear anything going on around me, and I kind of liked it like that. After their fights, my mom would be upset for a while, but all Spence had to do was come home with a gift or flowers, and she'd act as if nothing had happened, even if he had blackened her eye.

I kept in touch with Ava, but it was nothing like seeing her every day at school. She came over one time, but she later told me she probably wouldn't come back. She said that Will had made her feel uncomfortable by the way he was looking at us while we were playing basketball on the court that Spence had put outside. I told her that he was a little different, but she didn't have anything to worry about. She still chose to not put herself in an uncomfortable situation, and hated that I had to live there with them. She felt that the entire situation was strange, from my mom moving on with another man so soon, to leaving our house behind to buy a home with that man and his kids. I definitely agreed with that, but there was nothing I could do about it. I always listened to what Ava had to say about things because she was wise beyond her years, so I did take her concern about Will seriously. I began watching his actions closely, and paid a lot more attention to how he looked at me. I definitely began to notice what Ava was talking about, but he hadn't been disrespectful towards me in any way, so I kept it to myself.

Chapter Twenty

My mom and Spence left the house one early Sunday morning. Spence was wearing a suit, and my mom was wearing a dress. All they said was that they would be back later. I couldn't imagine that my mom was going to church, unless Spence was forcing her to, but he didn't seem like the type to go to church either. When they got back, my mom came in the door smiling, with her hand out in front of her.

Spence came in behind her, also smiling, and said, "Now introducing, Mrs. Lena Spencer!"

When I looked closer at my mom's hand, her wedding ring from my dad had been replaced with a ring that didn't even look like it was half the value of her other one. I couldn't believe my mother was being so impulsive. All of the decisions that she had made within the past few months had been huge, and I definitely didn't feel as though she was in her right mind. I looked at Spence's hand, and he also had another ring, but it wasn't on his ring finger. It was on his right hand. He was still wearing the ring from his previous marriage on his left hand.

"Spence, why are you still wearing your other ring?" I asked.

My mom hadn't even realized that Spence had put the other ring back on.

She looked down at his hand, and said, "You put it back on? It's time to let it go, Spence. We're married now!"

"This ring is attached to me. I'll never take it off. It's from my first love, and I've told you before, I'll always love her."

My mom's excitement completely diminished. She stormed through the house, straight to her safe haven, the bathroom.

I stuck around and continued to talk to Spence.

"So, what made the two of you decide this?"

With his arrogant demeanor that I couldn't stand, he said, "I have a buddy that's a pastor, so when I realized my anniversary with my ex-wife would've been today, I thought, why not ask Lena to marry me, and we get married on that same day? That makes fewer dates for me to have to remember," he laughed.

I couldn't even believe he had let that come out of his mouth without an ounce of shame. I was young, but I knew what should've and shouldn't have come out of a person's mouth, and that was one thing that shouldn't have left his lips. Will and Joey even looked at each other in disbelief. I'd heard enough for one day. I shook my head and went to my room. What I didn't know was that there would be more to come.

That same evening, Joey, Will, Spence, and I sat at the dinner table getting ready to eat Sunday dinner. After dealing with the emotional disappointment of her new husband telling her that he would continue to wear his wedding band from his previous marriage, my mom had been slaving over a hot stove for the rest of the afternoon. She had reverted back to what she knew by keeping herself busy all day in order to keep her mind off of how upset she really was. Joey, Will, and I fixed our plates, and my mom fixed Spence's plate, as usual. When she finally got to sit down, she looked around at everyone at the table. She didn't look right, and I recognized that emptiness in her eyes. I figured that she was probably still a little upset from earlier, but it had triggered a whole lot more than a little anger.

Without tasting a thing, she asked, "Is the chicken dry?"

Everyone began looking around at each other, then Spence, Will, and Joey looked at me, as though I was supposed to tell them what to say.

"No, mom. The chicken is good," I finally answered.

She looked around at the others and said, "So, why didn't anyone else answer?"

She then stood up over the table and pounded it with her fists.

"I said is the chicken dry?!"

"Lena, what's happening here? Spence asked, dumbfoundedly.

My mom answered her own question, and said, "Yes, the chicken is dry! You know how I know? Because I was so upset that I couldn't focus on what I was doing, and I left it in the oven too long. Now it's dried out. No one is honest anymore! If the chicken is dry, just say it!"

She began snatching up all of the plates from in front of us that we had loaded with food, and quickly began walking back and forth to the kitchen, throwing them in the sink. She then took the entire chicken and threw it across the table. It smashed into the wall, just missing Will's head.

"Mom, calm down," I pleaded with her.

"Little girl, who are you to tell me to calm down? You think I'm supposed to take orders from you?"

"Nadia, what's wrong with her?" Spence asked in desperation.

I thought for a second to tell him what was going on, but after all that he had put my mom through, I didn't feel like he deserved to know. She hadn't treated me the best, but I still loved her, and I knew that Spence really didn't have her best interest at heart.

I shrugged my shoulders. I had watched my dad handle my mom when she was like that, and I could've easily intervened, or given Spence some tips, but he was the reason that this had happened. He had triggered this response.

My mom grabbed the knife off the table that she had used to carve the chicken, and that's when Spence jumped up and quickly grabbed her and restrained her arms.

I grabbed her hand that was holding the knife, and began to caress it. "It's ok, mom. Just breathe . . . in and out . . ."

She finally began to calm down, but Spence was sure not to let her go too soon. Joey and Will had also jumped out of their seats and had their backs up against the wall. Their eyes were popping out of their skulls.

After getting my mom completely calm and into bed, Spence was still confused, but just assumed that she'd snapped because he had upset her. I decided to let him believe that, and not tell him that he would be dealing with that for as long as they were together. I was a little glad it had happened. Maybe in the future he would've thought twice about mistreating her. I went into the living room and laid across the sofa in front of the television. It had been an exhausting day. I was so tired that I fell asleep within minutes of laying down, as attempted to watch a movie. I suddenly felt someone sit beside me. I managed to get one eye open and saw that it was Will, so I just pretended to be asleep because I really didn't feel like talking. I really just wanted to be alone, and should've gone to my room. Will grabbed the remote and began flicking through the channels. As I attempted to fall back asleep, I heard Joey's voice as he walked into the room. He sat down in the chair and they began having a normal, brotherly conversation, mostly about what had transpired at the dinner table, when all of a sudden, I felt Will's hand on my leg. I tried not to think anything of it, until he began caressing it, which wasn't appropriate in any way.

"Dude. What are you doing?" I heard Joey say after he noticed what was going on.

"What are you talking about?" Will asked, acting as if he was doing nothing wrong.

"Keep your hands off of her."

"I knew you liked her," Will said, laughing. "Does this make you mad" he said as he put his hand on my thigh.

Before things could go any further, I jumped up and ran upstairs to my room. I didn't know what that had been all about, but maybe that was exactly what Ava had had a bad feeling about.

I never thought that Will would actually try to touch me, but I guess I had been just a little too naïve.

While trying to fathom what had happened, I ended up dozing back off until I was awakened sometime during the night by a loud squeaking sound. It was the sound that my bedroom door would make when I opened it. When I opened my eyes, I didn't see any light shining through my room, so I knew that my door was still closed. As I tried to go back to sleep, I suddenly felt someone hovering over me. I could feel their breath close to my skin. I began panicking, and tried to jump up, but I was pinned down to the bed and couldn't move. I tried to reach for the lamp to either turn on to see who was attacking me, or knock them upside the head with it. Whichever came first. I cried and screamed to the top of my lungs, but it was a waste. No one could hear me. My attacker never said a word, but they came in like a thief in the night, stole my innocence, and left me defenseless and disoriented.

As soon as he left, I struggled to get up, but managed. I limped down the stairs with tears streaming down my face, and blood running down my legs. I made it to my mom's room and the door was locked.

"Mom," I cried. "Please open the door."

Spence came to the door, barely cracking it open. "What's wrong with you? It's three in the morning!"

"He raped me!" I yelled.

"Who raped you?"

My mom then came to the door and pushed it all the way open.

"What's going on?"

I hugged my mom, and said, "Will raped me."

Spence said, "Will? He would never do something like that!"

Spence walked around the house, checking the windows and doors.

"Everything is closed and locked. No one came in here and attacked you."

"I know no one came in. They didn't have to come in because he was already here! Are you listening to me? Look at me!" I said, pointing to the blood on my legs."

After my mom looked down at me, she yelled, "Will!"

She headed to his room, and Spence grabbed her.

"You think my son actually did something to her?"

"Do you think my daughter is lying? She's bleeding!"

She continued walking to Will's room and we followed behind. When she opened his door, he was in bed, knocked out, snoring.

"Did you see him?" my mom asked.

I hesitated, and said, "No, but earlier today, he had his hand on my leg while I was sleeping on the sofa."

"Really, Nadia? On your leg?" my mom said.

"I told you," Spence said. "My boys aren't like that. I raised them right. She's just looking for attention! And that blood is probably just from her period, unless she wants to say that came from Will touching her leg!" he said, shaking his head.

I started walking towards Joey's room to see if he had heard anything.

"Where are you going?" Spence asked.

"Joey saw what happened earlier. I want to see if he heard anything."

All three of us walked into his room, and he was also sleeping.

"Nadia, I think you just had a bad dream, and like Spence said, you started your period, so go clean yourself up and go back to bed," my mom said, looking at me like I was the one who had the problem.

I knew what had happened to me, and they didn't want to do anything about it. They made me feel like I was crazy. I even asked them to call the police, and they asked me what they were supposed to tell them. I had come to the conclusion that I was in a house full of crazy people and God had to have a better plan for me. He had to be working on a way out for me. I tried to believe that in my heart, but sometimes it was so hard.

I spent the rest of the early morning showering and praying. I couldn't go back to sleep, and even after I'd showered for over an hour, I still felt dirty. I couldn't wash away what had happened. What had I done to anyone to be treated that way? Absolutely nothing.

Later that morning, I ran into Joey in the kitchen and asked if he had heard anything earlier that morning. He said he hadn't and asked me why I was asking. I told him what had happened, and even he looked at me like I was crazy. He asked if I thought maybe I'd just had a bad dream. I knew it wasn't a dream, and I knew Will had done this. There was no other explanation.

Will walked in shortly after. He had violated me, and I couldn't even look at him.

"You look like you had a rough night," he said.

Joey looked at him, and laughed. "Yeah, she did, in her dreams."

"It was not a dream!" I yelled.

I became so upset that I ran up behind Will and jumped on his back. I began beating him in the head with both fists.

"You did this to me! Just admit you raped me!"

Will began turning around in circles, trying to pry me off of him.

Spence then walked in and aggressively pulled me off of Will. He then threw me up against the wall and pulled back his fist as if he was about to punch me, when my mom stepped in and pulled him back.

"You better tell your daughter to stop telling these lies! I didn't sign up for this, Lena."

My mom knelt down, and I'll never forget what she said.

"Nadia, stop trying to be the center of attention! You were always like this, and your daddy did whatever you wanted him to. Your daddy isn't here anymore, Baby girl, so you have to accept that life doesn't revolve around you!"

"What is wrong with you?" I asked. "What kind of mother doesn't believe their daughter when they tell them something like what I told you? I was raped! Why don't you believe me?"

"I'm a great mother, especially for one who didn't want any children! I resent your dad to this day for making me keep you. You have done nothing but cause problems."

15 "Can a mother forget the baby at her breast and have no compassion on the child she has borne? Though she may forget, I will not forget you! 16 See, I have engraved you on the palms of my hands; your walls are ever before me."
– Isaiah 49:15-16 NIV

The kitchen became completely silent. I knew at that moment that my mom didn't love me. I was only around because of my dad. I slowly got up off the floor and thanked my mom for telling me how she really felt. I went up to my room and shut and locked my door. As far as I was concerned, I was on my own. No one stood up for me or supported me when I needed it most, so I did what I had to do.

I had thought about calling Miss Val to tell her what was going on, but I had begun trusting people less and less, and I thought that since Miss Val had been so close to my mom, she wouldn't have believed me either.

The next day, I left the house early, heading for school. I didn't want to see anyone. Not even Joey. I felt like he could've defended me, but chose not to. I had planned out exactly what I was going to do the night before. The hospital wasn't far from my school, so I took a chance of going there to try to find Nurse Grace. Something was telling me that she would be able to help.

Chapter Twenty-One

As I stood in front of the hospital, it brought back so many memories, but I had to refrain from thinking about that at that moment. I snuck past the front desk as the receptionist was helping someone else, and got on the elevator, heading to the second floor. I remembered that room 2115 was the room that Nurse Grace had taken us to, so I was hoping that I would find her somewhere nearby.

As I walked the second floor in the Intensive Care Unit, I walked past several nurses, but none of them were Nurse Grace. She could've been anywhere, even helping out with someone's surgery. Tired of walking the halls, I sat in a chair outside of one of the rooms with my head down. I felt like I had wasted my time, and it was time to just give up.

"Hello, there," I heard a familiar voice say.

I looked up with tears in my eyes and saw Nurse Grace. I was so happy to see her, I quickly jumped up and hugged her.

"Thank you so much," I said.

"Thank you for what, Sweetie?"

I looked up at her and said, "Don't you remember me?"

She squinted her eyes and said, "Yes! Karter Robinson. You're his daughter. What's your name?"

"Nadia."

"Yes! I'm sorry. I see so many people every day, but I most definitely remember you. You're a strong young lady. That day, I could feel the strength that God has blessed you with."

Feeling as though I was about to disappoint her, I said, "I'm not that strong. I need help."

Nurse grace began to look concerned, and said, "I was just about to head to the cafeteria and take a break. Come join me."

When we got to the cafeteria, Nurse Grace bought me and herself breakfast. While we ate, I told her everything that had happened since my dad had died, and how Spence had been abusing me and my mom. I left out the part about being raped because I was so ashamed of it. I never wanted to feel like a victim, but that was exactly what I felt like. I had been stripped of so much, and I didn't know how much more I could take.

I just wanted Nurse Grace to say that she would take me home with her, but she said she couldn't legally just take me.

"Nadia, I would if I could, but I could get in trouble. I believe everything you're saying, so what I can do is report this abuse and have the Department of Children and Family Services to come by the house and investigate the situation. Also, when this is happening, if at all possible, call the police."

I felt better just by letting a lot of what I had going on in my head, out in the open. I felt that same light that I did initially when I first met Nurse Grace. She said she could feel my strength, but I could feel her anointing, which in turn, helped to give me strength.

"Do you need a ride to school? I can take a few extra minutes to drop you off," she said.

"No, I'll walk, but thank you."

Nurse Grace then grabbed my hands and said she just wanted to pray with me. In the middle of the entire cafeteria, with everyone watching, Nurse Grace prayed for my entire situation. She prayed that everything would be handled accordingly by

God's will, and that he would continue to protect and bless me. I received everything that she said in that prayer, and I had faith that it would all come to pass.

As she walked me to the exit, she told me to remember to be completely honest when the time came. She gave me a big hug and reminded me that God was always with me and had my back.

Later that evening, the doorbell rang as I sat in the living room alone. When I heard it, I didn't move. I then heard Spence heading towards the door.

"I'm not looking to buy anything," he said as soon as he opened the door.

"Good, because we're not selling anything," the woman at the door said.

I then heard a male voice say, "Sir, we're from the Department of Children and Family Services, and there was an anonymous tip called in that there had been some things going on here that may be putting minors in danger."

"I think your anonymous tipster gave you the wrong address. There's nothing going on around here."

I got up and peeked around the corner as Spence spoke to the man and woman at the door.

"Well, Sir, because this was the address given, we are required to perform a formal investigation. I'm Chris Harper, and this is Carrie Miller."

They both handed Spence their cards and proceeded to enter.

"Lena, we have company," Spence yelled.

"Who lives here with you?" Carrie asked.

"My wife, two sons, and step-daughter."

As he said "step-daughter", I came from around the corner.

"And there she is."

"Hello, young lady. We're just going to be asking some questions, so we just ask that everyone is completely honest," Chris explained.

"Ok."

My mom came down the stairs, and said, "Oh, I didn't know we were expecting anyone."

"We weren't, but obviously people don't know how to mind their business. They're from the Department of Children and Family Services," Spence replied.

"Oh," my mom said, cutting her eyes at me.

Chris and Carrie first just walked around the house, checking to make sure there was nothing that looked odd. They even checked the cabinets and refrigerator to make sure there was food.

"You have a very nice house," Carrie said.

"Thank you. I bought it after my husband passed away suddenly."

Chris and Carrie looked at each other."

"I'm sorry about your husband. When did he pass?" Carrie asked.

"Back in May," she replied.

"Less than a year ago?" Carrie said, sounding as if she had become suspicious.

I could tell Spence wanted to tell my mom to be quiet, and that the information that my mom had just given wasn't sitting well with the investigators.

"Ok then," Carrie said." Everything here looks good. Now I need to ask some serious questions. Can you tell your boys to come down?"

Spence went and got Will and Joey. When they came down, they both looked a bit nervous.

"Ok. Since I have everyone here, I have to ask, does anyone feel threatened in the home by anything or anyone?" Chris asked, as Carrie took notes.

This was my opportunity to say something and possibly get out of this situation. Everyone looked around the room, but it seemed like all eyes ended up directly on me. Spence's eyes were whose I noticed the most. They appeared darker than usual. I wanted to say something so badly, but nothing would seem to come out, and I knew it was because he was looking at me. Nurse Grace had set this entire thing up for me, and told me to be honest, and now I didn't even have the nerve to say what needed to be said to save me from my misery. I was afraid. Every question they asked, I shook my head.

When they were done, Spence said, "I told you everything was good around here."

"I'm sorry, Mr. Spencer, but it's our job to make sure everyone is safe." Chris said.

As soon as they were about to leave out of the door, I ran towards them, and Spence tried to push me back.

"Did you need to say something?" Carrie asked.

I stood quietly for a few moments, then said, "No. I just wanted to tell you thank you, and have a good night."

"You too," they both said.

As soon as the door shut, I tried to quickly walk away. Spence grabbed me and slapped me so hard that I fell to the floor.

"You know she sent them, Lena. She needs to show some appreciation."

"I know," my mom said. "She'll learn. Won't you, Nadia?"

"No, I won't because there's no lesson to be learned on my part. Hopefully you'll learn who was really there for you, but when you do, it'll be too late," I said, as I stood up and ran to my room.

Just to stay away from home as much as I could, I would walk to Ava's house some days after school, whenever she didn't have basketball practice. It was a forty-five-minute walk, but it gave me time to get some fresh air, and pretend that life was good. Ava could tell that I was sad, and I wanted to give her all the details of what was going on, but being around her was my small ray of sunshine and I didn't want to ruin those moments. She was one of the few people who had helped me get as far as I had. I was just hoping and praying that one day I would be able to tell my full story to Ava and whoever else wanted to listen, and be able to smile knowing that God had brought me so far.

Chapter Twenty-Two

A few months had gone by since the rape that I had supposedly dreamt, and things hadn't gotten any better. I never again mentioned that night because I knew it was a waste. I had come to terms that my own mom didn't believe it ever happened, or just pretended not to believe it so she could hold on to her new family who didn't care anything about her. In addition to the mistreatment that I endured on a daily basis, I was sick every single day and all I ever wanted to do was sleep. When I was awake, I did everything in my power to always avoid crossing paths with Will, and it seemed that Joey had turned all the way against me, too. My mom only spoke to me when necessary, and I could tell that Spence had been keeping a close eye on me ever since the Department of Children and Family Services had shown up at the house.

As each month went by, I gained more and more weight. I was thin by nature, so it was very apparent that I was pregnant. I began to wear my clothes big and baggy, but knew that someday I wouldn't be able to hide it any longer. My mom and Spence became so angry when I told them about the rape, that I was afraid of what they might've done if they found out that I was pregnant, as a result.

All I could think about was the fact that just a year ago I had been living a pretty normal life, and in less than a week, I would be fourteen years old. My birthday was in four days. I was becoming emotional just thinking about it. Fourteen wasn't a milestone, but it would be the day exactly one year ago that my dad walked out the door and never returned. I wondered what he was thinking as he looked down on me. I knew that he probably would've come and saved me if he could have. I truly wished that he could.

I wondered if my mom would even acknowledge my birthday. If she did, I would've been extremely surprised. After she told me that she never wanted me, nothing about our relationship no longer felt special. I wanted to blame it on her mental illness, but I just couldn't believe an illness could wipe away all the love a person ever had for someone. I wondered if she had always felt that way, but tolerated me just to make my dad happy.

The morning of my birthday, my mom came knocking at my bedroom door. I had learned to now keep my door locked.

"Nadia. Come downstairs real quick"

I stood up and slipped on my robe. As I headed downstairs, I smelled a familiar aroma, and it made me sad. When I got to the kitchen, my mom, Spence, Will, and Joey were standing around the table. Balloons were tied to the chairs and there was a stack of my mom's special blueberry pancakes, that always smelled like she was baking a cake, sitting in the middle of the table with lit candles on them. They began singing happy birthday as I began crying like a baby. Even though I knew that the men in the house didn't care for me, it felt nice to pretend as though they did. My mom then handed me a small box. When I opened it, there was a necklace inside with a locket. I opened the locket and there was a picture of me, my mom, and dad. From that one small gesture, I knew that my mom loved me, and she was still deep down in there somewhere. I gave her a hug and we celebrated my birthday by eating my favorite breakfast.

After that, the months flew by, and no matter how hard I tried, I could no longer hide the life that was living inside of me. My teachers were even looking at me strangely, but wouldn't ask any questions. If I had counted correctly, I was about thirty-five weeks pregnant, so I knew that it was time to say something.

My mom was sitting on the sofa, alone, watching television when I got home from school. Spence was still at work, which was good because I wanted to tell my mom when there was no one else around, especially him.

"Mom."

Without looking at me, she said, "You don't have to tell me. I already know."

She then looked at me.

"How did you know?"

"You must think I don't pay attention at all. I've known for over a month and was wondering when you were going to say something, or what your plan was."

"I didn't know how to say anything. Everything I say around here, people think I'm lying."

"Well, maybe if you don't lie, people won't think you're lying. You have to earn people's trust. Now, whose baby is it? I didn't even know you had a boyfriend."

I rolled my eyes and shook my head. "What do you mean? It's Will's! I told you he raped me. I was a virgin!" I said, beginning to cry.

"Are you still sticking to that? I thought we had moved past that. You want to know why people don't believe you, but this is why! Stop lying on people! You make me look bad."

It never failed. Just when I had started having a little faith in my mom, she disappointed me once again.

"Does Spence know?" I asked.

"Of course, he knows. He's my husband, and we don't keep secrets. He said that he knew you would get pregnant. He told me that he sees you walking around in these streets being fast."

"What happened to you?" I asked, wishing that she would be able to give me a reasonable answer, but I knew she wouldn't.

She probably did me a favor by not answering me at all. I didn't know what was going to happen from that point, but I figured if they were going to do anything crazy, they would've already done it since they had already known.

Since they did know, I didn't feel the need to walk around the house all covered up anymore. Obviously Will and Joey hadn't gotten the memo because when I walked into the kitchen with my sweats and t-shirt on, they almost spit out their food.

"Wow," Will said with his eyes bucked and mouth hanging low.

Joey didn't say a word. He sat there, speechless, holding his spoon in his hand.

I hadn't said anything to Will in months. He knew what he'd done, and I just knew that one day he'd just go ahead and admit it instead of making people think I was crazy. I guess it was better for people to think that I was crazy, or a liar, than for them to think he was a rapist or child molester.

"You're really going to sit there and say "wow" after you did this to me?" I asked.

"Nadia, I didn't do anything! Stop saying that. I would've never done what you said I did!"

"What? Rape me? You can't even say it, can you?"

"You're fourteen years old. What would I possibly want with you?"

"I don't know! Ask all of the other pedophiles in the world!"

"This is too deep for me," Joey said, as he walked out and headed outside to the patio.

"Look, I didn't do it, so tell whoever's it is that I said congratulations," Will said, as he headed outside with Joey.

I stood there in disbelief, unable to understand how Will could still stand there and lie with a straight face after seeing what he had done. I was a child, and he had caused my entire life to change. He had no remorse whatsoever for what he'd done.

I walked past the patio door and saw Will and Joey sitting at the table talking. I wondered what they were talking about, and I was really curious whether or not Will had shared with Joey what he'd done to me that night. I went and stood on the deck, which was built directly above the patio. I immediately heard Joey tell Will that he didn't understand how I was pregnant and was only fourteen.

"It's possible," Will said. "I just don't understand why she would think that I would do that, or why she would lie on me for no apparent reason. Maybe she's crazy like her mother."

"Maybe someone got into the house," Joey said.

"Joey, Dad checked all the windows and doors. No one had gotten in. Plus, the alarm was on, so if anything had been opened, the alarm would've gone off."

Joey then began to tap the table with his fingertips.

"So, what do you think happened?" he asked.

Will looked Joey directly in the eyes and said, "If it did happen, I think someone in this house did it, but it wasn't me, and it wasn't Dad."

Joey began massaging his temples as if he was stressed.

"Baby Bro, is there something you want to tell me?"

Joey looked down at the table, and whispered, "I just couldn't help myself."

Will became angry and said, "So, you were just gonna let me take the fall for it?"

"No one believed her, so it didn't matter, but now she's pregnant and that presents another problem."

"Joey! You messed up."

"No one knows it was me, except you. The baby can be anybody's."

"God knows," I whispered to myself.

Will nodded, and said, "True. You just better keep playing dumb. My lips are sealed."

I couldn't believe what I'd just heard. Joey was the last person I thought would've done this. We had gotten along so well, and Will was always the one I was leery of. The sad part was that I couldn't let anyone know that I'd heard that conversation. If there had ever been any doubt in my mind, I now definitely knew that I could trust absolutely no one in that house, and I had to come up with an escape plan, immediately.

A few weeks later, which was a week earlier than I'd anticipated, I woke up in the middle of the night in excruciating pain. I knew it was time, and I was on a mission, so I had to push through it. I pulled the bag that I had packed weeks ago, from underneath my bed, and looked around the room to make sure that I wasn't leaving anything else that had meant anything to me. That's when I grabbed the framed picture that I had on my nightstand of me and my dad, and made sure that the locket that my mom had given me was around my neck. Holding my stomach, hoping it would relieve some of my pain, I then put on my shoes, threw my bag over my shoulder and headed down the stairs. I deactivated the alarm system and walked out of that house, vowing to leave all of the pain and suffering in which I'd endured, inside of that house that had never been a home.

Simone

Chapter Twenty-Three

I was a twenty-nine-year-old woman who had been left on a wonderful family's doorstep only hours after I was born. A note that read, "Her name is Simone", was the only piece of a huge puzzle that my birth mother had left me with. The only part of me that I ever felt was an authentic piece of who I really was, was my name. I knew that it had come from my mother, and it had to have meant something to her for her to take the time to give me a name. I never knew the circumstances as to why I was left on a doorstep, and I probably would never know. I was, however, grateful that my chosen family received me and raised me as their own. It was just hard to know who I really was, especially growing up with a family that didn't look like me. They did their best to make me feel like I wasn't different, but truth is, I was then, and I always would be.

I was different from them, but I knew there was someone out there who I was like. I wondered about my birth mom all the time. I wondered if she had the same caramel complexion as me, if her hair was as course and thick as mine, if she was as thin as me, if her vision was as bad as mine and had to wear ridiculously thick glasses, and if she had the same heart-shaped birthmark underneath her right eye. I just had so many questions. I wondered why she had been so adamant about naming me Simone that she wrote it on a piece of cloth that she must've torn from her clothing, and wrapped it close to me inside of my blanket.

I gained a sister after being adopted. She was a lot older than me, so she was only around on a regular basis for a short part of my childhood. She went off to college and became a psychologist. She became very successful, and had also raised a beautiful family with a husband and two beautiful children. Her husband was also very successful, becoming the first Black CEO of a well-known Fortune 500 company. Being a Black man, he had been the closest person to me, who I could relate to the most.

I was still trying to figure out my life. I wasn't exactly sure of what I wanted to do, but I did know that I wanted to help people. I wanted to one day be able to touch people's lives by just talking to them, but I was so shy and timid, I knew that anything that I wanted to do involving speaking in public was very far-fetched. I was currently a Certified Nursing Assistant, and I actually enjoyed the work, but I knew that it wasn't something that I'd be able to continue to do if I wanted more in life. For now, I had a studio apartment, which costed me more than one of my entire paychecks every month, and that didn't even include the rest of my bills. My adoptive mom did help, but I was an adult, and I didn't want to have to rely on anyone for any reason.

I'd had a few boyfriends in my life, but I'd started to believe that I was just not the type of woman that a man wanted long-term. My longest relationship had been eight months, and I always believed that lasted that long only because he felt sorry for me. I knew that I was the clingy type, so I came off as being very needy. It wasn't intentional, but knowing that I was left once before, I was always afraid of being left again.

6 "'Be strong and courageous. Do not be afraid or terrified because of them, for the Lord your God goes with you; he

will never leave you nor forsake you.'"
– Deuteronomy 31:6 NIV

"Good Morning, Miss Franny," I said to one of my favorite residents, Frances Stevens, who lived at the nursing home where I worked. She was one that was always so pleasant and had nice things to say. Some of them could be so mean, and I had a tendency of being very sensitive, so it was sometimes hard for me to handle. Working in a nursing home could have your emotions all over the place, anyway. Even when the meanest residents would pass on, I would still cry, even though they sent me home some days in tears because of something they'd said to me. I couldn't help but to love them all. I never had ill feelings towards anyone, no matter how badly they treated me. That was easily both a blessing and a curse, because, like Miss Franny would always tell me, it's ok to love everyone, and it's the right thing to do, but if I didn't learn to stand up for myself, people would run over me all the days of my life.

> 9 **"Don't just pretend to love others. Really love them. Hate what is wrong. Hold tightly to what is good. 10 Love each other with genuine affection, and take delight in honoring each other." – Romans 12:9-10 NLT**

"Hey, Baby," Miss Franny said in her sweet, high pitched voice, as I helped her out of her bed into her wheelchair.

Miss Franny had osteoporosis and couldn't move around very well. She was living at home up until a few years earlier. Her husband had been caring for her, but he passed away after suffering a stroke. After that, she didn't have anyone to stay in the home to take care of her. Her son lived on the west coast with his wife, but Miss Franny refused to move away from the area she knew so well. The only nearby relative she had was her grandson, Bryce, but he traveled a lot with his job, so he was unable to tend to her needs the way she would've needed him to at home.

I could remember when Miss Franny first came to live at the facility. I felt so bad for her. She and Mr. Stevens had been married for fifty-five years, and she had a pretty hard time adjusting to living without him. I could hear her crying and praying on several occasions, and I soon began going into her room with her, getting on my knees right next to her bed, praying with her. I could tell that it tremendously helped with her transition, and I began to see her smile more and more. She even had begun to share little cute stories with me about the times she and her husband once had. Instead of her shedding tears as she spoke about him, she would smile, and we would laugh together.

Bryce felt bad for having to leave her in a nursing home, but ever since she'd been there, he had visited her at least four times a week. He never missed a beat. I admired how dedicated he was to making sure that his grandmother was well taken care of, because there were several residents who didn't have anyone to check on them. Over the past three years of knowing Bryce, we'd had several conversations. Many of them were right along with Miss Franny. Bryce was a few years older than me, but I enjoyed talking to him, and appreciated the fact that he was a lot more mature than most men that were my age. I didn't know if Bryce felt the same way, but I had become very fond of him. I guess you could say I was crushing on him. A lot. He was tall, extremely aesthetically pleasing to the eye, successful, confident, and had a great sense of humor. Of course, I'd never tell him how I felt. That just wasn't in my character, so I was just happy with being able to have him as a friend, and with that, I would settle.

"So, what do you have on the agenda for the day, Miss Franny?" I asked.

"Well, Bryce said he was going to come see me today. He doesn't have to be a big hot shot getting on that plane today to see all of those famous people."

Bryce was a celebrity business manager. Before he told me what his title was, I had known that celebrities had managers, but I never thought of it as being an occupation because I'd never known one personally. All of the celebrities I had known of had just appointed a family friend, or relative to manage their assets. Apparently, some celebrities were a little smarter by not mixing business with friends and family, and sought after Bryce or another celebrity business manager to help create and manage their streams of income. I was truly impressed by everything about Bryce, not to mention, the fact that he was a man of God. On paper, I felt like he was the perfect man, probably not for me, but for a woman whose appearance and accomplishments matched his. I didn't fit under either category.

12 "We do not dare to classify or compare ourselves with some who commend themselves. When they measure themselves by themselves and compare themselves with themselves, they are not wise." – 2 Corinthians 10:12 NIV

"Comparison is the thief of joy." – Theodore Roosevelt

"That's nice! I know you'll enjoy his visit, as always."

"Yes, I love my Bryce. I just hope he doesn't regret putting work before building a family with someone," she said.

"Do you think he wants a family?" I asked.

"I'm really not sure, to be honest. It's been so long since I've heard him talk about a woman. He just doesn't have the time. I don't know if he would even want a family if he did have the time. I know how you young people are these days. You all like to have someone without the commitment so you can just walk away whenever you want, but that's not the way to live. The problem is, people live in fear of being hurt, but that's part of the beauty in love. The unknowing. Yes, love will hurt sometimes, but if it's real, that pain will go away, and the love will continue on for years to come."

"Yeah, I know," I replied.

"I haven't heard you talk about any men in your life. You're such a pretty girl, so I'm sure you've had at least a few show some interest."

Anytime anyone paid me a compliment, I would feel uncomfortable because I didn't know how to accept it. I never believed myself to be a "pretty girl". I didn't think I was ugly, but I was pretty basic compared to the women out there, and men wouldn't give me a second look. After each of my past relationships had ended, my exes seemed to have a new girlfriend right away, so I assumed they'd had someone else all along.

"Not too many men see me in that way, Miss Franny."

Miss Franny looked confused, and said, "Why not?"

"I'm flattered that you think I'm pretty, but most men don't."

"Well, they must be blind! I see very well. My eyes are about the only things that haven't given up on me, and I know pretty when I see pretty. I hope you don't let these men out here tell you otherwise. Don't you let them do that to you. You'll look up one day, and you're my age, looking back at your old photos, saying, 'Dang I was fine and didn't even know it. That Miss Franny told me I was pretty, and I didn't believe her. I should've taken advantage of all that beauty back then!'" she said, as she giggled.

I couldn't help but to laugh with her. She had such a beautiful spirit and only wanted the best for everyone, just as I did. That's one thing we had in common, and I wished that I could've had a grandmother just like her.

After helping Miss Franny get dressed for the day, I pushed her outside to get some fresh air. She always enjoyed being out in the sun, no matter how hot it was outside. That was always the best part of her day.

Later that day, while Miss Franny played Bingo with some of the other residents, I happened to be sitting at the front desk, filling out some paperwork that had to be done before the end of my shift, when Bryce walked in with a bouquet of flowers in one hand, and a bag in the other. As you could imagine, seeing a gorgeous man walk in with flowers, any woman would've loved to be the recipient. I knew better. Bryce brought Miss Franny flowers at least once a week. She always had a fresh set in her room sitting on the window ledge.

"Hey, Simone," Bryce said, as I tried to pretend that I hadn't noticed him come in.

"Oh! Hey there! I didn't even hear the door open. I've got so much on my mind," I said, not knowing exactly why I had said that, because I didn't know how to answer the next question.

"Oh, yeah? What you got going on?" he asked.

It's true what they say. When you tell one lie, you have to keep it going with another and another. I should've known better.

"Just some stuff I need to take care of with my family," I quickly made up.

"Ok. Well don't let it drive you crazy!" he laughed. "Where's Granny Franny? Is she in her room?" he asked.

"No. Give me one second and I'll take you right to her."

As I finished up the paperwork, I stood up and began leading Bryce to his grandma.

When she saw us come around the corner, she yelled, "Bryce!" excitedly, as if she didn't know he was coming, but she was always excited to see him.

Bryce knelt down and gave Miss Franny a kiss on the cheek and handed her the flowers. The other ladies were so in awe of Bryce and Miss Franny's relationship. They smiled every time they saw them together, and would always tell Bryce that they wished they had a grandson just like him.

"Are you hungry?" Bryce asked Miss Franny.

"You know what? I have been at this Bingo for a while and I think my stomach is telling me it's time to eat."

"I bought you some dinner."

"Miss Franny smiled and said, "You are so good to me!"

"Well, I'll leave you two. My shift is over in five minutes. See you tomorrow, Miss Franny."

As I turned to leave, Bryce said, "Wait. Why don't you stay and have dinner with us? I brought plenty."

"I don't want to intrude on your quality time!"

"You're only intruding if you're not invited," Bryce said. "And maybe it'll help free your mind of all of the family stuff you have going on."

"Family stuff? You ok, Simone? You didn't tell me about any family stuff!" Miss Franny said, sounding concerned.

My big mouth, I thought to myself.

"Nothing major, Miss Franny. I'm fine."

"Ok, now come on so we can eat," she replied.

I looked at Bryce, then back at Miss Franny. She sat there grinning from ear to ear and nodding her head. I couldn't have possibly said no to that.

"Ok. Let me just finish up a couple of things and I'll be right back."

After I finalized a few things and washed up, I returned back to Bryce and Miss Franny. They had already set up a spot for me with plates, napkins, and utensils.

"Wow, look Miss Franny. Your favorite. Chinese food!" I said.

"I know, right?" she said.

Bryce and I couldn't help but to laugh. As we laughed, we made eye contact, and I immediately became smitten by his dimples. If dimples were a deformity as science had claimed, Bryce made them seem like the most perfect deformity that ever existed.

"Miss Franny, who's teaching you that lingo?" I asked.

"I learn it all from you, Baby!" she laughed.

As we ate, we enjoyed a little conversation. Bryce told us that he was going out of town the next evening to meet with a client, so he probably wouldn't make it by the next day. I asked him if he ever got tired of flying all over the place all the time. He just said he had grown accustomed to it, so it didn't bother him like it had in the beginning. I thought I would mention something that Miss Franny and I had discussed earlier, only because I was curious what his thoughts were.

I looked at him and said, "Do you think that you'll ever want a family, or be able to have a family with your schedule and all of the traveling you do?"

He put down his chopsticks and looked directly into my eyes. My glasses slid down the bridge of my nose as I nervously looked back down at my plate, and began playing with my food.

"Everyone wants to have a family, or at least a partner to come home to, but I don't think that's in the cards for me."

I pushed my glasses up and said, "Why not?"

I looked over at Miss Franny and she had stretched her neck out to make sure she would be able to hear the answer to my question. I noticed she did that a lot when she was trying to secretly hear what someone else was talking about.

"Truth is, I'm so busy and have so much going on, I need someone opposite of me. I need someone who's not going to have a schedule that's all over the place, and not traveling, because when I'm home, I need to be sure they're home so that we can spend time together. I seem to attract the women who are the female versions of myself, and that just won't work, and I refuse to waste my time pretending like it would."

I nodded my head as Bryce spoke, because what he was saying made a lot sense. It seemed like he really did want the companionship of someone, but was afraid of it failing because of his lifestyle.

He continued, "Now adding kids to the equation would be something I definitely wouldn't want to do, because I don't want to seem like an absentee parent. If I'm a parent, I want to be there full force."

Bryce picked his chopsticks back up, and before he began eating again, he said, "Does that answer your question?"

As I took my glasses off to clean them, I said, "I don't think I could've asked for a better explanation, and it makes a lot of sense. We have to do what makes us happy."

"Very true. So, what would make you happy, Simone?" Bryce asked, catching me off guard before I could even put my glasses back on.

I looked at him, and he was just as much of big blur as my mind was at that moment.

"Um, at this point in my life, figuring out what really interests me and committing to it will make me happy. Once I do that, then I can move on to figure out the family thing."

"You seem to love working here. This isn't where your interest lies?" he asked.

"Yeah, Simone. I thought you liked being here with us," Miss Franny said, sounding disappointed.

"I do love it, and I love everyone here, but it only supports me to a certain extent."

"Oh, so you weren't completely honest with me," Bryce said.

I squinted at him and said, "Of course I was."

"No. You know what your interest is. Your true answer to my question is more money. If you were making the amount of money you needed to be comfortable doing what you're doing now, would you be happy?"

"I suppose."

From that experience, I knew to never ask Bryce anything that I wouldn't feel comfortable or prepared to answer. He really made me think about a whole lot in just a few minutes. I really needed to begin seriously figuring out my life.

"Don't worry. None of us have it all figured out," he said, trying to make me feel better.

We all sat quietly and finished eating. After we were done, Bryce and I cleaned up our area and sat back down.

"I had a good time with the both of you! Thanks for inviting me to dinner," I said.

"We enjoyed you, too, Simone. My pretty girl," Miss Franny said, winking at me.

Bryce smiled at his grandmother, and she said, "Bryce, isn't Simone pretty?"

I began shaking my head in embarrassment, knowing that Bryce definitely did not see me the way his grandmother did.

He then looked at me as if he was gathering his final answer to the question. Unexpectedly, he placed his hand on top of mine, smiled, and said, "She's beautiful."

Chapter Twenty-Four

fter Bryce returned from his latest business trip, to my surprise, he asked me out on an official date. I had never seen Bryce outside of the nursing home, and he had never seen me wearing anything outside of scrubs, so, of course, I was extremely nervous. When he initially asked me, my first thought was to turn him down. I had never been out with a man like him. He was highly intelligent and established, and to be perfectly honest, I had no idea of how to impress a man like him. I had never really done much to impress a man at all. I was the type of woman that, upon just looking at me, screamed, what you see is what you get. I didn't know exactly what he was looking for in a woman, but I was hoping that he wasn't looking for anything different than what he had already seen in me.

I did, however, attempt to switch things up a bit. I straightened my hair, which was something I rarely took the time out to do, so I normally walked around with my hair wild and natural. I had grown up with a white mother, who wasn't at all "Black hair" savvy, so I had become used to my hair looking however it decided to look on any particular day. There was never much effort. I found a black pantsuit in the back of my closet that I had worn to a family dinner, and a pair of flat dress shoes. I avoided wearing heels at all costs because I could be a klutz at times, especially when my glasses would unexpectedly slide down the bridge of my nose, causing me to lose sight of everything around me. When I looked in the mirror, I took a deep breath and hoped for the best.

My doorbell rang, and when I got to the door, Bryce was standing there, handsome as always, holding a bouquet of yellow roses.

He looked me up and down, and said, "Don't you look . . ."

Bryce put his finger to his chin, searching for the right thing to say. I would've helped him out, but I had no idea what he was trying to say. I didn't know what he thought of my attempt at trying to impress him.

As I waited for him to complete his sentence, he took a deep breath and said, "safe."

I raised an eyebrow, and said, "Safe? I don't know if that's good or bad."

Bryce handed me the flowers as he walked into my tiny apartment.

"This is nice and cozy," he said.

I shut the door behind him and asked, "Are you going to tell me what you meant by saying I looked safe?"

He looked at me again and said, "You just look like you're going to a business meeting, and not a fancy one. One of those boring ones. You act like you're afraid to standout. Why is that?"

"I've never been one to seek attention, so if that's the type of person you're looking to date, then maybe we should just cancel this whole thing."

I walked over to the kitchen to put the roses in water, waiting for Bryce to respond.

"Simone, the last thing I want is an attention-seeking woman, but I do want someone who has confidence in herself. You can do so much better than this. You heard what Granny Franny said.

You're a pretty girl. You just need to step out of the box a little bit.
. . or by the looks of the shoes, a lot!" he said, laughing.

I didn't find any of it funny at all. I began to think that this had
been a bad idea, and I should've known better. I knew that Bryce
and I had totally different personalities, so there was no reason I
should've ever thought that we would be a match made in
heaven. Bryce noticed that I wasn't laughing, so he quickly wiped
the smile off of his face, and cleared his throat.

"Come on. Let's go my little librarian," he said, as he grabbed
my hand and began walking to the door.

I stopped, and said, "So, you still want to do this?"

"I would've never even asked you if I didn't, and plus, I have a
surprise for you."

I didn't know what Bryce had planned, but I just kept asking
myself what could possibly go wrong. I had a man showing, what I
felt was a genuine interest in me, and there I was, ready to give
up on what might've been one of the best things that had ever
happened to me, without even giving Bryce a fair chance.

When we left my apartment, Bryce headed towards
Downtown. We pulled up in front of a clothing boutique, and
Bryce put the car in park.

"What are we doing here?" I asked.

"I just want to do something nice for you."

"What? Buy me clothes because you don't like the ones I'm
wearing? I can buy my own clothes."

Bryce had already offended me in so many ways, and the date
hadn't even begun.

"Bryce, just take me back home."

"Simone, I just want to show you how beautiful you can be."

"Take me home!" I yelled.

Bryce put the car in drive and didn't say a word the entire way
back to my apartment. When we pulled up in front, he tried to
say something to me, but I quickly got out of the car and slammed
the door. I heard his tires skid as he sped off while I walked
towards my apartment building. I couldn't believe he thought that
he was just going to insult my appearance, and then try to fix me
up the way he wanted me to be. Maybe I didn't have the most

confidence in the world, but I never tried to be something that I wasn't, and didn't plan on conforming to something that others thought I should be.

> **2 "Do not conform to the pattern of this world, but be transformed by the renewing of your mind. Then you will be able to test and approve what God's will is – his good, pleasing and perfect will." – Romans 12:2 NIV**

The next day when I saw Miss Franny, she couldn't wait to hear about Bryce's and my date. I was sure she had been hoping for the best and I hated to disappoint her, so I had to think of the easiest way to tell her that her grandson was not who I thought he was.

"Did you have a good time on your date, Simone?" she asked.

"I guess you haven't gotten the chance to talk to Bryce. We didn't go."

"What happened?" she asked, sounding disappointed.

"I just don't think I'm the woman for Bryce. I'm no showstopper, and I think that's what he wants, so I'm not sure why he asked me out in the first place. He's seen me several times over the past few years, and knows what type of person I am, so I was confused when he got to my house and outwardly judged my clothing. Then, he tried to take me to a clothing store to buy new clothes to wear."

Miss Franny sat in her wheelchair staring at me as she took in everything that I had told her.

She then said, "I'm so sorry. Bryce is a very honest person when he feels strongly about something, and it does come across as being harsh sometimes, but I've always appreciated honesty over someone telling me that everything is fine when they really don't feel that way. There were many times my husband had to tell me that something I was wearing wasn't flattering, and I had to tell him more than a few times that those checkered shirts and striped pants just did not go together," she laughed, "But we didn't get offended. We just took it as constructive criticism and got better with our choices of fashion. I know the two of you aren't even close to being married, but I'm just giving you an example of how relationships can sometimes work."

When Miss Franny explained it from her point of view, it didn't sound as bad as it had seemed the night before. I just felt as though Bryce wanted to change me, and I felt if someone needed to change me in order to be with me, we didn't need to be together.

Miss Franny then said, "Can I ask you a question?"

"Of course. Go ahead," I replied.

"What woman turns a man down when they offer to take them shopping?"

We both laughed hysterically. Miss Franny didn't realize it, but she made my day a whole lot better than how it had begun. What had happened the previous night was still on my mind as soon as I had woken up. I had no idea how I would even face Bryce when I saw him again, but I would soon find out.

When I got home that evening, Bryce's car was parked outside of my apartment building. When he saw me pull up, he got out of his car and stood on the walkway, as he waited for me to get out. I sat in the car for a moment as I tried to get my thoughts together. I didn't know why he was there, but I was hoping it wasn't to further insult my fashion sense.

"Hey, Simone," he said, as I walked towards him up the walkway.

"Hi, Bryce," I said coldly, as I stood directly in front of him. "What do you want?"

"Yeah, I deserve that. I just wanted to apologize for making you feel less than enough last night. Even if I had an opinion of what you were wearing, there was a better way to express it, or not express it at all. I thought I was saying it in a joking way, and thought that you would find it funny, too. That's the thing about dating. You get to know things about a person so that you don't make those dumb mistakes like I made last night. I really felt bad for the rest of the night and I almost called you, but I knew you wouldn't want to talk to me, so I decided to give you some time to cool off. I was actually hoping you would go to work today and talk to Granny Franny, and she'd shed some light on my not so debonair qualities."

I smiled, and said, "Yes, she did, and made me feel a lot better."

"I'm glad. I'm not perfect, but I also don't want to be horrible either. Do you accept my apology?"

I put my finger up to my chin as if I was contemplating, and said, "Yes, I do."

One year later, I said, "I do" once again, as I stood at the altar, marrying my best friend.

Bryce and I had realized that the separate pieces of our lives meshed well together. They were like puzzle pieces that fit together perfectly. I was able to still do what I loved at the nursing home, and at the same time, be there for my husband when he wasn't working hard. Bryce had also found what he was looking to add to his life. He wanted to know that when he stepped off of the plane from those business trips, that he had a wife at home anxiously waiting for his arrival. It was funny how sometimes a series of events had to occur in order for people to cross each other's paths. It was definitely no accident that Miss Franny ended up in the nursing home where I worked, and her grandson, Bryce, would end up being my life partner.

22 "The man who finds a wife finds a treasure, and he receives favor from the Lord." – Proverbs 18:22 NLT

18 "Then the Lord God said, "It is not good for the man to be alone. I will make a helper who is just right for him."
– Genesis 2:18 NLT

Chapter Twenty-Five

During my first year of marriage, I noticed, but tried to ignore the fact that I had quite a bit of mixed emotions. I wasn't sure if that was normal, especially so early in. On one hand, I felt like Bryce was exactly what I needed in my life to help me to come out of my shell and become the confident woman that I should've been. I was thrilled about the woman that I had started to become. I no longer hid behind the huge glasses and caterpillar eyebrows, or feared trying different things with my hair. I began to feel more confident in the clothes I wore, and realized I wasn't shaped like a box. I even got really risky and tried pigmented lip-gloss. At my own discretion, Bryce had helped me change all of those things that subconsciously made me feel insecure. He didn't force it like he had tried at the beginning. I only chose to make a change because I was able to see first-hand the type of people Bryce had dealings with, and with that, I knew that I would need to make a good impression when I would have to join him at some of his business meetings, in which the wives came along.

On the other hand, I knew that I shouldn't have needed anyone except God to make me happy, and empower me enough to love and accept myself. I shouldn't have needed to change for anyone under any circumstances. I began questioning whether our love was built on the right things, but I definitely knew that I loved, and was in fact, deeply in love, with Bryce. I grew up in church with my adoptive family, and I was raised knowing that loving someone wasn't always enough, and if I thought it would be, my marriage would be destined to fail if a proper foundation wasn't built around it. Bryce and I felt the emotion of love for each other, but I didn't believe we both had love within us. I wasn't certain that Bryce and I had built that foundation. God is love, and without Him, it is impossible to have love. I could honestly say that Bryce and I hadn't put God first in our lives, and that was our first biggest mistake.

16 "And so we know and rely on the love God has for us. God is love. Whoever lives in love lives in God, and God in them." – 1 John 4:16 NIV

I knew that Bryce knew God, but he hadn't been to church in years. When he shared that with me before we were even married, I ignored it because, sadly, it didn't mean anything to me at that time. I was listening to my flesh, and not God. When Bryce told me he just didn't have the time to go to church because of his busy schedule, I just let it go instead of trying to talk to him about incorporating some different ways into his life to give some time to God. I had always gone to church, and continued to do so after Bryce and I were married, but even if he wasn't working on Sunday morning, I still couldn't get him out of bed to join me. I realized I couldn't force it, and just continued to pray that God would speak to him, and bring Bryce closer to Him.

16 "So I say, walk by the Spirit, and you will not gratify the desires of the flesh. 17 For the flesh desires what is contrary to the Spirit, and the Spirit what is contrary to the flesh. They

are in conflict with each other, so that you are not to do whatever you want." – Galatians 5:16-17 NIV

The more time that went by, the more I found myself compromising my entire identity. The person who I didn't really know, but had become pretty comfortable with over the years, was no longer there. I had failed to remember that that person had been created by, and was loved unconditionally by God, and I had allowed her to be recreated by man. I may have never known where I came from, but one thing I did know about myself was that I had never been a people pleaser. That was one of my best, and strongest assets, and it had been destroyed.

Bryce never compromised on anything. He was who he was, and that's all he had to be. I felt like it was ok to be yourself, but there was always room for improvement. It seemed like he began to look at me to always improve, but it was never enough, and it never would be.

"Are you almost ready?" Bryce yelled from the bottom of the stairs as I got dressed for a very formal awards banquet, honoring some of the most prestigious men and women in Bryce's field of expertise.

Every time an event like that came up, I would begin to overthink everything, and become extremely anxious. This particular night was no different. I had bought a new dress for the event months before to coordinate with the suit that Bryce would be wearing, yet I'd changed clothes almost ten times. I ended right back in the dress that I had bought. Anyone else would've probably said that my hair, makeup, and dress were all flawless, but when I looked in the mirror, I looked a mess.

As I walked down the stairs, Bryce stood at the bottom, wearing a tan Brioni bespoke suit, smiling. "You look gorgeous," he said.

When Bryce said that, then I felt beautiful. I always needed validation from him, and I couldn't quite pinpoint when that had happened.

When we arrived at the banquet, the ceremony hadn't begun yet. We sat at the table with one of Bryce's friends who happened to work with him, named Ryan, and his wife, Ashley. They were both very down to earth and I always enjoyed going out, double dating with them. Watching them, and how well they seemed to complement each other made me wish Bryce and I could be like them.

"Hi, Simone! Ashley said excitedly, as she stood up wearing an off the shoulder wine colored gown that stood out against her perfect tan."

"Hey, Ashley! Good to see you!" I said as we hugged. I was just as excited to see her as she was to see me. It wasn't often that I got out to see anyone outside of senior citizens, or my family.

You look beautiful, Simone," Ryan said, as he also hugged me and kissed me on the cheek.

"Thank you," I said.

"Hey, Ry. You know you're the only man I'll ever allow to kiss my wife, right?" Bryce said, jokingly.

"I'm glad you're so generous because there's no man that I'd allow to kiss my wife! Not even you . . . Especially, not you. You're too handsome for your own good!" Ryan said, laughing.

Ashley and I looked at each other and shook our heads.

"You see how they talk about us like we're just property?" Ashley laughed. "Men! So, anyway, how's everything been, Simone?"

"Everything's good! How about you?"

Everything's great. Staying busy with the kids. Speaking of kids, when are you two going to work on some little Bryces and Simones?"

Bryce and I looked at each other, then Bryce turned back to Ryan to continue his conversation.

"Well, Bryce really doesn't want to have kids because he would want to be there for them all the time, and he just travels too much."

"It's doable. Ryan does it and still manages to spend time with me and the kids. Just give him some time, girl. He'll have a change of heart."

I heard what Ashley was saying, but I just shrugged my shoulders, knowing that was one of the things that Bryce was not going to compromise on. There was absolutely no negotiation when it came to that. The fact that she said Ryan was able to balance his work and family life did make me wonder why Bryce felt like he couldn't do it.

"How's work going?" Ashley asked.

"It's great. That's the highlight of my day. I love being around my patients and hearing their stories. Even the mean ones have grown on me. I'm so nice to them, that I break down a lot of their barriers. You know what they say about kindness."

"It definitely kills!" Ashley said. "I think you really have a gift for what you do. It takes a lot of love and patience to care for our senior citizens, especially in that type of environment."

"Yes! It doesn't pay the most, but I like what I do. Granny Franny makes the days so fun. You have to meet her one day."

Bryce had begun listening to our conversation and burst out with, "Simone, do you really think Ashley wants to hear about the world of diaper changing? No one else thinks that working in a nursing home, not getting paid even half of what you should be making, is interesting."

Ashley cut her sparkling blue eyes at Bryce and cleared her throat.

"Well, Simone, I think it's very interesting, and I respect you so much for all you do. Speaking of diapers, I live in a world of diaper changing as well, with fifteen-month-old twins running around. We definitely have something in common. Mine just don't talk back yet," she laughed.

Ashley always knew how to cool down the temperature in the room and smooth things over when Bryce would make one of his slick comments, as he did at least once on every occasion.

We then saw the MC come to the stage and grab the mic. The announcing of the awards was about to begin. Both, Bryce and Ryan had been nominated for awards. Ashley and I proudly watched our husbands walk across the stage to accept their awards and shake hands with some of the most important people in the entertainment industry. I couldn't deny that I was extremely proud of how hard Bryce worked, and what he'd accomplished due to his hard work.

After that part of the program, and all of the congratulations, Ryan and Ashley stood up to get ready to leave.

"You guys are leaving already?" I asked, hoping they would stay a little longer.

"I wish we could hang out a little longer, but mommy-duty calls. You guys have a good rest of your evening. They're supposed to have live jazz soon. I would've loved to be able to hear it, so enjoy!"

"Ok. See you next time," I said, with a sad face."

As Ryan and Ashley walked out, Bryce frowned at me and said, "Why do you have to act like that?"

"Like what?" I asked.

"You act so needy and desperate for a friend."

"Normal people are sad to see a nice evening end. Ashley and I really bonded."

"She needs to be trying to bond with her husband because he's doing a lot of outside bonding. I'll never understand how you cheat on a woman like that. Now that's what you call a woman! Even after having twins, she looks . . ."

"Bryce!" I said sternly.

I rarely talked to Bryce like that, but I'd had enough. I watched Bryce as he became excited talking and thinking about my friend, and his friend's wife, and it was disrespectful. I was disgusted by that, but what was more confusing and disturbing were the things that Bryce had said about Ryan cheating. I was so focused on that that I couldn't even get as upset as I should've been about the way he had been looking at Ashley.

28 "But I tell you that anyone who looks at a woman lustfully has already committed adultery with her in his heart."
– Matthew 5:28 NIV

After I said Bryce's name, he stopped talking, and looked at me furiously, as if I had done something wrong.

"What are you talking about? I've never seen a couple, besides my parents look so in love," I said.

"You look at them and think they're so perfect. No relationship is perfect. Sorry to break it to you, Baby. Ryan has been with every woman in our office."

I felt like asking him how many he had been with after experiencing the level of disrespect I'd just seen him display. At that point, I didn't put anything past him, but I was just upset, and I knew that. Bryce had never given me any reason to believe he was cheating, so I couldn't accuse him of anything that I had no proof of. I trusted Bryce to the fullest, and as long as I kept a positive mind, I would always have a positive life. I believed in my heart that if there was ever anything that I needed to know, God would always be with me to reveal the truth in perfect timing.

> 5 "So don't make judgments about anyone ahead of time – before the Lord returns. For he will bring our darkest secrets to light and will reveal our private motives. Then God will give to each one whatever praise is due."
> – 1 Corinthians 4:5 NLT

Chapter Twenty-Six

After getting home that night, I still had something on my mind that I wanted to talk to Bryce about, but I didn't want to have a conversation in the state of mind that I was in. At that moment, my mind was noisy, and I knew that I wouldn't be able to think clearly, or affectively express my thoughts and feelings the way that I wanted to. In the past, whenever I brought up the topic that I wanted to discuss, I was never able to fully communicate my emotions, but Ashley had given me some things to think about. I just needed to meditate and renew my mind so that I could hear God, and He could give me the right words to say. After all of the junk that I had just allowed to pollute my mind, I knew that renewing my mind was definitely necessary, so that I could be in a place of love, understanding, vulnerability, and peace when I talked to Bryce the following morning.

Bryce woke up before I did and had begun packing for one of his business ventures. He'd actually been home three days in a row, which didn't happen very often. When I heard him moving around, I knew I had to act fast.

"Good morning, Babe," I said as I sat up in the bed. "Can we talk?"

"Before you say anything, I know I had a little too much to drink last night, and I said some things that I probably shouldn't have said," Bryce said, sounding remorseful.

I crawled to the bottom of the bed where he was sitting, and said, "It's not even about that."

"Then what is it about?"

"I think we need to talk more about our family, and our marriage as a whole. It seems like I'm always open for compromise in this marriage, but you never are. You always seem to get your way, and I don't feel like it's fair. I've been putting one hundred percent into this marriage, but I honestly feel like I always get the short end of the stick."

"Are you serious?" Bryce laughed. "Do you realize what I contribute to this household? Everything! Do you think you would be living like this If it wasn't for me? So, you want to talk about "compromise", huh?"

"Bryce, I'm appreciative for everything that you do, but just because you contribute more financially, doesn't mean that everything has to go your way. I want to be a mother, and you're denying me of that opportunity. You blame it on your job, and wanting to be around, but Ashley and Ryan seem to make it work just fine, so why can't we?" I asked.

"You are forever comparing us to other people. We are very different from Ashley and Ryan. Look at Ashley. She does what she wants to do because, like I told you last night, Ryan is unfaithful, so to keep Ashley from becoming suspicious, he just goes with whatever. I'm not going to do anything I don't want to do. I feel like kids will complicate this marriage, and I already have enough to worry about. I don't need you calling me all day, every day, complaining about a crying baby, or telling me I need to change my schedule to help with the kid. Another thing is, I'm not paying for daycare, and your check won't cover it, so do you plan on quitting your job to stay at home all day with kids?"

I stared at Bryce realizing that the man I'd married had no real idea of what marriage was. It was supposed to be about give and take, and I was the one always giving. He thought money was everything, and could solve everything, but what he didn't realize was everything that I'd given him and put into our marriage was valued a lot higher than the material things that he had provided. I didn't want to give up. I knew deep down inside somewhere Bryce had to have some type of desire to leave a piece of himself behind. He knew how important it was to me. I'd expressed to him so many times, even before we were married, how I was adopted and had to live with the fact that I had no idea where I came from. I wanted to have the opportunity to help create another human being that came from me. I wanted someone else to have my DNA. I never had that, and it was hard walking around every day seeing people who looked similar to me, wondering if they were family. I just wanted my own little family, and to know that no one could take that from me.

"Bryce, you're being unreasonable and unsupportive. You know my background. You know how important this is to me."

Bryce took a deep breath as he stood up and grabbed his luggage. "I have to go, and Simone. . . I don't want to have this conversation anymore."

7 "In the same way, you husbands must give honor to your wives. Treat your wife with understanding as you live together. She may be weaker than you are, but she is your equal partner in God's gift of new life. Treat her as you should so your prayers will not be hindered." – 1 Peter 3:7 NLT

When Bryce walked out that morning, I knew that I had become too comfortable with depending on him. I had settled for the way life was, and was too accepting of whatever made everyone else happy. I no longer dreamed of being anything more than a CNA, although I'd always considered it to only be a short interlude in my life, at least until I figured things out. I had unintentionally become complacent during the process. I loved my job, but I knew that I was capable of more. My conversation with Bryce brought into the forefront, some of the things that I needed to concentrate on. Having kids with a man who didn't want any, even though he was my husband, didn't need to be my major concern at that moment, especially when there was really nothing I could do to change the situation.

"Good morning," I said as I walked into work that morning.

Whenever I would walk through those doors, even if something was bothering me in the depths of my soul, it always felt like a breath of fresh air, but not this particular morning. I felt defeated, and everyone I interacted with could tell a difference in me.

I always checked on Miss Franny when I got to work. She was always so happy to see me, and would treat me as though she hadn't seen me in years. There was a bright light always shining upon her, and after getting to know the side of Bryce that I had been getting small doses of, slowly but surely, it was unbelievable that the two were even related.

"Simone, what's wrong today? You seem a little down," Miss Franny said, sounding very concerned.

I didn't want her to worry about what was going on at home, so I told her everything was fine, but she kept digging.

"Is it getting a little lonely at home with Bryce being out of town so much?"

I sighed, still not wanting to share what was going on in my mind.

"Don't worry about us, Miss Franny. We'll be ok."

"Ok. Just remember, no marriage is perfect, and I know Bryce can be very stubborn, and he thinks he's more important than what he really is. He may hold a high position with that job, but you better believe they can replace him in a matter of minutes if they need to. None of that matters. He has always needed to have a reality check of who was really there for him. That's why he's not close to his parents. They tried to teach him right, but he always put everything before his family. When he got that job, he treated them like they were imbeciles, even after all they had done for him to get him through college and everything. They finally got tired of it, cut him off, and moved away. He's my grandson, and I love him dearly, but I know that he only took on the responsibility to look after me and pay for me to be here out of guilt. He felt guilty for the way he has treated people, and felt like doing this would make up for it. I still love him, though, and I do know he loves his Granny Franny. He just has some bad ways that he needs to be broken from.

3 "Because of the privilege and authority God has given me, I give each of you this warning: Don't think you are better than you really are. Be honest in your evaluation of yourselves, measuring yourselves by the faith God has given us." – Romans 12:3 NLT

Bryce had never talked too much to me about his parents. He just told me that they didn't agree on many aspects of life and he felt that it would be healthier for him to separate himself. I didn't really understand what that meant, but he didn't seem very comfortable discussing it, so I didn't push it. I was realizing that I'd decided not to push a lot of things because I didn't want to upset Bryce, and some of those conversations should've still been had to avoid any confusion later on down the line. I thought a lot about Bryce's feelings when I approached things, but he didn't seem to think about mine at all.

"Thank you for that, Miss Franny, because I honestly was beginning to feel like I was losing my mind. I just want a baby. Is that too much to ask?"

"No, it's not, but a selfish person doesn't like adding other people to the equation. They don't want to be forced to share what they think they've earned, but what Bryce fails to realize is that all he has is because of God! He didn't do any of that, and just like the Bible says, the Lord giveth, and the Lord taketh away, so Bryce better be careful!" Miss Franny said, nodding her head.

21 "He said, 'Naked (without possessions) I came [into this world] from my mother's womb, And naked I will return there. The Lord gave and the Lord has taken away; Blessed be the name of the Lord'." – Job 1:21

"I agree," I replied.

"You'll be ok. Just keep praying. God is working it out, and I know you already know that."

"Yes, Ma'am," I said.

I after I left from talking with Miss Franny, I walked to the front desk, and there was a man standing there waiting to be helped. He was average height for a man, slim, and looked as if he was of mixed nationality. If I guessed, I would've said he was Puerto Rican mixed with Black. I immediately assumed that he was there to visit a relative, although I had never seen him around before. We got new residents who moved in every day, so it was very plausible.

"Hi! I don't know where the receptionist went," I said as I looked around. "Can I help you with something?"

"Hi, are you a nurse here?" he asked, sounding extremely formal.

I then looked at his clothing. He was wearing a black button-down shirt, a black and gray tie, and gray slacks, which made me think that this visit was a lot more serious than visiting a relative. I began to think, perhaps, he was there to give our facility a random inspection, so I had to present myself in the most professional way possible.

Devaluing myself, as I often did, I said, "No, I'm just a CNA."

He looked at me strangely, and said, "Well, you still should be able to help me. I'm Dr. Noah Sullivan. I'm looking for one of my patients, Ms. Edith Smith."

"Oh, doctor . . ." I said, feeling embarrassed. "Yes, I know exactly where she is. You can follow me, Dr. Sullivan."

I would've never guessed that the man who stood before me was a doctor. He looked so young, so I couldn't imagine that he had been practicing medicine long.

During our walk to Miss Edie's room, I asked Dr. Sullivan if he had his own practice, or worked in a hospital. He told me that he was a cardiovascular surgeon, and his office was located inside of

St. Mary General hospital, which was a few miles from the nursing home.

When we walked past some of the other residents, they all spoke to him, knowing him by name, so I had to ask, "How long have you been practicing, If I may ask?"

"You may ask whatever you want," he said, smiling.

When he smiled, his entire demeanor changed. He went from overly reserved and haughty in appearance, to inviting and approachable. His smile could've lit up an entire room. "I've been a doctor for seven years, but I've officially been a surgeon for about three years."

"Since I can ask anything, how old are you?"

Dr. Sullivan frowned, and said, "Never ask a man his age."

"I'm so sorry!"

He began laughing, and said, "I'm just joking with you! Relax. You have to joke a little in this field. To answer your question, I'm thirty-three."

Dr. Sullivan was like a breath of fresh air. When we got to Miss Edie's room, he was so gentle with her, and his voice was so calming. I had never seen a patient seem so comfortable around their doctor, and I had seen plenty of doctors interact with their patients over the years.

From how the other patients responded to him, I could tell his reputation preceded him. I was just surprised that I had never heard anything about him before then.

While Dr. Sullivan examined Miss Edie, I assisted him with getting her medical chart updated, and went over her meal plan with him. I had never seen Miss Edie be so friendly towards anyone. If I hadn't known any better, I would've thought she was flirting with Dr. Sullivan.

When he was done, he told Miss Edie he'd see her again in about another month.

As I walked him to the door, he asked, "Can you do me a favor?"

"Sure. Did you forget something in her room?"

"No. This is more of a personal request."

I raised my eyebrows, and said, "I guess."

"No, I need you to say yes."

I was a little nervous about what he wanted me to say yes to, but I said, "Ok. Yes."

"You know how when I asked you if you were a nurse here, and you replied by saying, no, you're just a CNA? Please don't ever devalue your position like that again. You shouldn't be ashamed of what you do, or think you're any less important than anyone else here. Hold your head up high and say it with pride."

I hadn't even realized that I had done that until Dr. Sullivan mentioned it. I guess, subconsciously, I wasn't proud of where I currently was in life. I was about to be thirty-two years old, and still didn't exactly know what my goals were. I knew I needed to do more, just for myself, and that was a start.

"Thank you for bringing that to my attention, because I honestly wasn't aware."

"No, problem. I just like to help people realize their worth, and I noticed that you truly don't. Do you like it here?"

"I actually love it here, but I know I'm capable of more. I've just become stagnant."

"I'm just going to say, time waits for no one, so if you want to do something, get out there and do it. I think you'd make a great nurse in a hospital setting. We can actually use some CNAs right now at the hospital. You could go to school for nursing, if that's what you like, and apply for a position at the hospital to get some experience in that setting while you're in school."

"Hmmm. I may have to consider doing something like that. In all honesty, I hadn't even focused on my future long enough to even think about what the possibilities were."

"You have all the possibilities in the world. If you do decide to apply, just let me know. I'll put in a good word for you."

"Thank you so much, Dr. Sullivan. I truly appreciate you."

"You're very welcome, and call me Noah," he said as he handed me his card.

After Noah left, my mind was all over the place, but in a good way. I felt an excitement come over me that I hadn't felt in a long time. That excitement was motivation. In a matter of minutes,

Noah had motivated me to entertain some different ideas to get myself on the right path. He knew exactly what I needed to hear at that very moment, and that was confirmation that God had already begun working on my situation, and I needed to begin making some moves in my life. Whether Noah knew it or not, God had used him as a vessel in order to remove my tunnel vision, and open my eyes and my mind to the many wonderful things in the world that were available to me.

Chapter Twenty-Seven

I t was another lonely night of lying on the sofa with my blanket, catching up on my favorite shows. I kept having to rewind because my mind continued to drift away to thoughts of the future. I had never thought so much about it, not even as a kid, but this particular evening, I couldn't think about anything else. I finally felt like I could do anything. The confidence that I felt made my heart flutter. Little by little, I was beginning to learn new things about myself. Because of my past, and not knowing where I came from, I had allowed many walls to be built around me because I had never felt what I defined as true security. When I began my relationship with Bryce, he was able to tear down those walls because he made me feel secure in every way. He gave me a sense of purpose and confidence that I needed. I never thought he'd cause me to regress to feeling like I wasn't enough, but God wasn't having it. He hadn't brought me this far to leave me.

In the middle of my thoughts, my phone rang. It was Bryce. I hadn't spoken to him since our "discussion" earlier that morning before he left on his trip. He would normally call me as soon as he stepped off of the plane to let me know he had made it safely.

Since he hadn't, I knew that he must've still been upset, and I'd decided to let him have his time to cool off.

"Hey, Babe," Bryce said as soon as I answered the phone.

"Hey," I replied, without a notion of excitement in my voice.

"Was I interrupting something?" he asked.

"Not at all."

"Why didn't you call to check on me? You didn't know if I had made it safely or not, but I guess you didn't care."

"Well, obviously you made it safely, or you wouldn't be calling me right now, so why didn't you call me and let me know you made it, as you normally do?"

"I just wanted to test you to see how much you really care about me and my feelings, because from our conversation this morning, it seemed like you didn't care about them at all. If you did, you wouldn't have brought up the conversation of a baby again after you already knew how I felt."

"You know Bryce, you shouldn't have to test my feelings for you, and just because I want to have a conversation with my husband, whether it makes him uncomfortable or not, it shouldn't cause him to question my love for him. We should be able to talk about anything. I was just hoping we would be able to compromise on it."

The other end of the phone became silent. I gave Bryce some time to get his thoughts and words together before saying anything.

"Hello?"

"Yeah, I'm here. I'm just trying to figure out why Bryce would think I would compromise on something that I've already clearly expressed my thoughts on."

"Because I'm your wife, who you love. You know the desires of my heart, and I thought that maybe eventually you would have a change of heart."

Again, silence.

"Bryce, you sound like you really don't want to talk, so I'm glad to hear you made it safely. I'll talk to you later."

"Simone. Wait. What I really should be saying is I'm sorry. I know that you want kids. Truth is, I'm just afraid to fail as a parent. I don't want to have children and my relationship with them end up like mine and my parents. There's already a lot of pressure on me to be the man of the house. I have to support the household, and if I don't do what I need to do, everything goes downhill from there. With kids, there's even more pressure to be able to take care of an entire family."

Surprised with how much Bryce had just opened up, I was then silent. I wasn't expecting that at all. Bryce never talked about his relationship with his parents, or how he felt about it. I never thought about the fact that that might've had an influence on how he felt about having kids of his own, or how the pressure of being able to provide for his family may have been a concern. I now felt like I was partially at fault for not taking into consideration Bryce's past, and his relationship with his parents. I had been selfish minded to think about only my feelings.

"Simone, you there?"

"Yes, and I'm so sorry for not considering your feelings. I was only thinking about myself. I wasn't thinking about how much pressure you might've felt to be a good provider."

I suddenly felt like this was the perfect time to bring up what I'd been thinking about all day.

"Knowing the things that concern you, and the thoughts that have been going through my mind today, I think that I have a solution that may ease your mind, and alleviate some of your concerns."

Curiously, Bryce said, "Really. What's on your mind, Love?"

"Well, I know what I bring to the household isn't much, and I've become way too comfortable with being where I am in life, so I've decided since I love what I do so much, I might as well further my career in that field and go to school to become a nurse."

Bryce didn't say anything right away, but soon began laughing hysterically. I didn't understand what could've possibly been so funny, so I was hoping his laughter was due to the overwhelming joy that he felt.

Hesitantly, I began laughing with him, hoping it was for the right reason.

"I know! It's great isn't it? I finally know what I'm meant to do."

Bryce stopped laughing and cleared his throat. "So, you're serious?"

"Yes, I'm serious. What's wrong with that?"

"Simone, you're about to be thirty-two. You're about ten years too late. You've chosen your career. Remember when you told me you love what you do, and you would continue to do that if you could make more money? Well, that's where I come in. Just stick to what you do, and I'll do the rest."

I couldn't believe that Bryce was using what I'd said before we even got married against me.

"I was in a different place in my life at that time, Bryce. We weren't even dating! I feel like I'm a totally different person from who I was then. I thought you'd be happy that I wanted to do more with my life, to make life even better for us."

"You know what would make me happy? It would make me happy if you stopped trying to make life-altering decisions for us. Our life is just fine as it is."

"Yes, it is fine, but there's always room for improvement, and I really want this. If not for anything else, at least it will be an accomplishment towards self-improvement for myself."

"Simone, do what you want to do, but I'm not investing in what I already know will be a failure."

"So, what you're saying is you don't believe in me," I said, in a trembling voice, with tears in my eyes.

"Of course, I believe in you. I believe in all that you are right now. I believe in you so much, that you don't need to change a thing."

At that point, I knew that there was nothing else for me to discuss with Bryce. Every conversation that we ever had ended with me getting the short end of the stick. This conversation had begun badly, but had briefly turned around long enough for me to receive an apology. That had given me hope, but that hope quickly dissipated into thin air.

"Thank you for that. Your feelings really do matter to me," I replied.

"No problem. That's what I'm there for. To bring you back down to Earth."

"I know. I'll talk to you tomorrow."

"Ok. I love you."

"I love you, too. Goodnight, Bryce."

After hanging up the phone from with Bryce, I felt like I had been drained of all the energy, happiness, and motivation that I'd been feeling all day. I just knew our conversation about me going to school would've gone over smoothly, but I guess I'd been wrong. I loved Bryce, but unfortunately, we weren't on the same page, and I didn't know how to get us there. I began to think that maybe he was right. Maybe I was trying to do too much, and just needed to relax and enjoy the life that he was working so hard to provide for me. I began to wonder, myself, if I needed any kids, and imagined my life without them. I needed to be more appreciative for the things that I had in front of me, and stop worrying about what the future had for me. If I did that, I knew that there would be a lot less arguments between me and Bryce.

A couple of weeks went by, and there was no more talk of kids, or me going to school. It was as if none of it had ever come up. The more time that went by that Bryce and I pretended that the conversation hadn't existed, the more I realized that I wasn't at peace with my decision to just disregard the desires of my heart. There was nothing I could do about Bryce not wanting kids, but going to school was something that I wanted to do for myself. I knew I couldn't let what Bryce thought deter me from accomplishing my goals. If I did, I knew I would resent him for the rest of my life.

"Hello, is this Noah?" I asked the person on the other end of the phone.

"Yes, it is. How can I help you?"

I had finally gotten up enough nerve to call Noah after dialing phone his number, minus the last digit, at least ten times.

"This is Simone. The CNA from the nursing home. Do you remember me?" I asked timidly.

Noah laughed, and said, "Of course I remember you. Did you apply for that job I told you about?"

"That's actually what I was calling you about. I had decided against it, but after thinking about it a little more, I know I can't pass up the opportunity. I really feel that would be the perfect change for me right now.

"I wish you would've called and talked to me about it if you were confused, or having any second thoughts. I could've probably given you a few words of encouragement. Unfortunately, the submission deadline was a few days ago."

I sighed and said, "That's what I get for second guessing myself, or maybe it's just not meant to be. Everything happens for a reason, right?"

"You're absolutely correct, which means, I ran into you for a reason, so let me see what I can do, and I'll get back with you, ok?"

A smile immediately came across my face, and I said, "Thank you so much! I appreciate you."

"No need to thank me. I'll talk to you soon."

After my phone call to Noah, I could feel in my heart that I'd done the right thing. I knew that my choice to apply for the job at the hospital and register for classes to begin my journey of becoming a nurse was the right one. Even if Bryce wasn't going to support me, or help pay for school, I was determined to make a way.

While I waited for Noah to call me back, I went online and started the process of applying for school, and reviewing the schedule of courses. It ended up being a long day filled with talking to the student loan department, and the academic advisor that was quickly assigned to me. I had taken a day off from work, which I rarely ever did, to take care of some business. I didn't even tell Bryce that I was taking the day off. I wasn't keeping it from him. I just didn't feel the need to tell him if it wasn't necessary. I didn't need any of his discouraging words while I was on a mission to do what I wanted to do for once. I was finally putting myself and my feelings first.

Noah ended up calling me back, telling me that all I needed to do was email him my resume, and he'd take care of the rest. Everything was falling into place right before my eyes, and I wished so badly that I could've shared my joy with Bryce. He would find out sooner or later. If I got the job at the hospital, which I didn't see a reason that I wouldn't, I would have to tell Bryce that I was quitting the nursing home. My biggest concern was Miss Franny, and how she would feel about me leaving, but I'd have to wait to cross that bridge when I got there.

Chapter Twenty-Eight

"Bryce, there's something I need to talk to you about," I said, as I walked out of the bathroom from taking a relaxing bubble bath.

I took that time to mentally prepare myself for how our conversation may or may not have gone. I had been contacted by the hiring manager at the hospital, and was told that I got the job without even having an in-person interview. I would be starting in exactly one week. The fall semester of classes would also be starting within a couple of weeks, so now that everything had been set in place, I had to give, what should've been good news, to Bryce.

Bryce patted the empty space on the bed right next to him, gesturing for me to come sit down.

"Something's always going on in that mind of yours. What is it now?" Bryce asked as I sat down.

"I hate that I have to bring up past conversations, especially when they didn't go too well, but I have to fill you in on some decisions I've made for myself."

I paused, feeling like Bryce would probably interrupt me before I could even really begin, but all he did was nod his head.

"I've enrolled in school full time, but I'll still be working so I can continue to contribute to the household."

"Ok, and how do you plan to still work while you're going to school full time."

"That's another thing. I won't be working at the nursing home anymore. I'll be working at St. Mary General hospital. They'll be working around my school hours, and the pay is better."

Bryce began rubbing his chin. "Who's paying for this because I can remember me saying that I wouldn't."

"Yes, you did say you wouldn't. That's why I applied for student loans that I can begin to pay off once I graduate. You'll have absolutely no responsibility."

"Ok. If that's what you want to do. It's sounds like you have everything figured out, so why even talk to me if you've made all these decisions without me, or without even thinking of us?"

"I discussed it with you, and I tried to make the decision with you. You think I didn't think about us? I thought so hard about us that I almost forgot about what I wanted. The decisions that I've made will in no way adversely affect us. They will only make a better and brighter future for us. I've thought of all the pros and cons, and honestly, the only con I could find was that I would no longer be working with Granny Franny, but I couldn't let that stop me either. I would never do anything to jeopardize our marriage."

"I know you wouldn't," he said, as he grabbed and held my hand. "I enjoy knowing that my wife will be home when I'm home, and if you're not, I know you will be soon. With all this going on in your life, when will you have time for me?"

I knew that my new schedule would be a lot, but it was only temporary. I didn't have an exact answer for Bryce because he wasn't going to be happy with anything I said. The only thing he would be happy with was if I changed my mind about both, going to school and starting the new job. He was complacent with where I was because It was all predictable to him and he felt like he had control. I felt like this all would be good for our marriage. Change was good, and we had both became too comfortable in many aspects of our lives. He relied on me always being wherever he needed me to be, when he needed me to be there, and I relied on him to support me financially so that I didn't need to do anything else with my life.

"We'll make it work, and as long as we work hard to make it work, God will make sure He handles the rest," I said, before giving Bryce a kiss and rolling over, falling into a deep sleep.

When I told Miss Franny about all the new things going on in my life, she seemed sad, but she was also genuinely happy for me. She told me that I had a bright future ahead, and to not feel guilty for deciding to leave the nursing home because of her.

"Everyone has to do what's best for them, and I support you in that decision. I truly believe this is what's best for you, and there will be so many other doors opened for you because you're allowing God to order your steps. Don't let Bryce make you feel bad about that either, and don't you worry about him. Just keep praying for him, and I will, too. God will set him straight. That right there is not your battle."

"Thank you so much, and I promise I'll be here to check on you every chance I get, and when I can't, make sure you stay by the phone!" I told her.

My last week at the nursing home went by so fast, and it was all so bittersweet. I had met and been a part of so many of the resident's families, and seen so many of them spend their final moments with us. I had somehow become a permanent entity in their lives, and I would soon become a temporary entity in an entirely new group of people's lives. I didn't know how I would handle that aspect of working in the hospital, knowing that my patients would come and go, instead of being permanent residents, which was what I'd become accustomed to. I was sure that I'd adapt, but I also knew that it would take some time. So many things in my life were changing all at once, but I knew that someday I would be able to appreciate every change that I was going through, and everything they brought to my life.

Bryce seemed to be coming to terms with the thought of it all. I didn't think he really thought that I had the courage to do everything that I'd done on my own without his money or his blessing. It felt good to show him how strong I could be. It felt even better to show myself how strong I could be, but you better believe, as soon as I started believing in myself, and seeing how much God wanted to bless me, the devil was sure to go into attack mode.

My first day at the hospital, I was introduced to several of the nurses and CNAs on the heart floor. I didn't think it had been a coincidence that I would be working on the same floor where Noah's office was. He obviously had a lot of authority about who he wanted working with his patients. I looked around for him, so I could thank him again, but he was nowhere in sight. When I looked around at the CNAs, I saw a lot of kids. Most of them looked like they had just gotten out of high school, or in their early twenties. That right there confirmed that it was time for me to move on. I was assigned to work along one of the other CNAs, named Kenzie. She had worked at the hospital for around the same amount of time I'd worked at the nursing home, and she was currently in nursing school. The difference was, Kenzie was only twenty-two, which made me wish that I hadn't wasted so much time. I felt so foolish being trained by a twenty-two-year-old, which was exactly what Satan wanted, so I had to remember that things were working out exactly as they should've been.

The next week, I began classes. At eight o'clock, on the morning of September 1st, I walked into my first class of the day, and it happened again. I saw all children, besides one woman who looked like she was probably in her fifties. All I could hear in my head was the voice of Bryce telling me that I was too old to go to school. It was another one of Satan's attacks, and I immediately began to pray from the time I walked into the classroom, until the professor began instruction. I had given the devil access to my mind, and I was ready to quit after my very first day. I needed some loving support outside of Miss Franny, so it was clear that I needed to pay my mom a visit.

As soon as my final class of the day was over, I headed to my mom's house. I felt defeated, frustrated, and mentally exhausted.

"Simone! What a pleasant surprise!" my mom said as she hugged my neck. "Come on in. It seems like forever since I've seen you. I know we talk, but it's nothing like seeing your face!"

"I know. I'm sorry I haven't been to visit sooner. I've just been so busy," I said, feeling like I'd been neglecting the people who meant the most to me.

"It's ok. I was going to call you to see how your first day of class was today. Your dad and I are so proud of you."

I instantly became overwhelmed from the mention of school. There was no way I was going to be able to do this for the next four years.

After she had just told me how proud she and my dad were, I regretted having to say, "Mom, I can't do this. It was just too much. I realize now that Bryce was right. I am too old for this."

"Bryce said you were too old?" my mom said, looking disgusted. "Honey, you're still young! You are nowhere near too old. Don't you remember me telling you that I didn't go to college until I was thirty-two? I wanted to raise your sister before doing all of that because I knew I wanted to go to Law School and that would've taken a lot of time from her during her young years. Then, to my surprise, I was blessed with you soon after, but I was still able to do everything I wanted to do. Don't let anyone ever tell you that you're too old for anything. These are some of the best years of your life, so live them to the fullest! I have so much confidence in you, and proud that you've taken such a courageous step in your life."

I didn't know if I should've told my mom what Bryce had said. She never did really care for him, and she made it quite obvious whenever he came around. Before we got married, she always told me that it was something about him that she just didn't like, but never could tell me exactly what it was. All she ever told me was that he was too arrogant.

My mom had given me so much courage and hope. I knew that if she did it in her thirties, with two kids, I could do it, too. I just had to focus and remember that nothing was too big for God. I couldn't continue to allow what other people thought to affect my future. I had to believe in myself, and know that God was cheering me on.

13 "I can do all things through Christ who strengthens me."
– Philippians 4:13 NKJV

After I left my mom's house, I went straight home, and to my surprise, Bryce's car was parked outside in the driveway. He was never home that early, so I wondered what the special occasion was. Before I even walked into the house, I could smell that something delicious was cooking on the other side of the door. When I walked in, it was dark, but I could see candles flickering from the dining room. I could hear one of my favorite songs by Tamia playing through the speakers, and Bryce suddenly appeared from out of nowhere with a bouquet of rainbow-colored roses in his hand.

"Bryce, what is all this about?"

"I wanted to celebrate you. You've been working hard to better yourself, and I've been nothing but unsupportive. I'm sorry. Please forgive me. I want you to know that I see all you're doing, and I'm here for it. You deserve this and more, so let's make today all about you."

I ran up to Bryce and hugged him tighter than I'd ever hugged him before. He reminded me of how sweet and thoughtful he could be. The man that I'd recently been around, had not been him at all, but I was grateful for that moment.

"Of course I forgive you, and I'm sorry for anything I may have done and said in frustration."

"No apology necessary. Now let's sit down and eat while you tell me all about your new job, and your first day of class today. I have all night, just for you."

Chapter Twenty-Nine

The next morning, I woke up to a note on Bryce's pillow that read, "No matter what, remember I'll always love you. You are my world."

I was on cloud nine. The first thing I did was thank God for working things out in my life. Bryce had already left for work, so I was able to shout and sing praises to God in my worst singing voice all over the house as I got ready for work. I didn't know what had gotten into Bryce. Maybe it had been a revelation from God. Whatever it was, I was forever grateful. Last night had been the best night that Bryce and I'd had in months, and because of that, today was already a great day.

When I pulled into the employee parking lot at the hospital, I also noticed Noah pulling in as well. As we both searched for a parking space in the crowded lot, we drove past each other and waved. The past couple of weeks of working at the hospital, I surprisingly hadn't run into Noah, and each time I peeked into his office, his lobby would be full, and the receptionist would tell me that he was in with a patient. I had come to learn that he was a very busy man.

After finally finding a parking space, I got out the car and started walking towards the entrance.

"Good Morning, Simone!"

I looked back and saw Noah jogging towards me.

"Hey there! You're a hard man to catch!"

Noah finally caught up with me, and said, "You've been looking for me? Is there something wrong?"

"No, I dropped by your office a few times to tell you thank you, again. I can't tell you how much I appreciate everything. Also, did you request that I be placed on the heart floor?"

"You're very welcome, but you don't have to keep thanking me. You sold yourself that day I was at the nursing home. I saw your potential and knew where you were needed, and yes, I did request for you to be on the cardiology floor. I want only the best to be working with my patients, but if that's not where you want to be, I'll rescind my request and let them place you elsewhere."

"No, I like where I am. I'm just still getting used to working with patients of all ages, and not just the seniors."

I looked at what Noah was wearing, which seemed pretty odd. He was wearing jeans and a t-shirt. I knew I'd only seem him one time, but the one time I'd seen him, he wasn't dressed as casually.

"Is it dress down day today for the doctors?" I asked.

Noah laughed and said, "Not at all. I'm not in doctor mode today. I'm in daddy mode."

"Daddy mode?" I questioned.

"Yes. My wife gave birth to our baby girl yesterday afternoon. I was here most of the night with them. They should be ready to go home soon."

"Wow! Congratulations! You must be a happy man," I said with a big smile.

"I think I'm the happiest man on earth! My wife, Taylor, and I have been trying for years and it finally happened."

"What a miracle! I'm so happy for you."

As we stopped to wait for the elevator, Noah said, "Thanks, Simone. I really appreciate that. You have any kids?"

"Not yet. Not sure if I'll ever have any."

Before Noah could ask, why not, the elevator door opened.

"Bryce. What are you doing here?"

Bryce stepped out of the elevator, looking back and forth at me and Noah, seeming a little tense.

"I was looking for you," he said.

I looked at my watch and said, "Well, I have about twenty minutes before I start. Is there something wrong?"

Ignoring my question, Bryce asked, "Who is this?" pointing at Noah, who was still standing next to me.

As the elevator door closed without any of us inside, I said, "Oh, this is Dr. Sullivan. Dr. Sullivan, this is my husband, Bryce."

Noah extended his hand to Bryce, and said, "Nice to meet you, Bryce. You have a wonderful woman right here."

Bryce ignored Noah's courteous gesture, and just nodded his head. The tension was so thick, you could've cut it with a knife.

I didn't know why such an innocent situation felt so uncomfortable, and I was still pretty unclear as to why Bryce was at the hospital that morning looking for me, however, I still tried to break the ice.

"Noah actually helped me get this job."

Bryce suddenly looked at Noah with scrutiny and said, "So Noah, you're the one who put all those crazy thoughts in her head when everything at home was just fine."

I couldn't believe Bryce was back to this again. I guess the previous night was just for show. I thought we were finally on the same page, but I must've read everything all wrong. I was so embarrassed and just wanted Bryce to leave.

The elevator door opened again just in time, and as Noah stepped in without me, I said, "Noah, it was good to see you, and take care of your wife and that new baby girl!"

"Thanks, again, Simone. I hope the rest of your day goes well," he said, waving as the door closed.

I folded my arms and looked at Bryce.

"What was that about?"

"Is that why you wanted so badly to work at this hospital?"

"Did you just not hear me tell him to take care of his baby and wife? His wife had their first child yesterday, and he's ecstatic to be coming to pick them up and take them home. I have no interest in him whatsoever. What is wrong with you?"

"Nothing's wrong with me. I was coming to surprise you, and catch you walking in with another man, so maybe I should be asking you what is wrong with me? Am I not good enough for you? You need a doctor now?"

"Don't turn this around on me! Especially after you told me last night you were happy about everything that I was doing, but just told Noah he's to blame! Which is it? Are you happy or not?"

Realizing that we were still in public, I noticed everyone walking past, staring at us.

I stepped in the elevator, and as it closed, I said, "Bryce, just leave. We'll talk about this later."

I had claimed that my day would be great, and I couldn't let Bryce and his crazy antics steal my joy. He had caused me to be confused about everything that had happened the night before. I had never known Bryce to be the jealous type, so I didn't know where that performance had come from. He always acted as if he wasn't worried about me entertaining any other man, or another man looking at me, but now I wasn't so sure.

Before I started my shift, I decided to go to the maternity floor to see if I could catch Noah alone. When I got off of the elevator onto the floor, I immediately saw Noah from behind, walking down the hall.

"Noah," I whispered harshly.

He stopped, and after seeing it was me, he asked, "Is everything ok?"

I waited until I got near him and said, "Yeah. I just wanted to apologize for that. I don't know why he reacted that way."

"Does he not want you working here?"

"Funny thing is, he hadn't supported me in this transition until last night. He actually apologized for not supporting me, and told me he was proud of me, so I'm thoroughly confused."

"Hang in there. All couples go through things. He probably just needs to get used to all the changes happening in your life. It'll be ok."

"Ok. I just didn't want you to think that I had involved you in any type of drama. I need to get to work, so I'll see you later.

As I was walking away, Noah, said, "Hey, you want to see Amina Reign?

"Is that her name?" I asked.

"Yep."

"That's beautiful! Yes, I'd love to see her. I'm sure she's just as beautiful as her name.

We headed towards the nursery to see Amina, but when we got there, her crib was empty. The nurses had taken her to Noah's wife.

"I should've known she would be with Taylor," Noah said, smiling.

"Well, I'll see her another time," I said, as I began to walk in the opposite direction.

"Taylor's room is right down the hall. Follow me," Noah said.

"Are you sure your wife won't mind? She doesn't even know me."

"Not at all. Taylor's not like that. A friend of mine is a friend of hers."

When we got to the room, Noah tapped on the partially cracked door, and said, "Are you decent? We have company."

"Do we? Yes, come on in. Amina and I were just saying how we'd love some company," I heard Taylor say as we walked in.

"Taylor, this is Simone. She's a CNA on my floor. Simone, this is my wife, Taylor, and our baby girl, Amina Reign."

"Hi, Taylor! Nice to meet you."

"Nice to also meet you."

Taylor was beautiful. Even after just having a baby. I could've never imagined being so well put together after giving birth.

"She is gorgeous, you two! I can already tell she's going to be a daddy's girl," I said, as I watched Noah lift Amina up out of her mother's arms.

"You must've been a daddy's girl!" Noah said.

I smiled and said, "It's time for me to go and do some work. Thanks for sharing Amina with me."

The rest of my day went surprisingly well. Even though it had begun a little rocky, seeing Noah with his baby girl brought so much joy to my heart. I loved seeing other people happy, and Noah was a proud father.

When I got home that evening, Bryce wasn't home yet, and I couldn't wait until he got there so we could continue our conversation. I cooked dinner and fell asleep on the sofa as I waited. While asleep, I heard the front door open. I looked at the clock on the wall, and had to rub my eyes and look a second time when I saw that it said that it was one in the morning.

I sat up and said, "Where have you been?"

"At work," Bryce said nonchalantly.

"Please don't lie to me, Bryce. You're never at work this late."

"Well, never say never, because tonight I was."

"Whatever," I said as I snatched my blanket off the sofa and began folding it. I then headed to the bedroom to get in bed.

"What, now you're upset with me, Simone?" Bryce said as he stood in the doorway of the bedroom.

"Nope. If you said you were at work, then you were at work. You're my husband and I trust you. Can you say the same for me?"

"What do you mean?"

"I mean, can you trust me? You acted as if Noah and I had something going on today. And why'd you really come to the hospital? To see if I was really working there?"

"You know what, Simone? Maybe I was having some trust issues. Things with you are changing so fast. I just needed to make sure nothing was getting past me. Now I know I can trust you."

"Bryce, are you serious? I would never be dishonest with you, and one thing you don't have to worry about is me cheating on you."

"I know. I don't know what got into me. We had a great night, and I went and messed it up. I guess I owe Noah an apology, too."

"Don't worry about it. I apologized for the both of us."

The night before, and that particular night made it seem like things were headed in the right direction, but it seemed like things continued to be up and down. I knew that all marriages had their bumps in the road, but it seemed like we couldn't get a good straight week of everything going smooth. I wondered if all of this was caused by the changes I'd made and I'd started blaming myself. Was I not praying enough, and had God given up on us?

There were many more late nights for Bryce, and it seemed like he was away on business more than usual, but I honestly didn't know whether he was really away more often, or if it just seemed that way because I had so much going on in my life. There were several occasions when I just felt like giving up on school because it was so hard to concentrate knowing that things weren't acceptable at home, but I knew that wasn't the answer. As husband and wife, we should've been able to talk through any issues we were having and come up with a plan or resolution, even if only on a trial basis.

When we were both free, I began setting up date nights, and those were some of our best nights. We would laugh, talk, reminisce, and love on each other. I always wished that those nights would never come to an end, or that every night could be like that. I tried my best to make that happen. Even when Bryce was on business trips, I would try sending him random romantic texts throughout the day. Sometimes, he would text me back something romantic, and maybe even a heart emoji. Other times, I wouldn't get a response at all.

I talked with Bryce about seeing a marriage counselor, and he was completely against that. He told me that this was temporary, and things would turn around on their own. He would also even tell me that our situation wasn't as bad as some others. I didn't care about everyone else's relationship. I was worried about mine, and the sad thing was I was trying to do everything to fix it, but things weren't getting any better. I felt like I had done everything that I could've possibly done, and now all I could do was wait on God.

Chapter Thirty

"Hi, Taylor! Good to see you," I said to Noah's wife who was standing in the waiting room of his office when I walked in.

Taylor always looked so perfect. She was tall and thin. I never saw her in anything outside of heels, which made her tower over Noah since she was already taller than him, and she always had a designer bag that was bigger than her hanging from her shoulder. I didn't think she ever came out of the house without makeup, although I knew she didn't need it, after seeing her right after giving birth to Amina. Her hair was never out of place, and her nails and lashes were always done. If no one had ever told me that she was married to Noah, I would've never guessed. He was a lot simpler than Taylor, which made me think that his wife would've been a lot lower maintenance than what she was. Her only visible flaw was a nice sized scar on her chest that was only noticeable when she wore low cut tops.

"Hey, Simone. How are you?"

"I'm fine", I said as I knelt down beside Amina's stroller, and said, "Hey, Gorgeous."

Amina began giggling, and it just made my heart melt.

"We just stopped by to get some money from Dr. Daddy so we can go shopping for Miss Amina's first birthday," Taylor said.

Shocked, I said, "First birthday already? The year has gone by so fast."

"Yes, it has."

"Hey, Ladies," Noah said, as he came to the front after he finished examining a patient.

"Hey, Baby. You know what I'm here for," Taylor said, grinning in Noah's face.

"Can I at least get a kiss?" he asked, jokingly.

Noah and Taylor were the exemplary couple, and I loved seeing them together. The way that Noah looked at Taylor told an entire story. He seemed to love everything about her. He adored her, and she knew it. Taylor didn't work. She took care of home and the baby, and that was enough for Noah. I had never heard either of them speak of her past jobs or career, so I wasn't sure if she'd ever worked.

"And what did you need, Simone?" Noah asked as I watched him interact with his beautiful family.

"Oh, I was just letting you know that Martha Buchanan has been admitted. She's getting set up in room 3105 right now."

"Ok. Let me grab her chart and I'll be down shortly."

"See you later, Taylor. Have fun shopping for Amina."

"Simone, before you go, you and your husband should come to the party tomorrow. There will be lots of kids, and it'll be nice to have some extra adults around."

Noah and I looked at each other because we knew that the first and last time he and Bryce had seen each other, things didn't go so well.

"I'll check with my husband to see what he has going on, and if he's free, we'll definitely be there. I'll get the details from Noah later."

"Ok. Sounds good," Taylor said, as she waved goodbye.

On my way home from work, I thought about some of the couples that Bryce and I had hung out with in the past, and for the most part, they all seemed to have it all together. If there had been any major issues in their relationships or marriages, they had been very good at concealing it. The more I thought about it, the more I began to realize that others looking in on my marriage from the outside probably felt the same way about me and Bryce. Without me telling them, no one would probably know that Bryce and I struggled with all of the issues that we did. Those thoughts took me back to when Bryce told me that his friend Ryan was cheating on Ashley. I always felt like they were the perfect couple, and I definitely looked up to them. I just couldn't bring myself to believe that they had any major issues, especially not infidelity. There were absolutely no outwardly indications that there was any trouble in paradise, and I would never believe there was unless I heard it straight from the horse's mouth.

When I got home, Bryce's car was in the driveway, which I was excited about because it wasn't very often that he beat me home.

"Baby," I said, as I walked through the house looking for Bryce.

I didn't see him anywhere, so I figured he was probably in his office working on something. His office door was closed, so I knocked, hoping I wasn't disturbing him too much. I just wanted to make sure that I asked him about going to Amina's birthday party before it slipped my mind.

"Come in," he said.

"Hey! You're home early, but I'm glad to see you," I said, as I stood behind Bryce's chair and wrapped my arms around his neck.

"Yeah. I had a few meetings outside of the office today, so I just decided to come on home and finish up the rest of the day."

"What do you have planned for tomorrow?"

He stopped typing, and said, "What is tomorrow? I've been so busy I can't keep up with the days."

"Well, you need to slow down. Tomorrow is Saturday."

"Nothing for tomorrow, but I did want to talk to you about next week. I'll be gone for a few days."

I knew from prior experience that Bryce and I had two totally different definitions of "a few", so whenever he said that, I needed for him to specify.

"When you say a few, what do you mean?"

"Not for certain, but probably around five days," he replied.

"So, you're telling me you'll be gone for about a week."

Bryce looked at me as if I'd said something that irritated him.

"If that's what you're going with, then yes, I'll be gone for about a week."

"What do you have to do that's going to take so long, and where will you be?"

"I'm going to Atlanta, and you know that's my hot spot, so I have a few different clients I need to see down there, and I'm basically working around their schedule. I prefer to make one trip and get everyone out of the way, rather than making several separate trips. Do you agree, or do you have a better idea?" he asked sarcastically.

That was why I didn't like asking Bryce questions because he was always on the defense, but some things, as his wife, I just needed to know. He wasn't going to voluntarily offer any information without me asking, and he barely wanted to tell me when I asked. I just decided to get off of that subject and talk about what I'd initially gone in to ask.

"No, I don't have a better idea. It sounds like you have it all figured out, but what I came to ask was if you'd like to go with me to Noah and his wife, Taylor's daughter's birthday party. She'll be turning one tomorrow, and they invited us to come. Before you answer, I know you and Noah's initial introduction didn't go well, but . . ."

"I'll go," Bryce said without hesitation.

"Oh. Ok," I said, surprised that Bryce had agreed without me having to twist his arm. "I'll let you know what time once I hear from Noah."

"Ok," Bryce said as he stared at his screen and began typing again.

That had gone incredibly easy, but I wasn't complaining. It wasn't too often I could catch Bryce on a free day, and it definitely wasn't often he would agree to go somewhere where there would be a bunch of kids running around. Since Bryce was working, and didn't seem like he'd be coming out of that office anytime soon, I decided to go out before everything closed, and find a gift for little Miss Amina.

The next morning, when I woke up, Bryce had already left. He said he didn't have anything to do, so I didn't know where he could've possibly gone. I was going to call him, but I just figured something had come up, or maybe he just needed to go into the office to take care of a few things. With the fact in mind that I didn't even have to convince him to go to the party with me, I wouldn't have been surprised if he flaked on me. I wasn't going to stress over it. Noah had texted me and told me that the party would be at his home starting at three o' clock. If Bryce hadn't shown up by two-thirty, I'd be leaving without him. I really didn't want to go without him since we had both been invited, but if I had to, then that's what I was going to do.

I did a little cleaning and other things I needed to do before preparing to head over to Noah's house. Two-thirty quickly rolled around, and as I was headed towards the front door, carrying the gift bag containing the gift I'd bought, I heard a horn outside the door. When I opened it, it was Bryce, sitting in the driveway, waiting.

"You ready to go?" he yelled out the window.

"Yep. I was just about to leave," I said, as I shut the door behind me.

When I got into the car, I noticed a few bags in the backseat.

"What's all that?" I asked.

"I went shopping for their little girl."

Confused, I said, "I'd already gotten her a gift."

Bryce looked at the bag in my lap, and said, "That's all you bought?"

"Yeah. I didn't know we were going all out for other people's kids."

I wanted to add, "especially since you don't want your own kids," but I decided to zip my lips. I didn't want to start an argument before we made it to our destination.

When we pulled up to Noah and Taylor's house, I was amazed at how beautiful it was. It looked like we were the first to arrive, which was probably going to feel a bit awkward, but at least if there was anything that needed to be said to clear the air, it could be done before anyone else arrived.

"Now this is a nice house," Bryce said, as we walked along the long pathway to the door.

As soon as I was about to ring the doorbell, Taylor opened the door with her beautiful, bright smile, wearing a tank top which exposed her scar. Her ability to willfully display her flaw that most women would've been trying to relentlessly cover up, defined the high level of confidence that she possessed.

"Hey, Simone! I'm so glad you could make it."

"You know I couldn't miss this!" I said, as we walked in.

As we stood in the foyer, I introduced Bryce to Taylor. "Taylor, this is my husband, Bryce. Bryce, this this Noah's wife, and Amina's mom, Taylor."

Bryce gently took Taylor's hand, smiled at her, and said, "Very nice to meet you. He then kissed her delicate hand.

Taylor, blushing, said, "The pleasure is all mine."

I thought things would seem a little uncomfortable, but I never thought the discomfort would come from the way Bryce interacted with Taylor.

"So, where's the birthday girl?" I asked, breaking up Bryce and Taylor's own little party.

"Oh, she's in the backyard with Noah. Let's head on back."

We followed Taylor to the backyard, where we found Noah standing at the grill, flipping burgers, and Amina sitting on a blanket in the middle of the yard, playing with toys. When Noah saw us, he put down his spatula and began walking in our direction.

When he approached us, he said, "Hey, Bryce. Good to see you again."

I noticed Noah didn't offer a handshake this time, but surprisingly, Bryce did. When Noah saw that Bryce was trying to make amends, he shook his hand and smiled.

I was pleased with what I saw, and relieved at the same time. After they shook hands, I gave Noah a hug and stood around the grill talking to him and Taylor. That quick, I had lost sight of Bryce.

I looked around, and there he was, kneeling over Amina, talking to her, and grinning from ear to ear. I liked seeing Bryce interact with Amina. His fatherly instincts seemed to come so naturally, which made me feel like there was a bigger reason than what he had been telling me, as to why he didn't want any kids.

"He seems to be a natural with kids," Noah said, as we watched from a distance.

"Yes, he does!" I said, smiling.

Taylor then went over and sat on the blanket next to Amina and gave her a huge hug. The three of them looked like a happy family, and it was a picture-perfect moment. When I realized what I was looking at, my smile immediately disappeared.

"Bryce! Why don't you come help Noah out on the grill!" I yelled.

Bryce stood up and headed our way.

"You're making me look bad out there," Noah joked with Bryce. "If I didn't know any better, I would think you had kids of your own."

"Nah. I don't have any. I don't think I ever will."

"You should. It's truly a blessing."

"I'm sure," Bryce said.

I cringed when Bryce said he didn't think he would ever have any kids. I cringed each time he said it because even though I knew how he felt, it hurt every time I heard him say it. I could only focus on the moment and continue to pray that God worked on Bryce. Seeing Bryce with Amina definitely made me feel like there were some changes occurring.

Amina's party became more and more packed by the minute. Noah and Taylor had a lot of friends and family. Taylor's family even drove in from Chicago. I could see where Taylor got her looks. Her mom was also tall, thin, and gorgeous. She seemed to be extremely confident, just like Taylor. I was so fascinated with genes and how they worked. Anytime I was anywhere and saw a family in passing, I would literally examine their features, envious of the fact that they had the privilege of knowing where they got their eyes, nose, or high cheekbones. The younger generation would someday even have the privilege of passing on some of those same features to their children, which was something else, I probably would never have the opportunity to do.

I envied Taylor as I watched her, her mom, and her dad interact with one another. They all seemed so close. Her mom and dad displayed some form of public affection the entire time, whether it was by holding hands, a quick kiss on the cheek, or a loving smile. I could tell Taylor had grown up in a good home, and had been shown lots of love. She and her mom talked and laughed with each other like two best friends, which led me to believe that they probably told each other everything. Her mom was her best friend, and that was the type of relationship I also wished I could've had with my mother, whoever she was.

In the middle of observing everything that was going on, I managed to catch the perfect opportunity to get a picture of three beautiful generations. Taylor was sitting next to her mom with Amina on her lap.

"Say cheese!" I said, as I interrupted their conversation, holding my camera up in front of them.

They all posed and smiled for the camera, including Amina, who already loved taking pictures.

"Make sure I get a copy of that!" Taylor said.

"For sure!" I said.

When it was time to open gifts, I noticed that we had left ours in the car, so I told Bryce to go out and get them. He and Noah seemed to be having a good conversation, which was a good thing.

"Come on, Noah. I might need some help with these," Bryce said, as he stood up to get ready to go to the car.

Just a few minutes later, they were heading back with all of Amina's gifts.

"It looks like we only needed to invite Bryce and Simone!" Noah said, holding up a few of the bags of items Bryce had gone out and bought. I hadn't even looked through the bags to see what was in them, but just from seeing the names of the stores on the bags, I knew that Bryce had spent quite a bit of money.

Bryce handed the bag with the gift that I'd bought to Taylor.

"This is from Simone."

I couldn't believe Bryce had done that to me. We had gone to the party together, so whatever he had bought should've just been in addition to what I'd bought. He made it seem like a competition of some sort. Like he was trying to prove something.

"Awww! Thanks so much, Simone. I'm sure Amina is going to love whatever it is."

Bryce then snatched the other bags from Noah, and said, "These are from me. I went shopping bright and early this morning."

"I'm telling you, you're really good with this kid thing, Bryce. Simone, I think he's ready!" Noah said.

"Oh, are the two of you considering having a baby?" Taylor asked inquisitively.

Before I could get my words out, Bryce replied, "Absolutely not."

That comment was the last straw. I was tired of Bryce treating me like I was just any ole random woman on the street, and like he was disgusted by the thought of having a child with me.

I stood close to Bryce, and said, "I'm ready to go," loud enough so that only he could hear me.

Not so quietly, Bryce said, "You beg me to go places with you, and when I finally do without an argument, you want to leave early."

"Are you leaving?" Noah asked.

"Yeah, I think we should go. I'm suddenly not feeling very well," I said.

"Oh no! Am I that bad of a cook?" Noah laughed, trying to make me feel better.

"No. I just need to lie down."

"Well, don't forget to tell Amina goodbye," Taylor said. She's going back to Chicago with her grandparents for a little while."

"Don't remind me! I'm going to miss my baby girl," Noah said.

I gave Amina a kiss on the cheek as her mom held her, and said, "Bye, Amina. Have a good time visiting your grandparents." I smiled at her, and she smiled back, revealing her cute little dimples.

"Thanks for coming by, and we appreciate all of the gifts from the both of you," Noah said, with intent.

I looked at Noah, and he immediately winked at me. He knew that when Bryce split up the gifts, it had upset me, so Noah was just trying to let me know, the gifts were all accepted as coming from the both of us.

The car ride home was quiet. Bryce didn't even turn on the radio. I rolled the window all the way down so I could feel the nice breeze, and I closed my eyes. As soon as I'd found a peaceful place within my mind, Bryce had to go and ruin it.

"We could've at least stayed until they opened the gifts. You didn't even get to see what all I'd bought."

I opened my eyes and focused my attention on Bryce.

"You're trying to tell me what we could've done? You could've woken me up so that we both could've gone shopping. You could've just put all the gifts together and told them that they were from the both of us. Since when do we separate things? Whenever I buy something for someone else, whether it's for someone's wedding, birthday, graduation, or baby shower, I always put your name on the gift. What were you trying to prove today?"

"I thought you'd be happy that I was participating in the whole thing. I didn't even know you had gone out last night and bought a gift. I thought I was helping."

"Never mind, Bryce. You're missing this point, so maybe you'll understand this one. When someone asks us about having a baby, you respond as though you're disgusted. Do you really not want to have kids, or are you just disgusted at thinking of having kids with me?"

"Simone, not this again. I told you I don't want kids."

"Ok," I replied.

"Ok? What do you mean by ok?"

"You answered the question, and my response meant that I heard you."

"Ok," he replied, and that was the last of our communication for the rest of the night.

Chapter Thirty-One

That next Monday morning, I couldn't wait to go to work. I just needed some time away from Bryce. We hadn't spoken since our drive home from Noah and Taylor's house. I didn't even know what day he was leaving to go to Atlanta, and I wasn't going to even ask. I wouldn't have been surprised if he would've packed up and left without me even knowing. That's how distant I felt we were.

I felt so unhappy. It was the unhappiest I'd felt in a long time because I believed my marriage was failing. It seemed like I had tried everything to bring me and Bryce closer, but nothing was working. I prayed all the time, so I didn't want to give up the faith that I had that things would eventually get better. I really didn't know if Bryce even cared whether or not things got better. It seemed as if his job was the only thing that mattered. He was married, with the life of a bachelor, and I felt like he looked at me as a burden.

I thought about all of these things as I sat at the lunch table playing with my food. I was so deep in thought, I didn't even notice that Noah had come and sat down right across from me.

"Earth to Simone," he said.

"Oh, hey, Noah. I didn't even see you there."

"I see. What has your mind so far away?"

"There's just so much on my mind and it's getting so heavy."

"You want to talk about it? I have a little time."

"Sometimes I feel like giving up on my marriage, but I know it can be fixed. I'm just so tired of trying, and feeling like I'm the only one trying," I said, with tears welling up in my eyes.

"Simone, you know that no marriage is perfect, right?"

"Yeah, that's what people keep telling me, including Bryce, but the good is supposed to outweigh the bad, but it doesn't seem that way for me."

"Who told you that?" Noah asked, lowering his brows.

"Well, isn't it?" I asked, no longer confident in my statement.

"Every marriage is different, Simone. The beginning of yours just may be rough, and it is possible that the bad may outweigh the good, but you have to continue to work towards the goal of having the good outweigh the bad. Both of you have to work hard and want it, though. From what I've seen and heard from the two of you, there seems to be some conversations that weren't had before getting married. Conversations, such as, baby talk. Did Bryce communicate to you that he didn't want kids before the two of you got married?"

I took a deep breath and began playing with my food again.

"I'll take that as a yes, and I can tell because he is so adamant about not having any."

"I just thought once we got married, his thoughts on that would change."

"That's one of the number one mistakes people make when getting married. They find some things they don't like about that person, but feel like they can change their views or thoughts after they get married. You cannot go into a marriage counting on being able to change your spouse. They are who they are, and will only change if they want to change. For instance, Taylor loves to shop. She loved to shop before we got married, and I really didn't like it, but I had to ask myself if I would be able to tolerate it, or if it was a dealbreaker. A dealbreaker, meaning, it would be something that could possibly cause the demise of our marriage. I didn't feel it was a dealbreaker. We've been married almost six years, and she still loves to shop, and does it often, but it doesn't bother me, and I would never think to divorce her because of it. I met Taylor during my first year of residency, which was one of the most stressful times of my life. It didn't help that the way we met weren't under good circumstances, and those circumstances caused a lot of strain on our relationship early on. I knew that if we could get past all of what we dealt with, her shopping problem would be a piece of cake to deal with.

The way that Noah went around the subject of the circumstances that caused strain in their relationship, I assumed that he had no desire to talk about it, so I didn't stop him to ask any questions to try to dig a little deeper, even though I was extremely curious. I just listened as he continued to make his point.

"Now, this baby situation could possibly be considered a dealbreaker for many couples, especially where your feelings are with it opposed to his. You want a baby so bad, Simone, and I feel your pain because Bryce truly doesn't want one. The two of you need to sit down and have an adult conversation, because if you don't, you'll resent him for the rest of your life."

All I could do was nod my head because everything that Noah said was true. I knew that Bryce never wanted any kids, and I still settled because his feelings for me felt real, and I had never felt that type of love before. We definitely needed to have a real adult conversation, as Noah called it.

"I've tried talking to him about it, but I also realize those conversations have only consisted of me trying to force something on him that he doesn't want, and I knew that he didn't want from the beginning. I get upset with him about it, but what we've been going through is not entirely his fault. I've brought a lot of this on myself by doing exactly what you just said. Going in thinking I could change the things that I didn't like about him. The crazy thing is, I know he didn't like things about me when we got married, but I changed those things for him. I considered those things to be compromise, and I expected him to do the same for me."

"Things like what?" Noah asked curiously.

"My appearance and style of dress. I changed it all for him. I used to only straighten my hair every now and then. Now I have a relaxer. I never wore heels or fitted clothing. Now that's mostly what my closet consists of. I wore huge thick glasses because I'm blind as a bat, but he talked me into wearing contacts even though I was terrified to stick anything in my eyes."

I opened my wallet and took a picture out. "Here. Look at this," I said, as I handed the picture to Noah.

Noah's eyes became huge. "This is you?" he asked in disbelief.

"Yes. Terrible, huh?"

Noah looked directly into my eyes and said, "No. You were just as beautiful as you are now. All beauty doesn't look the same. You had your own unique type of beauty in this picture, and the beauty you possess now, is just an enhanced form of beauty that wouldn't even exist without your natural beauty."

Noah made me blush because I was always comfortable with being natural and ordinary, but I never felt beautiful. People would tell me that I was beautiful, including Miss Franny, but I just always believed they were saying it to make me feel good because they felt sorry for me.

"Thank you. I appreciate that."

"I'm just being honest, and while I'm being honest, I must say that you changing your appearance was not compromise. You sold your true self in exchange for who you are right now. You can only compromise on life decisions and choices. A compromise would've been Bryce telling you that instead of not having any kids, since you did want some, he'd agree to one. That's compromise. Don't ever think that changing yourself for someone is compromise. Never compromise who you are for anyone. I don't care who it is. If someone can't accept you for who you are, they don't need any parts of you."

"Do you think this marriage is even worth saving?"

"Simone, I can't tell you to leave your husband or get a divorce. Everything I'm saying to you right now is basically in hindsight. Now, you've stood before God and said vows to this man. Just because he doesn't want kids isn't a good enough reason to break that covenant."

As tears began streaming down my face, Noah pulled a tissue out of his pocket and leaned over the table, wiping my eyes.

"I'm so sorry," I sobbed. "I didn't mean to throw this on you."

"It's ok. I'm a friend, and friends are there for you to have a shoulder to lean on. I'll always be honest with you. Even when I feel you're wrong, I'm going to tell you."

"Thanks again, Noah. I have to pray about some things. He'll be going out of town soon, so I'll probably wait until he gets back so we can have a serious talk about everything going on."

"When you do, just express yourself to him just like you did for me. Let him fully understand your pain."

"I definitely will," I said as I stood up from the table to head back to work. "I'll see you later, Noah."

After my talk with Noah, I began to have a very different perspective on things. I had expectations of Bryce that would possibly be unachievable, and I had to accept that. I had to learn to respect the fact that he didn't want kids, because I accepted it when I said my vows and married him. He accepted me the way that I was when I married him. If I hadn't changed my appearance in order to adapt to his lifestyle, he would've had to accept that because that was who he had married. Noah had only been married for five years, but he was wise beyond his years. He had given me a lot of good, solid advice, and I appreciated him for that.

I felt like I was in a much better headspace than I had been in a while, so when I got home, I cooked dinner, set the table, and took a nice, hot bubble bath before Bryce got home. I knew he hadn't left for Atlanta yet because his luggage was still in the closet.

After I got out of the tub, I put on some comfortable pajamas and waited for him. As soon as I saw his headlights beam through the living room picture window, I quickly lit the candles at the dinner table, and ran and stood behind the door. As soon as he opened the door and shut it behind him, he saw me standing there. I smiled and wrapped my arms around him.

"I miss you. I don't like when we're not speaking," I said.

"I miss you, too, Baby," he said, as he gently kissed me on the lips. He looked towards the dining room, at the romantic ambiance, and said, "I see you've been busy."

"Yes, I have. I've been thinking about us all day. Go upstairs and get comfortable while I fix our plates," I said.

Bryce kissed me again, and said, "I love you," before going upstairs. By the time I'd fixed our plates and poured some drinks, he was on his way back down. I was already sitting, and he sat right across from me. Before we ate, I said a prayer, and in that prayer, I not only prayed over the food, but I also prayed over our marriage. I prayed that anything causing any feelings of anger, resentment, or unforgiveness in our marriage would be destroyed. I prayed that any dishonestly would cease, and any secrets would be revealed.

Once my prayer ended, I said, "I'm sorry for everything. I make everything out to be your fault and it's not. I tried to force something on you that you made very clear from the beginning you didn't want any part of. I don't want to ruin tonight by talking about all of it, but I just wanted you to know that I can now see your perspective of things. We can get everything out in the air whenever you get back from Atlanta."

Bryce looked down at his plate, then folded his hands underneath his chin and stared at me.

"Is something wrong? Do I have something on my face?" I asked, wiping my hand across my face.

"No. You're perfect, and I know I haven't been the easiest person to be married to. I know I'm stubborn and set in my ways, so I want to also say that I'm sorry. I also want you to know that I've been thinking a lot about the baby thing during these past couple of days of silence between us. I see how much you love Amina, and she's not even your own. You would make a fantastic mother. Any man would consider it an honor to have you as the mother of their child, and I'm blessed enough to have you as my wife."

My legs began shaking as Bryce was talking. "What are you saying, Bryce?"

"I'm saying I'm open to us discussing having a baby."

I couldn't contain my excitement. I wanted to scream. I wanted to shout! I jumped up out of my seat, ran over to Bryce and jumped into his lap, giving him the tightest hug I'd ever given anyone in my entire life. He had made me the happiest woman alive. Even though he didn't say for sure that we would be having a baby, I was happy with him just being open to discuss it. That was definitely a big step in the right direction.

Bryce told me that he would be leaving for Atlanta the very next evening, and we agreed to have a deep discussion about everything when he returned. He said there was a lot that he wanted to open up to me about, and he wanted me to open up to him about whatever I needed to. He wanted to start fresh and make it right. I was so glad that Bryce and I had actually been able to apologize to each other, and have a conversation without it ending in an argument. I was never even expecting an apology, but after I received it, I realized that I needed it. I had always felt like Bryce never thought that he did anything wrong, but by him apologizing with sincerity, he had taken accountability for his part. I had high hopes that taking that first step in recognizing and admitting that we'd both been wrong would be the beginning of something beautiful.

Chapter Thirty-Two

The next morning, I had class, but wished so badly that I could've spent the entire day with Bryce until he got ready to leave for the airport. This would be the longest amount of time we'd ever been apart, and I knew that it was going to be tough, especially with us just getting on the road to reconciling many of our differences. We were in a good space, so I hoped that our time apart wouldn't land us right back to square one.

"Bryce," I said in the softest voice possible as I gently nudged him while he slept peacefully.

Bryce finally stretched and opened his eyes. "Good Morning," he said, smiling at me.

I couldn't deny that I was loving every bit of what I was feeling. Everything suddenly felt so brand new, in a good way. Bryce seemed as though he'd made a complete one-eighty, and I was definitely there for it.

"I have to go to class, but I'll be back this afternoon," I said.

Bryce made a sad face, which tempted me a bit to skip class, but I knew how easy it was to fall behind in the classes that I was taking, so I had to make the responsible choice.

"I wish I had the whole day with you. I'm going to miss you so much while you're gone, but we'll have the rest of our lives."

"I'm going to miss you too, but the time will fly by. Just watch. And you know what they say. Absence makes the heart grow fonder, so be ready for me to be all over you when I get back," Bryce said.

"I'm going to hold you to that," I said before giving him a kiss goodbye.

While in class, I kept telling myself that I should've just stayed home, because I couldn't think about anything except Bryce, and how I was going to make without him for an entire week. We had wasted so much time arguing about frivolous things, when we should've been trying to sit down and work out our problems together so we could give all of our love to one another. When I was done with classes for the day, I couldn't think of one thing that I had learned.

I rushed back home later that afternoon, not wanting to waste one second of the time I had left to spend with Bryce before his departure. When I got home, he was dressed, and had his luggage waiting at the door.

"Wow! You look like you're in a hurry to get away from me," I joked.

Bryce laughed, and said, "No, I just wanted to be prepared by the time you got home. I was thinking maybe we could go out and have a nice dinner. Then, instead of me driving to the airport, maybe you can drop me off after dinner. That way, we'll have a little more time together."

"That sounds like a plan."

Bryce and I went to dinner at an Italian restaurant not far from the airport. He again expressed to me how sorry he was about how things had been going lately, and he really needed to have a serious conversation with me when he got back. He made me even more anxious for him to return, and he hadn't even left yet. Besides talking more about expanding our family, I didn't know what else he could've possibly wanted to talk about, but whatever it was, it seemed to be very important. I wasn't worried about it being anything devastating because of the place we were currently at in our marriage. Now, if he had told me he needed to have a serious conversation with me while our relationship was in the fragile state that it had been in recently, then I would've been extremely worried.

We prolonged dinner for as long as we could, and then headed to the airport. Bryce drove, as we cruised through the city and listened to some good music. When we pulled into the airport terminal, Bryce put the car into park and popped open the trunk to get his luggage. I quickly got out on the passenger side and walked to the back of the car and watched as Bryce pulled his luggage out of the trunk. He opened his arms wide as I fell into them.

"Please take me with you," I said in a sullen voice, as we held each other tight.

"I'll be back before you know it!"

He gave me a tight squeeze and a kiss before releasing me, then grabbed his luggage and started walking towards the sliding glass doors.

Before I got into the car, I yelled Bryce's name.

When he turned around, I said, "I love you."

"I love you, too, and I'll never stop," he said before winking at me and heading inside. I stood there until I could no longer see him, as the people in their cars behind me obnoxiously honked their horns.

When I returned home, the house seemed so quiet. What was strange was that the silence was nothing new to me since I'd often been home alone, but knowing that Bryce was going to be gone for an entire week made it seem so obscure, and the obscurity began to suddenly make me feel anxious. I turned on the television to try to ease my mind, and ended up falling asleep on the sofa. I must've awakened out of a very deep sleep because I had no idea of where I was. I looked around and realized I was on the sofa, and immediately looked at the clock, trying to determine how long I had been asleep. It had only been a couple of hours, and I knew it was way too soon for Bryce to be all settled in at his hotel, so I got up off of the sofa, and decided to go to bed and wait on his call.

The next morning, the sun began to beam in through my curtains, and shined directly in my face. I continued to lay in the bed, not realizing what time it was. I then remembered that I'd forgotten to set my alarm clock the night before, and quickly jumped up. I was already an hour late for work, and I was surprised no one had called me to make sure I was ok. I had never been late, or even called off sick since I'd been working at the hospital. I couldn't even remember a time that I was late, or called off while working at the nursing home. That was the reason that everywhere I'd worked, my employers loved me. They knew I was extremely reliable.

I quickly got ready for work and ran out the door. The morning had already been so hectic, I hadn't even thought about the fact that I hadn't talked to Bryce, but I'd call him once I got settled in at work if he still hadn't called. When I walked onto the floor, everyone looked at me strangely because they knew being late was not in my character. My co-worker, Kenzie, who had trained me walked up to me and discreetly asked was I ok. I told her I'd had a long day the previous day and just overslept. Noah hadn't made it in yet, and I was sure that if he had been there, and noticed that I wasn't there, he would've called or texted to check on me.

As I started my day, and checked on a few patients, I began to calm down and get back into rhythm. Just then, my phone rang when I was walking out of one of my patient's rooms, and I knew it had to have been Bryce. I quickly walked around the corner into a quiet hallway to take the call.

The phone number wasn't familiar, so when I answered, I said, "Hello," with hesitation.

"Good Morning. This is Gregory Youngheim calling from Assurance Airlines. Is this Mrs. Simone Stevens?"

"Yes, it is. Was my husband's luggage lost again?" I asked, immediately becoming irritated because it always seemed that somehow, at least one of Bryce's pieces of luggage became lost.

"I'm sorry, ma'am. I really wish that that was the reason for my call."

"Well, why are you calling?" I asked nervously.

"I regret to inform you that there was an accident during your husband's flight from Houston, Texas to Chicago, Illinois. Unfortunately, there were no survivors."

I began laughing hysterically, and then paused. "Wait, that's where you're wrong. You must have him mixed up with someone else because my husband was on a flight to Atlanta."

"I'm giving you the information I have. Maybe you're confused about the location that your husband was traveling to, but the investigators on the scene have collected all passenger's belongings, and your husband's identification was with his things."

"I don't understand. Why was he going to Chicago? Why would he tell me he was going to Atlanta? Bryce Stevens is his name. Is that who you're talking about?"

"Yes, ma'am."

I was in complete shock and couldn't even speak. My bottom lip quivered, and I had a million thoughts going through my mind. Kenzie walked past, carrying her clipboard, and saw something wasn't right.

"What's wrong, Simone?" she asked as the man on the phone continued to say "hello" to see if I was still there.

Tears began streaming down my face, and I broke down to the ground.

Kenzie grabbed the phone from me and said, "Hello. What's going on"

As Kenzie listened, she began writing on a sheet of paper on her clipboard. When she hung up, she knelt down in front of me and hugged me.

"Simone, I'm so sorry."

I continued to cry in her arms until I couldn't cry anymore. Kenzie asked me if I wanted her to call someone for me, and I told her to call my mom. While Kenzie talked to my mom, she walked me to the bathroom, so I could clean up my face. My mom told her she would be there soon to pick me up so that she could take me to the morgue to identify my husband's body.

Chapter Thirty-Three

Kenzie got someone to cover for her while she sat with me as I waited for my mom to get to there to pick me up. There was no talking. Just complete silence as we sat on a bench in front of the hospital. As soon as my mom pulled up and saw me, she jumped out of the car and held me tight as I began to cry again. I could always count on her support whenever I had anything going on in my life. I just chose not to share a lot of things because that was just how I was. I liked to be as private as possible. I could tell she had been crying, but she always tried to be strong in front of me and my sister, no matter what.

My mom thanked Kenzie for calling her and staying with me. Kenzie told her that it was no problem, and handed her the piece of paper that she had used to write down the information that the man from the airline had given her. She then gave me a hug and told us to let her know if we needed anything.

The heartbreak that I felt was so intense. I never could've imagined that there was an emotion such as the one I was feeling. The pain was so bad that I felt like I was dying inside, and nothing would ever be able to take that pain away. As my mom drove me to the morgue, she prayed aloud. I felt so bad that I didn't want to pray, and didn't want to hear anyone else's prayer. I just wanted to wake up from this bad dream. I wanted someone to tell me that this was a mistake, and that Bryce wasn't on that plane. I wasn't prepared for this, and definitely didn't feel like I could handle it. It was often said that "God gives His toughest battles to His strongest soldiers," but I was starting to feel like I would've preferred not to be considered one of His strongest soldiers.

After my mom finished praying, she said, "Simone, I can't tell you that I've experienced anything like this, but I know you're strong, and you'll get through this. I'm going to be there for you every step of the way to help you get through it. God never puts more on us than we can handle. I know you feel like you can't handle it right now, but you can, and you will."

I heard everything that my mom was saying, but I had nothing to say. I just kept playing back in my mind the last few conversations that Bryce and I had had. I thought about how things were starting to turn around for us, and I finally, again, had high hopes for our future. I thought about the fact that he had died on a plane going to Chicago when he told me he was going to Atlanta. We were working things out, so why was he lying to me? Was he just playing games with my heart, or were the things he said sincere? I just wanted answers, and the only person who could've answered me was gone forever. I would have to live with those unanswered questions for the rest of my life. I just didn't know if my love was strong enough to help me overcome the resentment that I would have in my heart towards Bryce once I got past the pain.

We finally pulled up to the morgue, and before we got out, my mom asked me if I was sure that I wanted to go through with that right then. I told her that I needed to get it over with because it had to be done, whether I liked it or not.

My mom held my hand like she did when I was a little girl as we walked up to the door. She opened the door for me as I walked in, and she followed behind. There was a woman sitting behind a window who asked us to sign in and have a seat until a morgue attendant came to get us. As my mom and I sat next to each other, she put her arm around me and held my hand. After a few minutes, we finally heard the doors swing open, and standing in the doorway was the morgue attendant, wearing a long white jacket.

"Hello. Is one of you ladies Mrs. Stevens?"

"Yes, and this is my mother," I said, nervously.

"Hello. Nice to meet you, but I wish it were under better circumstances. My name is Jake. Just follow me on back."

I nodded my head, and my mom and I followed behind Jake.

We walked through the double doors and headed down a long hall. As we passed the restrooms, I heard a door open and close. I looked back and saw a man who looked familiar walking the opposite way. I stopped in my tracks and continued to stare.

"What's wrong, Simone?" my mom asked.

"Noah," I said, trying to get the man's attention, still unsure whether it was him or not.

The morgue attendant noticed we stopped, so he also stopped, confused about what was happening. Then, Noah turned around.

He had one hand in his pocket, and in the other he held a tissue.

"Simone," he said sorrowfully, as he walked towards me.

"What are you doing here, Noah?"

He put his hand to his face and took a deep breath. "I came to do the same thing you're coming to do."

I wasn't following what Noah was saying. The first thought that came to my mind was why on earth he would be there to identify Bryce. I looked at my mom, and she looked confused as well.

"It's Taylor. I had to identify her body."

I gasped and said, "What happened to her?"

"Simone, I think it's best that you go and handle your business. I'll be out here waiting for you, and then we can talk more."

I nodded my head, still trying to make sense of things in my head.

"You guys ready?" the morgue attendant asked.

"Yes, I think so," my mom replied, questionably, looking at me as if I'd done something wrong.

We soon went through another door, and behind it were several metal tables that were lined up. Some of them had white sheets on top, in which I assumed Bryce's lifeless body was underneath one of them. The attendant led us over to one of the tables, and first looked at me to make sure I was prepared before he pulled the sheet back. I nodded.

There was Bryce, lying there looking as if he was asleep. My mom held me as I stood over him. I put my hand up to my mouth trying to hold back my shout. I had to have been dreaming. This couldn't be real.

I couldn't take it anymore. "Cover him back up," I said softly.

The attendant didn't hear me, and said, "What was that, Ma'am"?

I began shaking uncontrollably, and my mom yelled, "Cover him back up!"

He quickly threw the sheet back over and apologized. I had never heard my mom get that loud with anyone, but she was just trying to protect me. She then apologized for her outburst.

"Can I ask a question?" I asked Jake.

"Sure?"

"Can I see Taylor Sullivan?"

"I'm so sorry. I can't do that without the next of kin's permission."

"Well, can you tell me what happened to her?"

"I can't give you any specific personal information, but I can give you general information, such as, everyone who was brought in today were from the plane crash."

"So, they were on the same plane going to Chicago," I said, talking to myself.

"Here's his bag of belongings," the attendant said, handing me a clear plastic bag.

I then signed the paperwork to confirm everything and make further arrangements.

As my mom and I walked out, heading back down the long hall, I could see Noah sitting down in the distance. As he saw us approaching, he stood up and walked towards me. His eyes looked the same as mine. Bloodshot and puffy. He hugged me tightly, and I couldn't tell if it was his body or mine that was trembling. Under the circumstances it could've been the both of ours.

When he released me, I said, "Noah, this is my mom. Mom, this is Noah."

My mom said, "Nice to meet you, Noah."

"Pleasure is mine," he said, with sadness in his voice.

"He's a heart surgeon at the hospital. He's the one that helped me get the job."

As soon as I spoke of getting the job at the hospital, I thought about Miss Franny, and how I was going to possibly break the news to her. This situation just got worse and worse by the minute.

"Yes, I remember you telling me about Noah. I'm just sorry that this is how we had to meet, and I'm sorry for your loss as well."

"Thank you. I appreciate it."

"So, what did you have to talk to me about?" I asked Noah.

He looked at my mom, then back at me, so I knew he wanted to talk in private.

"Mom, I'll meet you at the car."

My mom nodded and headed towards the exit.

Noah took a deep breath before he began. "So, what were you told when the airline called you?" he asked.

"I was just told there had been an accident and there were no survivors. I'm just confused as to why Bryce was on a plane to Chicago when he told me he was going to Atlanta."

"Taylor was definitely going to Chicago, and Bryce was going with her."

"What? No! Why would you say that, Noah?!"

"Because it's the truth. I know the truth and you deserve to know, too. The man from the airline asked me if I knew Bryce because both tickets were bought by him, and he and Taylor were seated right next to each other. I called the hotel that she was supposed to be staying at, and they had no reservation under her name. I then checked if there was a reservation under Bryce's name, and there was. I loved and still love my wife, but she played me. I don't know how long this was going on, but they definitely knew each other before Amina's birthday party last weekend."

I sat down in the chair where Noah had been sitting. I was in total disbelief. I didn't want to believe anything that Noah was saying, but I didn't have anything to refute his accusations. Everything lined up, and different situations began to make sense. I thought about the confrontation between Noah and Bryce at the hospital, and how upset Bryce became. Then I thought about how he and Taylor interacted with each other at the birthday party. As I sat and thought about things more and more, my eyes grew wider and wider.

"What is it, Simone?"

I didn't want either one of us to feel even more worse than we had already felt, so I said, "Never mind. It's nothing."

"Look, Simone. We're going through the same thing right now, and I'm sure everything that you just thought about, or whatever's going through your mind, I've thought about it, too, so we need to just help each other through this right now, because I'm not going to even lie, I'm so messed up right now. I feel like my entire life was a lie."

Noah stood over me with his arms folded, waiting on me to tell him what I was thinking.

"I was just thinking about that day when we ran into Bryce at the hospital as he was coming out of the elevator, and he said he was coming to see me. Do you think that he was there to see Taylor and Amina?"

"I've definitely thought about it. I thought about all the gifts he bought Amina for her birthday. What man buys that many gifts for someone else's child? He was so good with Amina. I kept telling him that."

I nodded and a tear rolled down my face as I said, "But he didn't want any kids."

As Noah and I continued talking, we had pieced everything together. Amina had gone to Chicago with Taylor's mom after she had come in town for Amina's party. Taylor was going to visit for a week, and then bring Amina back home with her. Evidently Bryce had decided to join her to pick up their baby. Noah asked if I would be open to getting a DNA sample from Bryce so that a paternity test could be performed. He just wanted to know for sure, and so did I, so I agreed.

2 "There is nothing concealed that will not be disclosed, or hidden that will not be made known. 3 What you have said in the dark will be heard in the daylight, and what you have whispered in the ear in the inner rooms will be proclaimed from the roofs." – Luke 12:2-3 NIV

When I got into the car with my mom, I sat looking straight ahead, without saying a word. I could see her looking at me from the corner of my eye, waiting for me to say something, but there was just so much, I didn't even know where to begin. Since I wouldn't say anything, she decided that she would.

"They were together, weren't they?" she asked.

I remained quiet, and she shook her head in disgust, as she put the car in drive and pulled off.

Chapter Thirty-Four

After going home with my mom and crying on her shoulder for hours, I told her I needed to be alone, so she took me home. I felt so lost. I still hadn't fully comprehended everything that Noah and I had talked about, and I didn't know if I ever would. As I got to my front door, I trembled as I put the key in and turned the knob. When I walked in, I shut the door behind me and stood in the living room, just looking around. I looked at all of the pictures of me and Bryce on the tables, on the walls, and the one of our wedding day on the fireplace mantle. We looked happy. I thought we were happy, but I was beginning to think that maybe Bryce never was.

I needed to know everything. I wanted to know had I just wasted the last three years of my life. One thing was clear. Bryce had made a complete fool out of me, and that just made me want to scream. I screamed as loud as I could, trying to release all of the pain and confusion inside of me. I felt as though I was having a nervous breakdown. Where was I supposed to go from here? What was I supposed to do?

"God, what do you want from me? I can't take much more!" I yelled, as tears streamed down my face.

I went to my bedroom and stared at the bed that I would now lie in alone. I looked in my closet and began going through Bryce's pockets, feeling like I needed more proof, although I knew that all what Noah and I had discussed had been the truth. I still didn't want to believe it. I found nothing in his pockets, so I thought I'd look in his safe where he kept his gun. I never knew the code. He didn't tell me, and I never asked because I didn't like guns, and never felt that I needed it. I tried different dates, including, our anniversary, his birthday, and my birthday. I even tried Miss Franny's birthday, and nothing worked. I sat on the closet floor, thinking hard about what it could've possibly been, and I suddenly had an epiphany. I entered Amina's birthday, and I immediately heard the lock on the safe release.

I slowly opened the door to the safe and the first thing I saw was his gun on the top shelf. On the bottom shelf were several envelopes labeled with the names of different destinations. I opened the very top envelope, that had been labeled "Cozumel, Mexico". I pulled out a stack of photographs, unprepared for what I was about to see. I sat there looking at Bryce, with a smile bigger than I'd ever seen, holding Taylor close with his hand on her pregnant belly, as she smiled back at him. They looked more in love than we'd ever been. Those pictures were dated only a year back, and I'd remembered exactly when their secret escape had taken place. Bryce was supposed to be going to California for four days to meet with a client, of course. I never questioned his traveling because I knew that was what his job entailed.

I went through the rest of the envelopes, finding that he and Taylor had been to Florida, Nassau, Cabo, and Jamaica, all right up underneath my nose. The photos went a couple of years back, so the affair had been going on for most of, if not our entire marriage. The very bottom envelope was labeled "Family", and that's where I found family photos of Bryce, Taylor, and Amina within the past year. The sadness of suddenly losing my husband was overcome by the anger of being led to believe that Bryce loved me, and that we were working things out. I felt that everything he'd told me had been a lie. I just wondered what he had planned to talk to me about when he returned home. Was he going to tell me about Taylor, and leave me to be with his real family, or did he just want to come clean about everything, and start fresh like he'd said? That was something I'd never know the answer to, and it would probably drive me insane for the rest of my life.

I could've never imagined this to be my life. I knew that Noah had to have been also losing his mind over it all. I knew that he was also in love with Taylor. She and Amina were his life, and Noah and Amina seemed to be Taylor's life. I couldn't console myself, so I definitely wasn't going to try to console Noah, but there was something that I needed to do right away, and that was to tell Miss Franny about her one and only grandchild.

I didn't want to give Miss Franny that type of news over the phone, so I gathered myself, and headed to the nursing home. I tapped on her door a couple of times and pushed it open. She was in her bed watching television, which I assumed she would be doing at that time of the evening.

"Simone? What are you doing here?" she asked.

"Hey, Miss Franny," I said, as I sat next to her on her bed.

She sat up against her headboard and said, "Something's wrong. You don't look good."

"Miss Franny, Bryce is gone."

"He left? Let me call that boy! He just doesn't know what he has! He has everything he needs at home, and just always wants to run from people who love him!" she said, as she grabbed her phone.

I took the phone out of her hand, and said, "No, Miss Franny. Bryce died."

"What?" How?"

"He was killed in a plane crash," I replied, holding Miss Franny's hand.

"No," she sobbed, then looked up at me, and said, "Are you ok?"

"Don't worry about me. I'll be ok. I just want to make sure that you're ok right now."

Miss Franny and I held each other for what seemed to be forever, crying in each other's arms. I didn't tell her all of the details, and didn't plan to. The fact that Bryce was gone was already a lot for Miss Franny to take in, and I definitely didn't want to make matters worse. It was all too much for me to take in, and at that point, I didn't know how I was going to manage to press forward. Miss Franny told me that she knew I probably couldn't afford to keep her in that particular nursing home, with it being one of the best and most expensive, and she would try to find something that she could afford with her social security. I told her not to worry about that. Bryce always paid ahead, and she was paid up for the next year. After that, we'd just have to figure it out at that time.

The next morning, Noah called, just wanting to talk. I hadn't been to sleep, and I knew he could tell in my voice that I had been crying all night. He told me that he had also been up all night, going through all of Taylor's things, trying to figure out how he had missed this. I told him that neither of us were at fault, and Bryce and Taylor had hidden their secret lives very well. We trusted them, as we were supposed to, so we weren't even looking for the signs.

I didn't tell Noah about the pictures I had found, but asked him if he wanted to come over for coffee, and he accepted my invitation. I knew that I looked a mess, but I was sure that he would, too, so I just threw on sweatpants and a wrinkled t-shirt, and attempted to tame my unruly hair. I put on my big, thick glasses because with all of the tears I'd been shedding, my eyes kept rejecting my contact lenses. As I waited on Noah, I turned on the coffee maker and pulled out two coffee mugs. Soon after, the doorbell rang.

"Hey," I said, after opening the door.

"Hey there," Noah replied, as I welcomed him inside.

When he got inside, we hugged, and he then looked at me strangely.

"You look . . ."

Noah seemed to be at a loss for words, so I helped him out by saying, "A mess?"

"No. That's not what I was going to say. You look like you. I remember the picture you showed me of yourself before marrying Bryce. You look like that person again. Beautiful."

Trying not to blush, I tried to disregard his compliment, and said, "You had perfect timing. I just turned on the coffee."

Noah followed me into the kitchen and sat at the island as I poured the coffee.

"How do you like it?" I asked.

"Black," Noah replied.

"Oh, yeah. I think all doctors like it black."

"It's a requirement," he replied.

We sat quietly sipping our coffee, looking into our cups as if we were waiting for something spectacular to happen.

"I have something I need to show you," I said to Noah, as I grabbed the envelopes off of the counter and placed them in front of him.

He looked at me and asked, "Do I really want to see what's inside?"

"I don't know if you want to, but it did give me some clarity."

He slowly opened the first envelope, pulled out the stack of photos, and paused.

He shook his head and said, "When I met you, I could've never imagined going through something like this with you.

He continued going through the pictures and other envelopes without any emotion. He then opened the last envelope, and that's when I saw a tear.

Noah put his hand up to his mouth and said, "Well, this right here says it all, but we'll have confirmation whether or not Amina is his tomorrow. Her grandmother is bringing her from Chicago tonight, and I'll be taking her in to give her DNA sample. Taylor's mom isn't doing well at all, and I know it's only going to get worse once she gets here. Taylor and her mom were extremely close. Taylor was her only child, and I know she'll be lost without her, just as I will. How can I console her when I'm dealing with so many different emotions? It's even worse knowing that she probably has been going along with this tomfoolery the entire time."

Noah took a deep breath and exhaled. He was still hurting, just like I was, but he wanted to be strong.

"Anyway, I'll cross that bridge when I get there. Thank you so much, Simone, for allowing the DNA test to even happen."

"I wouldn't dare try to keep you from getting answers that you need. I need to know just as much as you do. I wish that I knew what Bryce wanted to talk about when he got back."

"What do you mean?" Noah asked.

"He told me that we needed to have a serious conversation when he got back. He wanted to start fresh. I'm just wondering if he was going to tell me the truth."

"That's strange. Taylor told me the same thing," Noah replied.

I could tell by the expression on his face that he had the same thoughts that I had. He had begun thinking that Taylor was going to tell him that she was leaving him for Bryce, and that Bryce was Amina's father. That could've been the case, but, as I said, we would never know. All we would ever be able to do was speculate.

Chapter Thirty-Five

B y the time we'd had services for Bryce and Taylor, the results of the paternity test had come back, and indeed, Amina was Bryce's daughter. It seemed like Noah was more devastated by that news than the fact that Taylor was gone. To be honest, Noah had been doing quite well. A lot better than I had been. Although Amina wasn't Noah's biological child, he would raise her as his. He said that blood didn't mean anything to him, and Amina was his daughter.

We had been the latest gossip at the hospital. It seemed as though every time I walked into the building, there were whispers and stares. When people saw me and Noah walking together, there were even more whispers. I couldn't wait for the whole thing to die down, but Noah didn't make that very easy. He wanted me to also be a part of Amina's life, since in actuality, I was her stepmom. I couldn't bring myself to commit to that, and the more Noah brought it up, the more of a rift it caused in our friendship. He would try to throw a guilt trip on me, telling me how Amina needed a mother, and reminding me of how much I wanted a baby.

One afternoon after class, Noah popped up at my door with Amina, after I'd had a long conversation with him the previous night, explaining to him, once again, that I did not want to have anything to do with forming the type of bond with Amina that he wanted me to. I honestly couldn't see how he was doing it with such an open heart knowing the circumstances behind her conception.

"What are you doing here, Noah?" I asked, as I stood in my doorway with my arms folded.

"Can I come in?"

"Why would you bring her, Noah? You know exactly what you're doing, and I don't have time for games."

"Please, Simone. Just let me in so we can talk."

I exhaled and pushed the door open as Noah walked in with Amina in his arms.

"Have a seat," I said.

Noah sat down, and sat Amina right next to him. I watched as he opened her diaper bag and pulled out a snack to keep her occupied while we talked.

"Simone, I know you're still heartbroken, and you're tired of me bugging you, but believe it or not, I'm heartbroken too, but I have to keep going because of her," he said, looking at Amina. "I really believe all of this happened for a reason. Everything from me meeting you at the nursing home, to helping you get the job at the hospital, and you starting school. Bryce and Taylor had a relationship that we knew nothing about even before then, but God placed us in each other's lives, and it wasn't by coincidence. He knew all of this was going to happen before it happened. We formed a healthy friendship for a reason, and now, this child needs a mother and a father. I can only be a father. She didn't ask for this, and I truly believe we're here to help so she doesn't have to suffer in any way due to the sins of her parents."

"Now you want to put God in it," I said.

Noah knew how strong my beliefs were, and I felt as though he was trying to use it against me.

"I've never been anything except real with you, Simone, and that's what I'm doing now. There is no price that we can put on what we can do for Amina. I mean, if I have to raise her without help, that's what I'll have to do, and I'll definitely do my best, but I think her life would be so much better with you being a part of it as well. I told you, I'm not asking to be with you, or have any type of relationship outside of continuing a friendship with you. I'm just asking that you be a constant in Amina's life."

"Noah, you have an obligation to Amina. Not me. She is your wife's child . . ."

"And she is your husband's child. Your point?"

"You had to sign the birth certificate."

"But you know you love Amina! You've loved her since she was born."

Amina looked at me smiling as she ate her fruit snacks that Noah had given her. I smiled back at her, and I suddenly saw Bryce all over her.

"Yes, and I still love her, but I can't be around her the way you want me to be. She brings back too many memories. Even right now, so just leave it alone, and please don't ask me anymore."

"But Simone . . ."

"Noah, I don't have the type of love in my heart that you have."

"Yes, you do. You just don't know it."

"I know that I don't. I've walked around my entire life not knowing who my mom or dad is. I was left on a doorstep, and instead of believing that I just wasn't loved, and my mom abandoned me, I've worked hard on trying to convince myself that my mom loved me so much that she thought that leaving me outside someone's door was the best option for me. I've felt rejection all my life, so no, I don't have the type of love in my heart that you have. We are completely different. You grew up with both of your parents. You know who your family is. They showed you love all of your life. Poor Amina will never know who her parents are, just like I won't. I want no parts of that. It's devastating, especially, like you said, for a child who didn't ask for this."

I could tell that Noah was caught off guard with what I'd just confessed to him, and he wasn't sure what to say next.

"I didn't know. I'm sorry."

"You didn't know from seeing my white mom that I was adopted?" I asked.

"Remember, when I met your mom, I had just found out about Taylor. My mind wasn't all the way there, and I honestly hadn't thought about it anymore. I am sorry for everything you've gone through, but your story should motivate you even more to want to give Amina something that she may not otherwise have. You don't know what things you might've been subjected to if your mom hadn't decided to leave you on that doorstep. From what I can see, you've turned out to be a wonderful woman, and I'm sure your adoptive parents had a hand in that."

Noah reached over and grabbed my hands. "Simone, let me help you."

"Help me what?" I asked, loosening my hands from his.

"I want to help change your paradigm of love."

I stood up and said, "Noah, please leave. I don't want to talk about this anymore."

Noah took a deep breath and gathered up Amina's things. He picked her up and headed towards the door.

Before walking out, he said, "Thanks for at least letting me in and hearing me out."

I nodded, and watched Amina as she watched me while Noah carried her to the car.

A couple of weeks went by without me saying a word to Noah. It was so uncomfortable that I'd even considered applying to a different hospital. I constantly thought about him and Amina, and I continuously asked God to tell me what He wanted me to do. I felt like I knew what He was telling me, but I didn't want to believe that it was God talking to me, because I was against what He was saying.

Before leaving work one evening, I went to see if Noah was in his office, just so we could talk. I didn't know what I wanted to talk about, but it was in my heart to check on him. He had already left for the day, so I got in my car and headed home. I was almost a block away from my house, when I turned my car around and started heading in the other direction. I soon found myself parked in front of Noah's home. His car was parked in the driveway alongside another car. I paused before getting out, not sure if I should go to the door. Noah might've had company, and I certainly didn't want to interrupt. I could've called him, but I decided to just take my chances.

As I stood at the door, waiting for Noah to answer, I recalled the day that Bryce and I had stood in that very spot. Then Taylor opened the door with her big, bright smile, and he smiled right back at her.

"Simone," I heard as my thoughts were interrupted.

"Noah," I said, not prepared one bit. I didn't even know why I was standing there.

We stood there just staring at each other until an unfamiliar voice said, "Noah, I got Amina to sleep, so you get you some rest, ok."

Suddenly, I saw a beautiful older woman, who was very small in frame, and had beautiful gray hair that was braided up in one long braid that hung down her back.

"Oh, who is this?" the woman asked.

"This is Simone."

"Oh! This is Simone. Noah, let the girl in! Didn't I teach you better than that?"

The woman had the sweetest voice, but I could tell she was a force to be reckoned with. Noah quickly gestured for me to come in, and we all stood in the foyer.

"Well, I guess I should introduce everyone. Simone, this is my grandmother. I call her Granny Gi-Gi. Granny, as I said, this is Simone."

"Nice to meet you, Ma'am," I said as I offered my hand to shake.

"You call me Granny Gi-Gi, too. I've heard so much about you, I feel like you're family already."

Noah looked embarrassed. Granny Gi-Gi had basically told me that Noah talked about me often, and it didn't seem as though he wanted me to have that information.

"I don't do handshakes either. We give hugs around here," she said as she pulled me down to her height and hugged me tight.

When she released me, she stared at me and said, "There is something so familiar about you. Have I met you before?"

"No. I'm sure I'd remember you."

"I never forget a face. I'll let you know when I remember."

Noah interrupted, and said, "Granny, it's getting kind of late. You know I don't like you driving in the dark."

"Let's go sit down for a little bit. I want to get to know Simone a little better," she said, as she headed towards the living area, disregarding what Noah had just said.

"Ok. I guess we're sitting," Noah said as he followed behind his grandmother.

After we all were seated, Granny Gi-Gi kept staring at me, trying to pinpoint where it was that she recognized me from.

"What brought you by?" Noah asked.

"I really don't know. Amina, I guess. I miss seeing her face."

"You know I don't mind you dropping by to see her whenever you want. I told you that."

I wasn't comfortable with having that conversation with Noah's grandmother in the room, so I looked at him and shook my head.

"She knows, Simone. I talk to my grandma about everything."

"He sure does, Simone, and you may not be sure why you came here tonight, but God obviously put it on your heart, and you obeyed, so there's something that needs to be discussed between the two of you," Granny Gi-Gi said.

"Do you want to talk about it?" Noah asked.

I nodded my head.

"I'm going to say one thing, and I'm going to leave. That little girl upstairs is a sweet little girl. She was brought into this world because God wanted her here. Now, she has some wonderful people at her disposal, and she's going to continue to need wonderful people in her life to make it in this cruel world. It's easier to be selfish than it is to be generous, and that's because it's sometimes hard to open our hearts up to people in fear that they may abuse it, especially when it has happened in the past. Sometimes that's a risk worth taking, especially for a child that just needs a chance at a good life. We sometimes have to put our own emotions aside, because those are temporary, and we have to look at the bigger picture."

Noah's grandmother was so wise. Her words captivated me, and truly made me see things in a different light. Noah had tried to tell me the same thing, but it was just different coming from her. After she gave her speech, she headed home. After she left, Noah told me that she had been helping with Amina while he worked. He said that he hadn't realized how much help it was having a partner in the home to help take care of the kids.

"Well, maybe I can come by and relieve your grandmother sometimes when I have time," I said.

"Simone, you don't have to do that, and I definitely don't want you to do anything out of pity or guilt. I'll make it work."

"I know you will, but this is not about pity or guilt. I love Amina, and I realize that I am her stepmother, and I do have a responsibility to her. I not only need to help, but I want to help. I need to get over how I feel, and be more considerate of Amina and her life."

At that moment, I remembered that I had something that I wanted to give Noah.

"I have something for you," I said as I reached in my purse and pulled out an envelope.

"More pictures, Simone? I don't want to see those. Just burn them. I've seen enough," Noah said.

"They are pictures, but not what you think. I think you'll want them. If not, I'll keep them until you're ready."

I had forgotten that I'd gotten pictures developed from Amina's birthday party, and had planned to give them to Taylor so that she could put them with the rest of her memories from Amina's first birthday.

Noah took the envelope from my hands and slowly reached in, pulling out the photos. The photo on top was the one that I'd taken of Taylor, her mom, and Amina. It was beautiful, and I was sure that if Noah didn't want it, Taylor's mom would.

"Thank you, Simone," Noah said, without going through the rest of the photos.

After that day, I became very acquainted with Granny Gi-Gi, and began becoming closer and closer to Amina. As much as I had fought the thought of forming a special bond with Amina, I was loving every minute of it, although, I would still have my moments of asking myself what I was doing, and asking God if this was the life he wanted for me. Whenever I had those moments, I found myself pulling myself back from Noah and Amina for weeks at a time without explanation. Noah wouldn't address, or try to force me to come back around. He knew I was really trying, and was just grateful for that, but I knew that by me not being consistent could cause more damage than anything, so I needed to decide whether I was going to be all in, or all out. I hoped that one day soon I'd stop questioning what God was doing, but it wasn't easy after all I'd gone through.

Chapter Thirty-Six

My mom, sister, and I had planned a mother and daughter's day out since those were few, far and in between. My sister and my schedules were so hectic, it was hardly ever that we could both get together with our mom at the same time. We'd had spa day and a late lunch. Afterwards, we decided to go back to my mom's house to pop some popcorn and watch a movie like we used to do. When I was around my mom and sister, it always seemed as though I had two moms because my sister definitely treated me more like one of her kids than her sister.

While I was in the kitchen waiting for the popcorn to finish popping, my mom and sister sat in the family room trying to agree on a movie. I was never picky about what to watch. I just liked being in their company.

I suddenly heard the doorbell, and from the kitchen I yelled, "You want me to get that?"

"No. I'll get it," my mom said.

The popcorn was done, and I pinched the top of the bag with my fingers, trying to be careful not to burn myself. As I shook the bag, and walked out of the kitchen, I saw my mom opening the front door. I stood in the hallway watching, trying to see who it was.

"Hi. Can I help you?" my mom asked.

My sister then walked past me, heading to the door.

"Mom, who is it?"

"I'm here to find my daughter," the woman said.

"I'm sorry. I don't know who your daughter is," my mom said.

"You don't recognize me, Mrs. Kelly?"

"It's you!" my sister said.

"Ava!" the woman said, smiling as my sister.

"Mom, it's Nadia!" my sister said, as she grabbed the woman and hugged her.

At that point, I was very curious as to who this mystery woman was. Her name was obviously Nadia, but I'd never heard anyone talk about her, so I wanted to know more. As I approached the door, the woman looked up at me as she hugged my sister, Ava.

"Simone," she said softly.

I looked at the woman directly in the face. She looked very familiar. I felt like I already knew her. She looked like me.

Ava released the woman, and said, "Wait, how do you know Simone?"

"Ava, look at us," she said. "She's my daughter."

I dropped the bag of popcorn, and my mouth almost hit the floor.

My mom looked at Nadia and said, "Your daughter? But you would've only been . . ."

"Fourteen. I know. It's a long story."

I walked slowly towards the woman and said, "You're my mother?"

"Yes," she said, smiling, with her eyes welling up with tears.

She was so beautiful, and there was no denying that I came from her. I stood directly in front of her, wanting to remember that moment forever. Nadia could no longer resist, so she wrapped me tightly in her arms, and couldn't stop crying. She was everything that I'd convinced myself that she was, and more. She hadn't just left me on some stranger's doorstep. She had left me on her best friend's doorstep, knowing that they would take good care of me. My mom had always been with me. She had been in every part of the home where I had grown up, and I had no idea. What was even more ironic was the fact that my adoptive mom and sister had known my biological mom for years, and never had a clue that they were raising her child. There were so many questions that we all had, so our movie night turned into something a lot more interesting and fulfilling.

After getting past the initial shock, Ava and my mom invited Nadia inside. Everyone had a smile on their face, including me. I just couldn't stop looking at her, but I couldn't help but to wonder why she had waited so long to come for me. I could tell that she and Ava had been really close. I had never seen Ava so excited.

"Nadia, what happened? Where have you been all these years?" Ava asked curiously.

Nadia took a deep breath, and said, "Well, it's a really long story, but I'll just start with saying my mom had put in me in a very bad situation, and if I hadn't run, I don't know what may have happened. Ava, you were right to not want to come around after my mom and I moved. You felt something wasn't right, and your intuitions were right on point," she said, holding Ava's hand. "I never wanted to leave you, Simone, but I wanted you to have the opportunity to have a life that I wasn't able to give you," Nadia said, looking at me with apologetic eyes. "I knew that Ava's family would take very good care of you, because they took care of me whenever my mom wasn't around."

"Do you know where my dad is?"

"No, and to be honest, I have no desire to know where he is."

We all waited for my mom to continue.

"He was my stepbrother, and he raped me. No one believed me, which is why I had to go. I refused to remain in that environment, and definitely wasn't going to allow my child to live in that environment, just to become another victim."

"I knew there was something strange with that boy. I'm so sorry, Nadia. I wish I'd tried to help you," Ava said, as she consoled her.

"You knew something wasn't right, but it was actually Joey, not Will, that I had to be worried about," Nadia replied.

Ava, looking shocked, said, "And he seemed so nice. I would've never guessed it would've been him."

Changing the subject, Nadia said, "Enough of the sad stuff. This is a joyful moment. Simone, I want to know all about you. I know I've missed so much! Are you married? Do you have any kids?"

My adoptive mom looked at Nadia and shook her head. Ava held her head down.

"What's wrong? Did I say something?" Nadia asked.

"It's ok. We can talk about it," I said.

I told Nadia about my marriage to Bryce. I had never really discussed my marriage out loud in detail with anyone, and as I did, I realized how toxic it really was. Living it was one thing, but talking about it after living it was on a completely different level. I also talked about Noah and Amina, telling her that I was still unsure about where I wanted to stand in Amina's life.

"Simone, just from seeing you today, and hearing your story, I can tell you're a very strong woman, and it's evident that strength runs in the family. You've endured so much, and you can and will do anything you put your mind to. You know what your heart is telling you, so just follow it."

I appreciated hearing Nadia tell me that I was strong. I had begun looking at myself as being weak. I would think of all the things that I allowed Bryce to do to me, and I would tell myself no strong woman would've ever allowed a man to treat her that way. I had to look at my strength in a different way. Throughout my trials, I had remained strong in my faith in God and withstood a lot of pain, mental abuse, and disappointment.

"It sounds like the two of you have a lot of catching up to do. Why don't the two of you go enjoy the nice weather. We can reschedule this for another day, right Ava?" my mom said.

"Definitely! We all have some catching up to do, but first, you and your daughter," Ava said.

Nadia and I thought that would be a good idea. I walked out of the only childhood home I'd ever known with the mother who had given birth to me and left me on the doorstep of that same home. When we got into Nadia's car, she looked at me and gently rubbed my face underneath my eye where my heart-shaped birthmark was.

"My mother had that same birthmark," she said, with a slight grin.

As she began driving, she asked, "Is there anything you want to ask me? I'm sure there's so much you want to know, right?"

I hesitated at first because I didn't want to seem ungrateful that she had finally come to look for me, but I needed to know what had been holding her back. If I'd known who she was, or where she was, I would've been looking for her the first opportunity I got.

Hoping I didn't offend Nadia, I asked, "What took you so long?"

Nadia nodded her head, and said, "I was expecting that. The truth is, after everything I'd gone through, I was severely damaged. I was broken. I knew you were in good hands, and I didn't want to cause you any unnecessary damage. I honestly didn't think that I would be able to love you the way you needed to be loved at that time. I didn't love myself. I rode past your house on several occasions throughout the years. I even watched you play outside. Simone, I wanted this moment so badly, but I never thought it was the right time. I know I've missed out on a lot, but this right here, right now, feels perfect."

"Have you ever thought that maybe even through all of your hurt and brokenness, it was me that you needed to help you heal?"

Nadia held my hand and said, "You're very wise, and to answer your question, now that we're finally together, I do believe that could've been the case. I also believe that everything happens in God's timing, and this is all a part of His perfect plan for us. Since you grew up with the Kellys, I know you know all about God, which is a big part of the reason I was so confident with my decision to leave you with them."

"Definitely," I replied. "I don't think there was ever a Sunday when we didn't go to church, and if it wasn't for that firm foundation, I don't know how I would've made it through my marriage to Bryce and all of the circumstances behind his death."

"I want to apologize for that," Nadia said.

"For what?"

"I was trying to protect you from being hurt, and you ended up being hurt anyway. I guess it's true that parents can't protect their children from everything. At least you didn't allow it to break you."

"I've had a strong support system. It's helped having Noah around since we're basically going through the same thing. His grandmother is wonderful as well. I think you'll love her."

After we rode around talking for a while, Nadia pulled over in front of a restaurant that happened to have a huge sign that read, "Simone's Place." I had heard of it, but had never been there.

"You hungry?" Nadia asked.

"Just a little. I had a pretty big lunch."

"Well, it's dinner time now!" she smiled.

When we walked into the restaurant, it smelled amazing. The food must've been good because it was jam-packed.

"Hi, Ms. Robinson!" the host at the door said, greeting Nadia."

"Hey, Brandon."

"Who is this? Your sister?" he asked.

"No, this is my daughter, Simone."

"Oh! This is Simone!" he said with a huge smile. "It's a pleasure to meet you, Simone," he said, as we shook hands.

As Nadia and I walked straight through the restaurant, everyone stared. We finally sat in an empty booth near the back, and as soon as we did, someone came to hand us menus, and asked what we'd like to drink.

"You must eat here often," I said, assuming so, since everyone was basically treating her like royalty.

"I actually do. It always reminded me of you."

"How did you manage to find a restaurant that you absolutely love that's named after me?"

"Well, this place used to be called Nora's Diner, and my mom used to work here when she young. The owner's name was Miss Val and she really looked after my mom until she married my dad. Your grandfather was a wonderful man, but I'll tell you all about him another day," she said with a sudden hint of sadness in her eyes as she grabbed and held the locket that hung around her neck. After a brief pause, she continued her story. "The night I gave birth to you at the hospital, I snuck out with you in the middle of the night. That's when I took you to the Kelly's, and then I found myself on Miss Val's doorstep. She took me in, saving me from living on the streets, and let me work here. After finishing Grad school, I received my MBA in Business and opened my own restaurant in Downtown Houston, and named it "Simone's Place", after you. I then bought this restaurant from Miss Val when she became older and ready to retire. With Miss Val's blessing, I changed the name from "Nora's Diner" to "Simone's Place, also. I wish you could've met Miss Val. She was a good woman, but she passed on.

I looked at Nadia in awe, and said, "You have two restaurants named after me?"

"Yes, and they will both be yours someday. "Simone" was always a special name to me. I wanted to give you a name that had a special meaning."

"What does my name mean?" I asked.

"It means, 'God has heard', and God has definitely heard my prayers."

After everything Nadia had gone through, she had persevered, and done so much with herself, always keeping me in mind. I couldn't believe she had two restaurants named after me. I had only known this woman for a couple of hours, but there was nothing bad anyone could've ever told me about her, and no one definitely could've told me that she didn't love or care about me. She was amazing, and she was definitely my mother.

Chapter Thirty-Seven

I enjoyed every single moment that I spent with Nadia. I could see so many similarities between the two of us, it was sometimes scary. One thing that I would've never been able to tell about her just by looking at her was that she had been through hell and back. She held her head high, and that was because she had worked so hard to get to where she was. She didn't get stuck in the wilderness. It may have taken her some years to get out, but she never gave up, and kept moving until she made her way out. I had so much admiration for her.

I hadn't given Noah the good news yet, but I knew that he felt something was going on, especially with me not coming around as much as I had been. When I would see him at work, he would ask me if everything was ok, but I would just tell him that I was still just trying to sort out my life, which wasn't really a lie. I had to get acclimated with having Nadia around, and was still trying to convince myself that I wasn't dreaming. Now that I had her in my life, I didn't want to lose any more time with her, so any free time I had, I tried to spend with her. We had done a lot of things that we would've probably enjoyed doing together while I was growing up, and Ava joined us on several occasions. We had shopping dates, movie dates, and days we would just go to the park or beach and enjoy the weather. Nadia even went along with me on a few of my visits to see Miss Franny, and just as I thought, they hit it off well. I could actually imagine Nadia to be a lot like Miss Franny when she got her age. The happiness and fulfillment that I was experiencing was all so surreal.

While Nadia and I were out to dinner one evening, Noah kept calling, and I kept ignoring his call.

"Do you need to get that? It might be important," Nadia said, as she heard my phone ring for around the tenth time.

"No. It's just Noah."

"You told me you had been going to see Amina on a regular basis. I haven't heard you talk about her. Have you been to see her lately?"

In shame, I said, "No, actually I haven't been in a few weeks. I've just been wanting to enjoy my time with you, and spend as much time with you as possible."

"Simone, you had your own life before I came in the picture and I don't expect you to give that up. Please don't use me coming into your life as an excuse to not do what you know in your heart is the right thing to do. From what you tell me, Noah seems like a great person and has been a good friend to you. Return that favor."

"You're right. It just causes a lot of pain and memories when I see Amina. She makes me think of Bryce."

"That's natural, but it'll get easier. Put yourself in my shoes for a moment. I told you that I became pregnant with you after being raped by my stepbrother. Do you think when I saw you it didn't bring back some of those bad memories?"

I sadly looked down at my food, not realizing how Nadia felt every time she looked at me.

"I'm not going to lie to you. It brought back lots of bad memories, but the desire I have to make beautiful memories with you is much greater than those past memories, and the more time that I spend with you, the more those memories fade away. So, let's do this. Let's go pay a visit to Noah and Amina."

I looked up at Nadia and my eyes lit up. The thought of having such wonderful people in my presence all at once made my heart smile.

"That sounds like a wonderful idea."

Nadia and I finished eating and then headed to Noah's for a surprise visit.

When we pulled up to Noah's house, both Noah and his grandmother's cars were in the driveway, which was perfect because I really wanted Nadia to meet Granny Gi-Gi.

As Nadia and I walked up the long path to the front door, Nadia said, "Noah must be really good at what he does. It seems like he's doing well for himself."

"Yes, he's become a very well-known, reputable cardiovascular surgeon in a very short period of time. He was in the top of his class in his medical program," I smiled proudly, as I spoke of Noah's accomplishments.

Nadia, noticing, said, "You seem to think very highly of him. That's what makes a great team. Encouraging and complementing one another. The icing on the cake is that you'll be a nurse, probably working right in the hospital with him. How much more perfect does that get?"

"This isn't what this is about. We don't see each other in that way."

Before I could ring the doorbell, Noah opened the door.

"I thought I heard some chatter out here! We don't see each other in what way?" he asked, looking extremely pleased to see me.

"And he's handsome. You left that out," Nadia said, not at all trying to be discreet.

Nadia had truly taken on the role as a mother by embarrassing her child in front of a man.

I cleared my throat and said, "Surprise!"

"Nice surprise. I thought you were avoiding me for a minute," Noah said, as he welcomed us inside.

"And who is this young lady?"

Nadia, blushing, said, "And he's charming."

"This is my birth mother, Nadia."

Noah's eyes became as large as saucers, and his mouth almost hit the ground. "Wow! How did I not know? The two of you look identical."

Nadia and I both looked at each other, smiling.

"When did this happen?" he asked inquisitively.

"A few weeks ago, she showed up at my adoptive mom's house."

"That explains why you've been so short with me, and haven't been coming around."

"I'm so sorry!" I remorsefully said.

"You're forgiven. This is great! I was beginning to think it was me."

"Believe me. It's definitely not you!" Nadia said, grinning.

"Nadia!" I said, becoming more embarrassed, but loving it at the same time.

"Noah, where's Granny Gi-Gi?" I asked.

"She's upstairs giving Amina a bath. They should be down soon."

As we waited, Nadia and Noah did a lot of talking, getting to know more about each other. To my surprise, Noah knew all about Simone's Place and how good the food was. He told Nadia that he and Taylor used to go there often, and spoke of some of his favorite entrees. It felt a little uncomfortable hearing him talk about Taylor, but I knew he would always have those memories, just like I'd always have memories of me and Bryce.

We soon heard Granny Gi-Gi coming down the stairs with Amina. We all turned towards the stairway as Granny Gi-Gi held Amina's hand as she carefully walked down the stairs. Nadia suddenly stood up and squinted her eyes.

Granny Gi-Gi stopped halfway down the stairs, and said, "Nadia?"

"Nurse Grace?" Nadia said, as tears came streaming from her eyes.

Noah and I looked at each other and shrugged our shoulders.

Nadia met Granny Gi-Gi at the bottom of the steps, and they embraced each other without wasting any time. I walked over and picked up Amina, and Noah followed. I didn't know how Nadia knew Noah's grandmother, but it seemed as though they were very special to each other.

"I knew that I knew that face from somewhere when I saw Simone. I just couldn't place it, but I could never forget the face of that pretty little girl who I had the pleasure of meeting on her thirteenth birthday," Granny Gi-Gi said.

"And I could never forget you, Nurse Grace. If it hadn't been for you, I don't know if I would've had it in me to get out of my situation. God literally gave me grace to get me through it, and that grace was you. I've thought about you all my life, and how you tried to help me. You might've thought that you weren't able to do much, but from the first prayer I heard you pray in that bathroom in my daddy's hospital room, you helped me enter into a relationship with God, and from that point on, that relationship continued to grow stronger and stronger."

Noah, Amina, and I sat on the sofa, as Nadia and Granny Gi-Gi sat across from us, telling us their story. It was beautiful. The entire thing was beautiful how Noah had come into my life, and the entire time, we had been connected in so many ways, and had no idea.

As they told their story, Granny Gi-Gi asked Nadia how her relationship was with her mom.

Nadia shook her head and said, "I don't even know if my mom is still living. Even if she was still living, I don't think we'd have much of a relationship after everything she caused me to endure. I never could understand how a mother could allow their child to go through so much pain and suffering."

She then fiddled with the locket around her neck, as she did anytime there was any mention of her mom or dad. I was curious of what was in it, but I figured if she wanted me to see, she would show me in due time.

"I know you had it hard, but you have to forgive her in order to completely heal. You may not realize it, but there's still some pain inside of you that you haven't dealt with," Granny Gi-Gi replied.

"I know, but like I said, I don't even know if she's alive. I drove past that house years ago, and there was an entirely new family living there. I even took the time to pull up the information on the house and I found out that it was lost to taxes. My mom had received so much money after my dad died. I just don't understand how she lost the house."

"Nadia, that man took advantage of your mother. She wasn't in her right mind. I was still working at the hospital years ago when she was admitted."

"Admitted?"

"I would fill in on the psych floor many times, and I happened to be filling in that day. She had attacked her husband, and they brought her in wearing restraints. I remember her screaming your name and your dad's name. I cried out for her, and prayed for her. After they medicated her, and got her calmed down, I even tried to talk to her, but she remembered me, and you know she didn't like me very much. She did, however, tell me that she didn't know where you were, which made me worry, but I knew you were a smart girl, and I prayed for you, too."

"Do you know what happened to her?" Nadia asked.

"Last I knew, that man had put her in a facility. That's how they lost the house. He took all the money and left. She just may still be in that same facility."

Granny Gi-Gi gave Nadia the information and the next day, Nadia asked me if I would go with her to try to reunite with her mom. I agreed to go, and I hoped that if she was still there, that it wouldn't be too much for Nadia to handle.

When we pulled up in front of Living Way, which was a residential mental health facility, I was about to open my door to get out when I noticed that Nadia was still sitting in her seat with her hands on the steering wheel.

"Nadia, what's wrong?"

"I don't know if I can do this."

"Yes, you can. You came and found me, and that took all of the courage in the world, so I know you can do this. You need to do this."

"You're right, Simone. Let's do this," she said, as she put her locket up to her mouth and kissed it.

"Before we go in, can I ask what's inside of that locket? I've noticed that anytime you talk about your mother and father, you reach for it."

"I had never noticed that I do that, but yes, I'll be happy to share it with you," Nadia said, as she took the necklace from around her neck and showed me what was inside of the locket.

"This is the last happy memory I have of my life before my family was destroyed. It was when I felt like no one could've ever taken away my happiness."

When Nadia opened the locket, I saw my beautiful family. It was her and her parents. They were the people who I had come from, and they looked like a normal, happy family that I would've loved the opportunity to have been a part of. I could tell from the picture that Nadia's dad loved his family. He looked like a very proud and caring man, and I couldn't wait to hear more about him, but at that moment, it was time to meet the woman in the picture. The woman that had the exact same birthmark as me.

When we entered the building, we stopped at the front desk.

"How can I help you, ladies?" the woman at the desk asked in a high-pitched voice with a deep southern accent.

"I'm here to see Lena Robinson."

"I'm sorry. There's no Lena Robinson who lives here. We have a Lena Spencer."

"Yes, I'm sorry. Lena Spencer."

It had slipped Nadia's mind that her mom's last name had changed when she got re-married.

"Lena has a visitor today! How nice. Lena is one of our sweetest residents and I've always wondered why she never had any visitors." Looking at the both of us, the woman said, "I don't even need to ask if the two of you are family!"

"Yes. I'm her daughter, and this is her granddaughter."

"Wow. The genes are definitely strong. Here are your visitor's passes. Her room number is 1091."

Nadia asked, "So, no one has to supervise, or anything?"

"No. There's no reason for that. Lena's no threat, and she's actually here by choice."

"How long has she been here?"

Well, I've only worked here for about five years, but Lena had already been here for about twenty years."

Nadia grabbed the passes off of the counter and told the woman, "Thank you."

When we made it to Nadia's mom's room, we stopped and stared at the door. It didn't seem as though Nadia was going to knock, so I did it for her.

"Here I come," a woman's voice said from the other side of the door.

As soon as the door opened, the woman gasped. She looked as though she'd seen a ghost. She was Lena, Nadia's mom, and my grandmother. She was the epitome of beauty. Looking at her, I felt as though I was looking at myself about thirty-five years into the future.

"Nadia!" she said, putting her hands to her face. "Come in, come in!" she said eagerly.

Nadia and I walked in, and I could tell Nadia didn't know how to respond to her mother's joy.

I stood in front of Lena and said, "Hi, Mrs. Spencer. I'm your granddaughter, Simone."

She stared at me with tears streaming down her face. She gently took my face into both of her hands, and said, "My granddaughter? I'm so sorry. I dreamt of you. You've been through so much, but it's getting better."

Her words were anointed, and they touched me tremendously. When I looked at Nadia, she was holding a Bible that she had grabbed off of the table. She couldn't stop staring at it.

Lena walked over to her and said, "My beautiful Nadia, I'm so sorry. Please forgive me for everything I did to hurt you," she cried.

Nadia hugged her, and whispered, "I've already forgiven you, and I never stopped loving you. Mom, we're taking you home."

They continued to hold each other, and my grandmother continued to cry.

"I've been praying that this moment would come. I used to look at my life and see only the things that God hadn't done, causing me to not believe, but looking at my daughter, and my granddaughter, I can clearly see that God was always been busy working in my life, even through the bad times when I didn't even believe He existed." She released Nadia, and dropped to her knees, raising her arms up in the air. "Thank you, Jesus, for hearing my cries!"

Nadia stood over her mom, crying tears of joy.

I stood next to Nadia, and said, "I love you, mom."

That same day, Simone and I packed up Lena's things and moved her into Nadia's home, where she lived alone. That was the day my family became almost complete. One year later, Noah and I married. We then completed the adoption papers, and I was then, officially, Amina's mom. We, of course, couldn't forget about Miss Franny. We took her out of that nursing home and moved her in with us. We had plenty of room, so she had her own space on the main floor, and Noah hired a nursing staff to come in and take care of her while we were away. This all had been a part of God's will and His plan for each of us involved. I knew without a shadow of a doubt that it was His will because my mind was finally in perfect peace.

My grandmother, mother, and I had all been held in bondage due to things that happened to us in the past, just as many people are at some point in their lives. Some of the things didn't happen directly to us, but still ended up affecting us directly. When we confront our fears, apologize to the ones we've hurt, forgive the ones who have hurt us, and open our hearts completely to God and allow Him to order our steps, we can overcome anything. Our wounds had become chains, restraining us, hindering us from doing what God wanted us to do. In the midst of it all, although we hadn't been physically present in each other's lives, my grandmother, mother, and I still managed to BREAK EVERY CHAIN.

Break Every Chain

Qiana Rae

Beautiflaw Books

www.ingramcontent.com/pod-product-compliance
Lightning Source LLC
Chambersburg PA
CBHW050354260626
47156CB00003B/729